Constructing Churchill

Cover file sourced from:

Constructing Churchill

Contents

Warning: this book may contain scenes of socio-political commentary. If afflicted by feelings of rage at the woke lefty immigrant atheist PC Muslim Marxist trans gay agenda within, please follow the recommended cure; open the nearest right-wing newspaper or TV channel and smother the contents thickly over the cerebrum. Side effects may include impaired social skills, diminished empathy, and significantly reduced intelligence.

With thanks to Duncan Dicks and Martin Randall for the supervision; the novel would have been a lot worse without your joint input.

Dedication:

To the woke lefty immigrant atheist PC Muslim Marxist trans gay agenda.

Long may it continue.

Reader's Abstract:

Constructing Churchill is a satirical meta-novel investigating how national mythology is used by the English Establishment to perpetuate itself down the generations, with the specific focus being on the populist rendering of Winston Churchill the man into Winston Churchill the Myth, a figure beyond all mortal criticism. However, before any knuckle-dragging "patriots" explode in diarrhoetic outrage at this gross disrespect to their right-wing pin-up of choice, be assured the tight, white, hegemonic underpants of the nation are safe; traditional narratives such as "We'd all be speaking German if it weren't for Winston!" are never going to be overthrown by snippy plebeian novels such as this.

This fact is reflected within the structure of the book, as the official Establishment account is laid out like holy writ on the main pages in the traditional format of numbered, sequential chapters, while any alternative history or fact is relegated to the undigestible footnotes at the bottom of the page, where they will probably be ignored by everyone. However, the literary conceit of splitting the narrative between the page and the footnotes is an idea that can only go so far, given the book must also function as a piece of readable literature, and a smidgeon of mockery does therefore occasionally intrude (in the spirit of conventional unconventionality) upon the main pages, but only in the Reader's Abstract.

And the Author's Note.

And the Forward

And the Prologue.

But after this, the derision is safely contained in the chapter headings, muzzled away from the official story.

Except for a few light comments in Chapter Two.

And Chapter Eight.

And Chapter Nine is made up almost entirely of snark, given it features a hero named 'Zatman' and villains called 'the 1%er' and 'Flag Shagger'. Nevertheless, the scorn for the trustafarian right-wing public-school parasitical wankers and their boot-licking arse-kissing knuckle-dragging supporters in the real world is only ever alluded to via a series of subtle metaphors, so no real harm is done, and academic impartiality is maintained throughout.

Apart from when it isn't.

The story itself follows Yvonne Jones, a young Black woman from a nouveau (comparatively) riche family who finds her dream of success in the world of publishing is curtailed as she isn't part of the Establishment, which means she will never be given the same opportunities handed out by the elite to its own members.

The Establishment is represented by Michael Vansittart, the old Etonian inheritor of Clavier and Coldwell Publishing; his friend and fellow old Etonian Sebastion Featherstonehaugh, now enjoying his inevitable career in politics; Terrance Rogerson, a younger old Etonian and "journalist" looking to launch his inevitable career in politics, and finally Rupert Hutchinson-Cockburn, a fledgling old Etonian parachuted into Vansittart's business by the Old Boy Network as a precursor to his inevitable career in politics.

Finally, please be mindful that *Constructing Churchill* was written for my PhD in Creative Writing. This means the book was created primarily for my own amusement and edification, while the intended readership consisted entirely of university lecturers.

10

Which, I'll admit, may limit the book's appeal just a teensy-weensy bit on the open market.

Even in this lightly modified version.

Author's Note

It is the convention at the start of a serious novel for the author to beg the forgiveness of the reader for the sin of creating false locations – be they countries, counties, neighbourhoods, streets, or even specific buildings. Often, the writer will admit to having "lifted" or "borrowed" some elements of real geography, in which case an apology is usually tended toward those who live in or know the areas involved. PD James is a good example of this sort of thing, as shown in her author's note for *The Black Tower*. And *A Taste for Death*. And *The Lighthouse*. And *The Private Patient*. And *The Murder Room*. And *Gaudy Night*. Though the last one was by Dorothy L Sayers. But the point still stands, hence this carefully constructed (and somewhat meaningless) apologia.

Quite why authors should continue to do this is anyone's guess. Except this sort of false modesty, and the asking of forgiveness for something carefully planned, written, revised, submitted, and edited, is now an established publishing tradition – especially if the book in question is a populist piece which therefore stands outside the acceptable literary canon. Which presumably explains why the apology so often reoccurs in detective fiction.

With that in mind, I have nicked the exterior of Virginia Woolf's old house, 34 Paradise Road, Richmond, to use as the outer shell of Clavier and Coldwell Publishing, though I have rejiggled the inner layout for artistic effect while also translocating the entire building into the fictitious adjunct of Kensington Manor. I've also taken the liberty of slapping down a railway line in Hauz Khas, Delhi, again purely for artistic effect, and so I must now adhere to the ritual and appeal to the reader's kind indulgence in taking such presumptive steps with their beloved communities etc etc.

And while I'm on the topic, some of you may recognise the offices of the Daily Crier Magazine as well …

Having got that out of the way; welcome to my serious literary novel! Though it isn't that serious, to be honest. Or at least, it is serious, but only in a very unserious manner. And I'm not entirely certain if it's literary, either, because defining 'literary' is not a simple as you might think; literary fiction can be described as any work examining the human condition while breaking with conventional narrative and prose techniques. Then again, you could also describe literary fiction as being pretentious and a bit boring.

It's almost as though the supposed 'rules' to literature are little more than areas of (dis)agreement now labelled as tradition, in which merit is assigned by the dominant status quo to its favoured authors and practices. Which, incidentally, is pretty much what the rest of the book is about, albeit on a larger social scale. And so this digression, and pointing out the point of the digression, does serve as an apt introduction to the narrative.

But the book will at least *try* and be literary.

By which I mean it will be both pretentious *and* boring.

And will employ many a sesquipedalian word.

Forward, and a caveat.

This book is concerned with Winston Churchill, but it isn't really about Winston Churchill. It examines the construction of history and biography, but it is neither historical nor biographical. It is set during the shambolic premiership of Boris Johnson, (24th July 2019 – 6th September 2022), but it is not about Johnson himself.

Instead, the novel is concerned with *how* – how English society works, how it maintains itself, how it repeatedly offers prime opportunities to the aristocratic and capitalist elite who are already at the top of the pile, and how it denies any real prospects to those at the bottom. The narrative is, in short, about the people who make up the Establishment, though it features only a few fictionalised examples of them.

I should note here that I, the ill-bred author, have no experience or contact with posh society. This means I have no idea of the codes used within that society; see, for example, the oblique references in a certain 2014 Establishment biography to Churchill's mother using her charms on men to advance her son's career, which I *think* means she was shagging the aforementioned men, though I can't be certain. Though shagging is definitely something the Establishment indulges in whenever possible, (you can look it up on the Internet), and yet rarely do the newspapers condemn them for this. Unlike when working class women behave in the same way, and then get shredded for their promiscuity.

Odd that ...

If you're wondering what all this has to do with Churchill, bear in mind Churchill's story is the story of class, and hence the examination of the man is an examination of the nepotistic system that created him while excluding everyone else. After all, if I turned up at a bank/ business/political party/media firm expecting to be given jobs and opportunities while in possession of nothing more than a common name, an obscure background, and a respectable mother, (thus conspicuously lacking a title, social connections, and a mother enthusiastically screwing scores of influential men), I'd be told to piss off.

And this is pretty much the whole point of the novel: nepotism rules. And the class system wouldn't work without the support of the quisling English media coupled with society's deference to posh power.

Finally, it should be noted that while *Constructing Churchill* is critical of Churchill the man, the novel acknowledges it is possible to admire the art but not the artist, or the achievements but not the achiever. I can therefore admire Churchill's part in defending Britain while also criticising his motives in doing so, given the suspicion he was defending aristocratic power and wealth rather more vigorously than he was defending the liberty of the lower orders. (See footnotes #48 and #50 for evidence of his loathing and contempt for the workers).

Should the reader feel outraged at this lack of deference toward Churchill and his kin, then take comfort that they won and their values are maintained to this day; we *still* live in an oligarchical society with virtually no opportunities for those born outside the upper and wealthy classes. And you are playing your part in upholding the status quo by raging about the woke lefty immigrant atheist PC Muslim Marxist trans gay agenda from your kneeling position of deference down on the cold, hard ground.

Congratulations.

Prologue

The prologue is a construct much despised by some literary professionals, but given the work you hold in your hands is a self-reflexive novel bedevilled by the very notion of the construct, we can surely extend our indulgence toward this particular humble prelude – especially as this sort of preamble is useful when introducing characters who are vital to the back-story while remaining little more than supporting players throughout the work. So, let us be kind to this prologue which has, after all, served the purpose of establishing the place, plot, and themes of the novel.

Except, of course, it has done no such thing. This is because writers are liars. *All of them.* Trust no one. Instead, it will be down to the humble footnotes to explain how we are all constructs of class, education, and socialisation.

Churchill is an excellent focus for this as he was/is a construct; he had the means (via his Establishment background and contacts) to push a fictionalised version of himself into the public consciousness, and this image was then taken at its own value by the hordes of Establishment sycophants who came thereafter – see footnote #110 and Helen's comments in Chapters Fourteen–Sixteen for further particulars.

But how does the Churchillian (and other Establishment myths) keep going? What keeps them alive? Why does the public seemingly fail to understand they are looking upon a careful selection, presentation, and even distortion of facts whenever they open a biography or watch a documentary? Why do they accept and then regurgitate supposed "facts" even when they have no reason to do so? Why do they not question that which they are told to believe?

The short answer lies in the stranglehold of power held by the UK Establishment (political, media, and cultural) over the rest of the country, while deference, stupidity, and English exceptionalism provides the necessary support for this situation to continue.

History, after all, is moulded by those who hold the means of cultural production. Those born to wealth, leisure, and opportunity have the necessary access (via family, friends, and peers) to top positions within business, politics, publishing, the media etc, while everyone else must slave all day just to pay bills.

Which is a depressing way to end the prologue.

But it does sum up the book reasonably well.

Chapter One

... and the commencement of the Establishment narrative! Which is appropriate, as the entire concept of a "Chapter One" is a facile tradition in literature which suggests that everything starts from this one point, whereas in truth everything is in motion long before we enter the world. The Lovecraftian tentacles of social ossification reach out from the past to entwine around the present and future, ensuring that nothing will ever change, as this novel will now attempt to demonstrate. And so:

Chapter One

... and the commencement of the counter-culture footnotes! Please be aware the plebeian footnotes will surge exponentially from this point forward, deconstructing everything from education to convention to fondly held beliefs, thus demonstrating how the Establishment narrative is just that – a narrative.

Have fun wading through them all.

Chapter One

Actually, before we do get onto Chapter One, I would like to come clean and admit this idea of using footnotes to deconstruct a narrative is one I have used before, albeit in a different form, with my Poppy Orpington Steampunk series. And so having got that off my chest, we begin with:

Chapter One

Though, come to think of it, I suppose I should explain the main difference with the Poppy series was that each book (starting with Full Throttle, *available on Amazon, as is the entire run) was written as though a biographer, James Birkin, was telling the (real-life) story of Poppy Orpington, a 6'2" flame haired working class racing driver who lived over a century beforehand. The footnotes were therefore presented as being rather more academic and explanatory in tone, a bit like an Oxford or Penguin Classic reprint, meaning there is a little bit of difference between the Poppy books and* Constructing Churchill *as the former is a "straight" historical, albeit one set on an alternative Steampunk timeline, whereas the latter operates purely as a piece of meta-fiction.*

And so finally:

Chapter One

Mind you, it's quite interesting to see where I went wrong with the Poppy series; I wanted the footnotes to hint that the biographer (Birkin) was very carefully selecting and presenting scenes from Poppy's life to proffer an acceptable view of her character, a process Birkin found distasteful as he didn't want to lie, but he also knew full well that Poppy's character, already vilified by the Establishment, had to be carefully filtered for publication in an unforgiving patriarchal society.

This, however, was exceedingly difficult, as Birkin would hardly be able to reveal he was being selective with the facts without raising some awkward questions, meaning he could only give himself away by mistake, which was extremely unlikely in a book he was writing and editing. Regrettably, this was a dilemma I never managed to solve, so I can only hope I have succeeded better here given that Constructing Churchill *is, as mentioned above, a work of metafiction.*

But anyway, please enjoy:

Chapter One

In which we will meet one of our secondary (though important) characters, Michael Vansittart, owner of Clavier and Coldwell Publishing, who through inherited wealth is a powerful man in the publishing industry. Or at least, he is powerful within Clavier and Coldwell. We also meet Sebastian Featherstonehaugh, a government minister also born into a wealthy and well-connected family – yet he (like Vansittart) honestly believes his success is down to his own undisputable talent and sheer hard work...[1]

---

[1] This is the Dunning-Kruger effect, in which people significantly overestimate their abilities. See also Churchill's belief in his own

Michael Vansittart's eye glanced from corner to corner of his computer monitor, taking in the nervous, self-conscious faces of the unknown people sharing the online meeting, as well as the untidy clothing of his fellow guests; although the men were wearing shirts and ties, there was a sense this was not their usual apparel. Probably he was looking at people who more commonly wore hoodies and T-shirts in their daily lives. Slovenly.[2]

Vansittart checked his own camera feed, the image reassuring him with its carefully knotted silk tie, well-pressed shirt, and lightly laundered ironic smile. He wouldn't have dreamed of dressing in any other manner on a workday, but especially not when meeting his old friend, the Right Honourable Sebastian Featherstonehaugh MP, Deputy Minister of Culture (Regions) and self-proclaimed rising star of the government, for they both knew the code; they had, after all, been at Eton together.

The minister, however, was conspicuous by his absence, his camera feed showing the empty £12,999 taxpayer-

---

specialness and then contrast with the many, many errors, mistakes, and complete fuck ups littered throughout his life.

[2] At Eton, Vansittart would have worn a morning suit every single day. For him, and those like him, this was the norm. Is he intelligent enough to realise the enforced wearing of the morning suit is an applied convention to mark him and his peers out as being special and different? For the long answer, continue reading this novel. The short answer, however, is "no".

funded office chair and the golden £840-a-roll taxpayer-funded wallpaper behind.[3]

With time to kill, Vansittart lazily studied the backgrounds behind his fellow attendees. Like him, all seemed to be working from home. Unlike him, all seemed to have set up their laptops in their living rooms, (Vansittart refused to call such poky squalor sitting rooms), though one woman's feed seemed to hint at the edge of a bed in the very corner of the shot. Vansittart's lips twitched disdainfully; he alone seemed to have a proper office to work from, for he had long ago converted the fourth bedroom of the five-bed house into his own private space.[4]

'Hello, er, have we started yet?' asked a nervous voice afflicted with a Birmingham accent as another camera feed appeared on the screen, this time showing a middle-aged woman in a cheap blazer and blouse.

---

[3] Not that the taxpayers were aware of these costs; the government felt such information was not in the public interest.

[4] That no one else at the meeting had a spare bedroom, and therefore had to work from whichever room was free of other household members, was not a thought likely to encroach upon Vansittart's assumptions. His lack of self-awareness is an issue shared by practically all his contemporaries born into wealth and ease; they live in a world made for them, meaning their lives (and thoughts) all run on pre-laid regulation tracks, stopping at every station of opportunity while speeding by the sidings of deprivation. They never question their assumptions of superiority in much the same way that a fish (to change metaphors) doesn't think to question water.

'Not as yet, no,' replied Vansittart, his upmarket accent intimidating the woman still further. 'Although the feed is on for the Minister, Sebastian himself is not yet here.'

'Oh, er, you know him, then?' asked the woman in a flustered manner.

'We've met at a few social functions,' smiled Vansittart, glossing over their shared schooling and social advantages. 'The occasional soiree.' He paused, wondering if anyone else on the screen knew what a soiree was; they all looked like the sort to eat chips in a pub rather than attend an exclusive Garden Party. They also seemed to be somewhat uneasy, but talking to the great and the good was probably not their métier.[5] Vansittart supposed there wouldn't be much opportunity for such things out in the provinces. No wonder they all gave the appearance of a group of schoolchildren in their Sunday best.

'All right, Kerry, how you doing?' boomed a Black Country accent as another figure appeared on the shared screen.

'You all right, Jason?' responded the newly identified Kerry.

'All right, everyone?' continued Jason Allen, beaming at everyone on the screen. A chorus of greetings echoed back, ranging from the enthusiastic to the polite to the pained, at

---

[5] Vansittart – like many of his ilk – believes poverty to be both a choice and a moral failing on the part of the lower orders. He is open in his disdain when no one is monitoring his behaviour, but in public he is aware of the need to appear tolerant – a documented hypocrisy of the middle classes. Have a look at Jarness & Friedman, 2017, for more.

least on the part of Vansittart, who was wondering how a human voice could produce such an unmelodic noise so painful upon the ears. 'Ah, you're Mr Vansi-tart, of Coldwell books?' asked Jason. 'I saw your interview in the paper, not long back.'

'Van-sittart,' replied Vansittart, wincing at the mutilation of his name while hastily issuing the correction. 'Which paper was this?'

'The Folio Literary Supplement.'

'Really?' coughed Vansittart in surprise.

'Good morning, Michael, how are you?' tally-hoed another figure as she materialised on the screen. This was Cassandra Harrison, of the Chelsea Musicology Academy.

'Very well, thank you, Cassandra; and how are you?' beamed Vansittart at the cut glass-tone of his eldest son's extra-curricular headmistress, so unlike the uncouth, inarticulate hollering from "Jason".[6]

Vansittart looked with approval at Cassandra's glossy hair held back with a broad Alice band, cream blouse, light yellow scarf, tweed jacket and discreet make-up. His eye then slipped disapprovingly to the other women on the screen, all of whom probably bought their clothing from

---

[6] Vansittart would enjoy sharing his impersonations of Jason for several weeks thereafter with friends and family around various Chelsea supper tables, eliciting waves of laughter followed by hasty assurances that no, they weren't snobs, for that was an alien concept and quite old hat, and no one thought that way anymore, and anyway, what even is snobbery, it's all simply rather amusing, yah?

supermarkets and who wore noticeable shades of lipstick and foundation. *Less is more,* thought Vansittart, recalling his grandmother's oft-repeated mantra on feminine appearance, as well as differentiating between a lady and a mere woman.

'How are you finding all these online meetings?' hooted Cassandra, causing those who didn't know her to adjust their volume controls in the mistaken belief the sound levels were too high. Vansittart, however, was long acclimatised to the tones of the Cheltenham Ladies' College; his grandmother, mother, and aunts had attended there, as had virtually all his own female friends.

'It's not too bad, once you get used to it,' smiled Vansittart, who in fact was unable to even find the meeting icon on his home computer, never mind open it, without the aid of his wife, Heather.[7] And when working from the

---

[7] Incidentally, should Vansittart ever have a biography written about him by a fellow member of the Orthodoxy, his marriage to Heather would be rendered as: "The union was duly solemnised in a full church wedding attended by many famous and influential names from the publishing world, a satisfactory end to a brief yet genuine courtship." Nowhere would we discover that Heather had been Vansittart's PA before their affair was discovered (sans-trousers, over his office desk), after which the original Vansittart marriage was discreetly dissolved, the new nuptials quickly arranged, and the painful and distressing business laid to rest. This is how things are done by the Establishment; with delicacy, tact, and refinement.
And no one ever had the ill-breeding to mention the affair out loud.
At least in Vansittart's presence.
Unless it was done quietly.
Behind his back.

Kensington Manor office, Vansittart simply relied upon the latest unpaid assistant to ready the computer for his arrival.

'I say, it's terribly exciting, isn't it?' continued Cassandra as she adjusted the small but expensive earrings inherited from her great-grandmother, noting in distaste the hoops of false gold dangling from the ears of a woman in a cheap jacket and blowsy lipstick. 'The chance to ask Seb for an extra bit of funding, yah?'

Vansittart was spared the need to reply to this sightly indiscreet revelation of their close friendship with "Seb" by the arrival of the Deputy Minister of Culture (Regions) himself, sliding into his seat while frantically clicking his mouse before glancing at the screen. 'Ah, are we already on?' he asked, relieved to find his PA had already set the link up for him.

Featherstonehaugh smiled urbanely into the camera. 'I do apologise for being a little late; just a few last details needing to be dealt with on another matter. Now, are we all here?" He peered at his screen, giving the impression of a fish staring out of a small tank, noting the presence of Cassandra and Vansittart before counting the other camera feeds. 'Yes, we seem to be. Excellent.'

'Now, as is common knowledge, the government recently decided to award extra funds to certain organisations within the arts industry, as we recognise the arts are a vital part of modern Britain.' In truth, the government had only grudgingly agreed the extra funding after an article in a

———————————————————————

popular newspaper had decried the lack of support for the arts outside London,[8] but by glancing at his notes Featherstonehaugh was able to reassure himself of the truth of his words, for the words were written down on an official document and consequently they held equal – if not greater – authority than Holy Writ.

---

[8] The paper in question, edited by old Etonian Finley Anthony Wolfson, had printed the opinion piece to remind the government of the paper's power, not because Wolfson cared in any way about the arts outside London, or indeed anywhere.

Featherstonehaugh and Wolfson had enjoyed a gentlemanly laugh about the article in the private Chummo Club the following evening, though Featherstonehaugh had gently pointed out the government had dropped a point in a popularity poll that afternoon, leading him to tactfully remind Wolfson who was in charge of the country (though each man knew the answer to that).

Then, after a few more taxpayer-funded drinks and a meal spread over several courses, Featherstonehaugh and Wolfson jointly completed the paperwork which would ultimately see public money used for repairs on the Chummo Club's roof, for both men sat on the Chummo Building Committee.

And this came *after* Featherstonehaugh had rejected funding for the charitable Acton Soup Kitchen because – as he explained later in Parliament – feeding the poor and homeless would only encourage dependency. Besides of which, the Urban Development Corporation had some exciting plans to use the Acton site for office blocks, and as Featherstonehaugh happened to sit on the board of the aforementioned company, the decision was a no-brainer.

This, incidentally, is why decency and democracy has already lost. The Establishment holds the power. The people do not.

And nothing will ever change that.

'A sizeable allocation of funding, amounting to some three million pounds, has been earmarked for those artistic groups or organisations who, in our opinion, are doing the most for modern Britain,' continued Featherstonehaugh, his upper lip curling at the paltry sum of three million, though he reminded himself this was more money than most of the applicants in the North would see in as many as fifty lifetimes thanks to their feckless, lazy lifestyles.

'To this end, you have all submitted applications explaining how your own individual organisations best represent modern Britain through artistic endeavours.' Featherstonehaugh paused, wondering how a dance school in Nottingham could ever justify its submission, but he had to listen to the personal appeals from each applicant, as dictated by the rules, for then everything would be open, transparent, and democratic – and then he could get on with allocating the funds to Vansittart's publishing house and Cassandra's Musicology Academy, at which the minister's own daughter was studying the flute every Tuesday evening and Saturday morning.[9]

'We have now read your written applications,' continued Featherstonehaugh, moistening his lips as he recalled some

---

[9] This sort of personal cronyism in the upper echelons is nothing new, with jobs, favours, opportunities, and contracts flowing freely between them. For example, it was revealed in 2014 that around 1.36 billion pounds worth of NHS contacts was handed over to a company which had gifted the Conservative party 1.5 million. That is one hell of a dividend in anyone's financial returns.

of the awful presentations he had encountered,[10] 'and now you must make a short verbal pitch for your organisations, as explained in section four, subsection three, paragraphs five to twenty-six inclusive.' His voiced droned on, the soothing flow of words eroding responsibility from any potential future recriminations.

Vansittart and Cassandra nodded along, very much at their ease, in contrast to the ordinary supplicants who all gave the appearance of being intimidated or even, astonishingly, bored by the minister's restating of the known facts. Vansittart continued to smile and nod, showing he was participating fully in the ritual of belonging.

'This, then, is the summation of our role and purpose here today,' continued Featherstonehaugh, triumphantly winding up his brief (sixteen-minute) introduction. His attention had barely wandered as the oiled words rolled smoothly along, though thoughts of his discreet mistress did intrude once or twice. 'As well as justifying your organisation, and your organisation's role in the community, you must also show how the funding will be beneficial for all of Britain. As such, I now call upon you all to make your pitches, starting with Kerry Turner.' He peered suspiciously at the poor people on his screen,

---

[10] As of 2021, schools had suffered a decade of chronic underfunding, as identified by a school union, yet Featherstonehaugh – being rather dim – was unable to see the connection between poor educational standards in society and his government's political devastation of the education sector.

wondering if they were articulate enough to give any form of answer.

'Oh, er, right, thanks, Mr, er, Mr Feather-Stone-Huff,' stuttered Kerry. 'We at the Turner Dance School in Nottingham have worked for years in helping local kids get into dance, as it's a great way for them to learn new things and, er.' Kerry's confidence fled under the supercilious gaze of the wealthy elite, causing her to falter over the notes hidden on her lap. 'And, er, meet new things, I mean new people, and learn things, like dance, er, and meet new dancers.'

'Yes,' drawled Featherstonehaugh, the faintest hint of a well-bred sneer appearing around his full lips at the mispronunciation of his name, the uneducated voice, and the idea there were any dance institutions worth watching outside London. The minister had his family ticket for the English National Ballet, (always claimed back on expenses – and rightly, too, in his opinion – as he attended not as a private individual but as the face of the whole Government), and he knew what good dancing was. 'And how does this benefit the country as a whole?'

'Er, well, I suppose giving local lads and girls a way off the streets is good for everyone, isn't it?' wavered Kerry. 'It helps the community, doesn't it? Getting kids off streets, getting them meeting new people, making new friends?'

'Thank you,' murmured Featherstonehaugh before glancing at the man in the top left of the screen. 'Next is Mr Jason Allen; you represent the Black Country Poetry Press, yes?'

'Ar, that's right,' said Jason, his colloquial response and broad accent provoking a fleeting wince on Featherstonehaugh's face. 'The press was founded back in 1987, to give a voice to Black Country poets who was being discouraged from trying poetry by those who said writing verse wasn't for the likes of us.'

'Indeed,' said Featherstonehaugh, making a small cross on his paperwork; he could not comprehend how anyone of Jason's type could ever appreciate true poetry, the beautiful form of Shakespeare and Shelley and Spenser. *It would be a positive boon to literature*, he thought, *if the Black Country Poetry Press collapses forthwith.* 'Thank you, Mr Allen,' he smiled, tuning back into the meeting as he saw the low-born lips stop moving. 'And now you, Mrs Sheena Griffith, of Newcastle Amateur Theatricals.'

Featherstonehaugh glanced down at his notes, giving an excellent impression of deep concentration, though he had no need to focus here, at least; Newcastle was currently a marginal seat and a byelection was looming, so funding would be pushed forward – though only on the understanding the right candidate (i.e. from Featherstonehaugh's own party) got in at the election.

Hopefully, that would be enough to swing support their way. The minister certainly didn't want to have to visit the place. No doubt it was full of seedy people living in sordid terraced houses who spent each evening drinking brown ale in some awful local pub. He really couldn't understand why anyone chose to live that way.

Featherstonehaugh nodded and smiled and grimaced on automatic pilot as each applicant made their case for the funding until finally, just as his secret doodle of his mistress' breasts was nearing completion, there were just two applications left. 'Thank you. And now over to you, Mr Vansittart, of Clavier and Coldwell Publishing.'

'Thank you, Mr Fanshaw,' purred Vansittart, correctly and conspicuously pronouncing Featherstonehaugh's name and thus eliciting a nod of approval from the minister, as well as a series of uneasy blushes from the other participants.[11] 'Now, as you know, Clavier and Coldwell was founded in 1931 on the back of the Bloomsbury movement, with a commitment to finding the best artistic voices who understood the essential need for truth and decency in society.[12] With this in mind, and in order to qualify for the

---

[11] Note how the faux pas is used to shame those on the outside of the Establishment club. Then consider how this sort of social shaming, replicated throughout society, helps maintain social compliance and control over a deferential population. Sinister, isn't it?

[12] Vansittart didn't mention how this commitment to truth and decency owed more to cultural arrogance than anything else for the founders, Bartholemew Clavier and Tarquin Coldwell, refused to believe that any writer beneath the wealthy middle classes could have anything true or decent to say – a business decision which eventually resulted in the owners selling up in alarm as their family wealth gurgled down the drain of socio-literary snobbery. Note that Vansittart is glossing over this inconvenient fact even in his own mind, for it does not fit the Establishment narrative of posh people always being successful in everything they do.

most generous allocation of funding from the government,' (*grovelling little turd,* thought Jason, glumly; *wish I'd thought to say that),* 'I have determined the best way we can serve the community is by inspiring the community.

'As such,' continued Vansittart, 'we plan to launch a call for a brand new, innovative retelling of the greatest hero this land has ever produced; we are seeking a new biography of Winston Churchill!' Vansittart smiled as he laid down his trump card, for he had no fears on Seb being in any way displeased with the truly original proposal.[13]

'What an excellent idea!' enthused Featherstonehaugh. 'Churchill was as much an inspiration and unifying figure then as he is now, no doubt about it![14] Oh, and do you both have a commitment to equality in all areas of your business?' he asked of Cassandra and Vansittart, poised to tick off another box and completely forgetting the existence of the other applicants for the funding. 'You do consider

---

[13] You can pop onto the Internet and type 'Churchill Biography' to see just how "original" the proposal for a new Churchill biography is. Note: it isn't. At all.

[14] In fact, recent research into Churchill's war speeches reveals a distinct lack of public approval; several contemporary listeners even thought he was drunk while speaking. See also the many contemporary (and non-Establishment) commentators asking critical questions about Churchill the man, which undercuts Featherstonehaugh's belief in Churchill as a beloved unifying figure. But then, Featherstonehaugh's world is small, insular, and informed by Establishment dogma.

NINeW[15] – Non-Indigenous and Non-White persons – in your hiring processes?'

'Oh, yes!' hooted Cassandra. 'Why, we interviewed three people only last week for the post of caretaker, and we are giving serious consideration to giving the job to Mr Samuels, who is West Indian. His family came over here just after the war, apparently.'

'And you, Michael – Mr Vansittart?' murmured Featherstonehaugh. 'You also employ an NINeW?'

'We do, for we are a truly diverse and inclusive organisation,' beamed Vansittart in multicultural pride. 'After all, a publishing house has a duty to be a reflection of society.'[16]

---

[15] Pronounced "Nin-ooh". Featherstonehaugh was able to smoothly and professionally insert the latest governmental placebo to inclusivity into the proceedings, despite his private contempt for the acronym and the people it covered – though his feelings were, naturally enough, buried beneath layers of plausible deniability. He knew how to play the game.

[16] Vansittart's genuine sincerity was coupled to a total lack of self-awareness, for his "diverse and inclusive organisation" consisted of just one Black individual, Yvonne Jones, who worked on the voluntary (i.e. unpaid) intern programme. And this was only as a grudging favour to Yvonne's mother, an old neighbour and casual acquaintance, who had overheard Vansittart talking loudly about the internship programme while queuing in the post office a few weeks previously. Vansittart, upon turning and realising Mrs Jones had heard the entire conversation, could not avoid the suggestion that maybe her own daughter could benefit from the scheme.[*]
Vansittart, however, was on firmer ground with his belief that Clavier and Coldwell was a reflection of society, though not in the way he

'Excellent,' smirked Featherstonehaugh as he ticked the relevant boxes on his paperwork, going over the light marks he had placed there earlier for Cassandra's Musicology Academy, (which would benefit the nation as the students came from good families), Clavier and Coldwell Publishing, (which would benefit the nation by the publication of their new biography of the greatest Englishmen ever), and the Newcastle thing. He wasn't quite sure how this last would benefit the nation, but he'd get one of his assistants to fill in that section.

This was when Featherstonehaugh enjoyed his work the most; in maintaining tradition and excellence across the land. The power, huge salary, vast expenses, and constant networking opportunities were, he reassured himself, mere irrelevances. After all, he had gone into politics to help people. That he helped himself first, his peers second, and no-one third, was a truth never allowed to cross his

---

imagined; research in 2019 noted how career opportunities in writing favour those from posh white moneyed backgrounds, (for creativity is a luxury of privilege), hence his publishing list is indeed a reflection of his society – almost all his authors were white, middle-class, and Oxbridge-educated, with only a few token non-white/middle-class/Oxbridge authors included for reasons of public relations rather than genuine commitment to equality.

*This fortuitous post office encounter is the closest Yvonne (who we will meet properly in the next chapter's final footnote) will ever get to the Establishment practice of handing out opportunities to its own kind. And she does so only because of a pure fluke.

complacent mind, for he truly believed himself to be a Great Man of History.[17]

---

[17] The 'Great Man' theory of biography needs some explanation, and here is as good as place as any. The basic idea seems to have taken root with Thomas Carlyle and his 1840 lectures, later adapted into a single book, *On Heroes, Hero-Worship, and the Heroic in History*. In brief, the Great Man theory consists of two basic components; Great Men have special qualities that others lack, and these Great Men step forward when the world needs them. This describes Churchill perfectly, at least as far as his supports are concerned, given they believe Churchill – and only Churchill – could have guided us to victory in World War II.

This goes some way to explaining the trope's popularity with the Establishment, as against the narrative presented above, any questions against Great Men become encoded as unpatriotic, socialist, and just plain wrong. Even if the questions have perfect validity such as "what about all the other nations and peoples involved in the fight against the Nazis?" or "Why do we laud a man so obviously racist, sexist and classist?" or "Is this selling of the Great Man Myth merely another means of keeping us all compliant?" But then, this is most likely the point; if "we" all share a narrative of "our heroes" and "our way of life", then any questions against this narrative become difficult to contemplate, and even more difficult to say out loud.

This groupthink is nothing new; Louis Althusser noted in 1970 how the state is not a means to an end but is instead the end in itself, replicating its own oppressive structures via the Repressive (i.e. explicitly violent) State Apparatus and – of more interest to this book – the Ideological State Apparatus (RSA and ISA for short). Althusser notes almost all institutions (including schools, the church, the family etc) are inherently Ideological State Apparatuses, for they all enforce codes of ideological beliefs upon us concerning how to think, how to behave, what to expect from our futures and so on.

The ISA of Churchillian Mythology is clear to behold; Churchill as Hero is the dominant ideological discourse and all other views (concerning Churchill's racism, imperialism, corruption etc) must be attacked and devalued as being false and unacceptable, for such questions are dangerous to the Establishment. After all, if people suddenly started questioning the Myth, they could then question reality, and where will that end? Presumably with questions like "Why do the corrupt bastards at the top have everything while we have nothing?"

This helps explain why we have so many media stories screaming about the dangers of anyone (i.e. immigrants, lefties, progressives, intelligent people) who aren't invested in Establishment myths, for these groups will have their own views on history, society, equality, justice etc, meaning they may be difficult to control. And this may explain the deliberate Establishment stifling of the humanities in schools, colleges, and universities as education, it seems, is not an ongoing life journey of exploration, self-realisation, and honest knowledge, but is instead concerned with corporate conformity and training the plebs into viewing employment (aka economic servitude) as being their only outlet for achieving personal and nationalistic pride.

The last is important, for nationalistic pride is an essential aspect of the Establishment. For nationalism to work, it requires some form of myth concerning a common past; in the case of Churchill, (and thus, by extension, the entire UK), we have the myth of Our Finest Hour when we – and we alone – stood up to the Nazi tyranny and saved the entire world, a myth repackaged down the generations until it has become reality. At least as far as Establishment historians, racists, politicians, the mainstream media and other idiots are concerned. Just don't mention the pivotal roles of America and Russia in the war. Or the millions of people living under the British Empire who suddenly found they were fighting the war as well ...

Having looked at the cultural imperatives behind the Great Man theory, let us now examine some of the more personal reasons for the persistence of the theory within Establishment circles. Firstly, it must surely play directly into the egotistical narcissism of many individual members of the Establishment, for a belief in the general theory of the Great Man entwines neatly with the specific belief of their own Individual Greatness. Certainly, Vansittart and Featherstonehaugh both feel they have worked hard for, and thoroughly deserve, their success,

---

and neither man has any patience with alternative historical theories such as the 'history from below' approach.

Of course, it is hardly surprising that overprivileged public school elitists who have everything handed to them from birth onwards should believe they are Great Men Destined for Greatness, but in truth, Churchill and his class are not that great, but simply have the chance (denied to others) to acquire greatness. Though the Establishment seems to be permanently unaware of this simple truth, and instead believe they are, one and all, Great Men.

The second reason for the Establishment's adherence to the Great Man theory is, again, purely self-serving, as Great Men are allowed to get away with truly appalling behaviour and beliefs. This could be termed the 'Mythic Fault'; if forced to criticise your hero, do so in a manner which reinforces their Brobdingnagian character, further bolstering their status as being above the mortal herd. Many who "criticise" Churchill do so through this 'prism of greatness,' emphasising the Mythic nature of the man and excusing his mistakes/flaws as being almost beneath notice. Who else but the Great Churchill could make such Great mistakes such as the slaughter at Gallipoli, his handling of the Bengal famine, the gold standard debacle etc? As such, the Greatness of the Great Man in emphasised, keeping him in the realm of the Gods and beyond all mortal criticism.

Interestingly, it was Churchill himself who created his own myth. Accounts of the Second World War could be controlled in the UK by vetting memoirs or restricting documentation, to ensure no dissent was ever raised. In America, however, serious attacks were made on Churchill's conduct – and this prompted Churchill in 1946 to begin his own narrative of the war years. In doing so, he laid down the official track (Churchill as War Hero and Great Man) which others then obediently followed, never once thinking that perhaps they should step off the path of blinkered orthodoxy and dig through the potato patch of honest truth. (See, for example, how Churchill's actions in bringing Japan into the war have been kicked into the long grass of historical amnesia; Churchill decided in 1941 that America would only enter the war if attacked themselves. He therefore encouraged America to

39

---

invoke an oil blockade against Japan, thus precipitating Pearl Harbour.
The British ambassador to Japan at that time, Sir Robert Craigie, was in
no doubt the country could have been kept out of the conflict).
And this myth bleeds into England's perceptions concerning its (real
and fictitious) past and its (real and fictitious) present, making Churchill
an excellent micro-example of modern-day cultural mythology, for his
image is now a deliberate and recurring construct. 'Churchill the man'
is now truly 'Churchill the Myth'.

Chapter Two

"The Old Grange looked down upon the village, the bare, bleak windows almost like disapproving eyes from which the spirit of the old squires could grimace at all aspects of the modern while thinking back with longing to those long lost days when the Lord of the Manor could ride with English pride down the high street and thrash a worker for his insolence and a hussy for her decadence as he collected his hard-earned rents, tithes and percentages, before enjoying a slap-up meal at the Olde Inn on Jericho Street and finally moving on to a full evening of fortified conversations and business with the true blue of old England at the Rich Man's Clerical Conservative Landlords' Political Club."

Sir Flatulent Wedge Marsh-Warbler IV, The Journey of Young Master Cedric Fanthorpe-Wickstiffe *(Snobly & Uppity Publishing, 1798).*[18]

---

[18] Using a quote at the beginning of a chapter is a tradition used by writers to show how well read and authoritative they are. It's pretty much the literary equivalent of posing on the beach in your swimming trunks, flexing your muscles in the hope of appealing to busty blondes in bikinis. Ideally, the excerpt should be from the classics (Dickens, Shakespeare, etc) though an extract presented in the original Greek/Latin/French/Scandinavian Camel Trumpeting is equally desirable – especially if there is no accompanying translation.
Back in the old days, it could take hours of scouring encyclopaedias or reference books to find a suitable passage. Today, a quick search on the Internet brings up innumerable suggestions within seconds. The one above, however, is faked, (as are several others throughout the book), as I can't afford to pay a publisher/author for the rights to quote from a real work. This, of course, is not an issue in academia, where you can quote (in moderation) under the fair use law.

Having set up the story in the previous chapter, we should now set the scene also, to give the reader some idea of the world they are now inhabiting. To do this, the plebeian author will be allowed to hog the main pages of the chapter as he gives a lengthy and somewhat ornate description of Clavier and Coldwell House,[19] for while in practical terms it's a simple building in which our main characters lose their humanity in serving both mammon and social expectation, it is also a symbol representing the world of Vansittart and his ilk, meaning the house of privilege must serve a dual purpose within the narrative. Or in this chapter, at least. So, please enjoy the following portrait of a place, which exists only to prove I can do description, given this is a novel about the conceptual spaces we carry around in our heads, not the geographical spaces we live in.

Built sometime in the 1750s as two separate dwellings but later joined into one, 34 Paradise Road, Kensington Manor,

---

As such, all quotes from real people have been removed from this, the published version of the novel, though I do still occasionally refer to the real people and the points they make. If you want to see the quotes I originally used to back up my points, you will need to look up the PhD manuscript at the University of Gloucestershire's Research Repository.

[19] The description of the house, in line with its sociological and marketable value, is embedded into the chapter. In contrast, the full introduction of our main character, a young Black woman on the outside of the Establishment, will be relegated to a footnote because she isn't – in society's terms – anyone important.

is a four-level construction of hope and confidence[20] which appears to have stood firm against the passing armies of time, for the house has changed little – at least externally – within living memory. True, the centrally placed front door is a late addition, as are the accompanying respectable white pillars on either side, but all seem to be in keeping with the original design – as do the double-glazed windows peering down at the busy main road which links the town hall, the library, the police station and, in one nod to modernity, the tube station (built 1927, extended 1967, and referred to locally as "the pit").

Those allowed entry through the front door find within a wide hallway with two reception rooms on either side, now utilised as the general office and board room respectively, the latter of which remains largely unchanged since 1931 and contains a large dark wood table, eight matching chairs, and twin portraits of the original founders of the business, Bartholomew Clavier and Tarquin Coldwell. (Clavier and Coldwell, incidentally, eventually sold out to Harrison Humphries, who in turn sold out to Charles Donahue, and finally Donahue sold out to the Vansittart family who were riding high on trade while fervently wishing for respectability, hence four generations later we arrive at

---

[20] In what way is the house a construction of hope and confidence? Hope and confidence on whose part? The town planners? The builder? The first owner? Beware passages such as these, for they corral the reader into the enclosure of predetermined conclusions. See also histories, biographies, newspaper articles etc.

Michael. He keeps the portraits for the sake of tradition, as well as for the tone they add to both the room and the business, a consideration especially useful when meeting important clients).

The general office, in contrast, is made up of flatpack furniture, cheap shelving sagging under the weight of hundreds of box files and thousands of books, and a few second-hand office chairs. Although this office abuts onto the kitchen, the staff are strongly discouraged from entering therein, and indeed Vansittart has gone as far as providing the office with a tiny galley area to keep the main kitchen free from outside contamination.

The kitchenette consists of a miniscule sink, barely large enough to hold the single dripping tap used for filling the office kettle, (possible only if the kettle is held at an angle approaching 90 degrees and filled via the spout), while a small, mildewed fridge just about allows the storage of one carton of milk, two bottles of juice, and a few sandwiches.

Upstairs is little different; three of the four bathrooms are strictly out of bounds to the staff, though in any case they are virtually inaccessible owing to the innumerable boxes of books shoved into each room in defiance of the fire insurance policy relating to the storing of flammable materials. The five bedrooms are also used for storage, and are similarly impenetrable to all except the most agile who can contort themselves through the hundreds of boxes containing an entire library of remaindered books which represent a dusty archive of Vansittart's bad business decisions, poor management, bad timing but also – on more than one occasion – pure bad luck in the publishing world.[21]

---

[21] To Vansittart, the house represents his heritage, his family, and his place in the world. It also represents his security, both ideologically and financially. Alas, the property doesn't sit on weakened foundations or suffer from drastic subsidence, but then, a metaphor can only be carried so far before it falls under the strain of disbelief, meaning there can be no gothic collapse of the building (and all it represents) at the end of the novel. Though the plaque on the front door is, it is true, somewhat stained around the four rusty screws holding it in place, so there at least we can find an artistic representation of the moral decay to be found within.

To Yvonne Jones, the young Black woman sitting in the office and whose lot in life is dealing with the mundane aspects of the business such as sorting the mail and cleaning the bathrooms, the house represents the first step in her desired literary career; Yvonne is the volunteer mentioned in chapter one, working for no pay in order to break into the publishing/corporate world. (See the following chapter for further details on Yvonne's ambitions; for now, we must contextualise her existence via a laborious backstory).

Given the unconscious prejudices and assumptions running through *Clavier and Coldwell*, the reader may be wondering how a young Black teenager is able to take an unpaid post there and survive. The reason is simple; Yvonne has relatively wealthy parents who happen to know Vansittart by virtue of living down the road from him.

Barry and Gloria Jones set up a childcare day centre in one of the poorest neighbourhoods of London in the 1990s, taking advantage of the nursery funding offered by New Labour for four-year-olds, then set up another centre and ultimately followed this up with five more, all still serving the poorest areas until Barry and Gloria were able to divest themselves of the business, as well as their old friends and neighbours, by selling up and moving into a wealthy (white) area.

Barry and Gloria found their new neighbours warmly welcoming as the community publicly embraced the Jones' to their collective bosom – albeit while holding them at arm's length, especially if the door to the silver cabinet was unlocked when the Black family came round for a

---

visit. One of these neighbours was Vansittart himself, meaning it was through the established British method of social connections rather than merit that Yvonne's mother found out about the voluntary scheme at *Clavier and Coldwell* designed (so Vansittart had it) for young people to learn about publishing from the bottom up. In truth, the opportunity has more to do with Vansittart's cost-cutting than anything else.

And if the reader considers this to be a clumsy literary contrivance to place an outsider (Black, no social contacts, no Oxbridge networking, no generational wealth, or social breeding) on the inside of our mise-en-scène – well, they're probably right. But then, Yvonne would never get this close in real life, as shown in a 2019 survey which revealed the publishing industry is mostly run by posh white people who favour posh white writers. Which explains why there are no poor or working-class characters in the novel; the poor and working class can't get close to the cultural/political elite even in a work of fiction. Even our main character, Yvonne, is only there by chance after an overheard conversation (see footnote #16) – and she has had to wait until Chapter Two to even appear, while Vansittart and Featherstonehaugh, important but secondary characters, were introduced immediately in chapter one. Such is the power of privilege.

But to return to the footnote. Vansittart was genuinely delighted to have Yvonne aboard, though not for any intrinsic qualities of her own; rather, Yvonne's presence meant Vansittart could congratulate himself on his impeccable cosmopolitan credentials in having a Black around the place. In short, Yvonne unknowingly became the public face of Vansittart's ethno-credibility.

Having read the above, the reader may be forgiven for thinking Yvonne is going to be our identifying character, the person we can cheer for as the narrative progresses, living vicariously through her innate integrity, experiencing her hopes when she rises and experiencing a cathartic sense of safe proxy grief (for this is only fiction, after all) when she falls. Alas, this is a work of bitter fiction based on the misery of reality, in which hardly anyone can be laudable or even vaguely pleasant, and hence our central character is herself problematic – for Yvonne is a deeply prejudiced individual.

Despite having suffered from many racist incidents and attitudes over the years, Yvonne still actively detests Indians and Pakistanis (who she considers to be one and the same) for their supposed laziness, dirtiness, and religious extremism. She has been challenged (off page) on this bigotry and yet she sees no paradox, no immorality, and no hypocrisy in her attitude, for the character of "the Indians/Muslims" are (supposedly) well known to all.

And on the rare occasions Yvonne has been pressed further, she has made use of the argument that racism is not prejudging someone based on the supposed characteristics of their race, skin colour, or place of birth, but is instead a system of political, social, and economic power designed to oppress non-white people – which means she cannot possibly be racist as she doesn't benefit from that system.

This does risk causing the novel's main character to lose sympathy with the readers, but it also raises the issue of how people in general can be messy and complicated, with bigots revealing unexpected kindness and empathy, (at least within certain sociological groupings), or pleasant people unexpectedly demonstrating repugnant moral views.

It would be natural if the concerned reader is now pondering the ethics of the author (a white, male, failed writer from the West Midlands) creating and using a character like Yvonne (a young, Black, London-born woman from a much wealthier background) in his PhD project. Is the validity of a novel destroyed if it is written by an outsider? Does the fact that Yvonne's worldview has been partially adapted from two real-life sources, (a Black woman I met some twenty years ago who hated Indians, coupled with an actual statement of belief from a former university diversity officer), make any difference? Does the fact that Yvonne only exists because my PhD supervisor told me I ought to be writing about characters from outside my own ethnicity change how we view the novel? Does the need for intersectional works demonstrating how every outsider is being screwed by the elite override the issues of authentic authorship? And what is authentic authorship, anyway?

This last question needs careful consideration, especially as Yvonne's thoughts and experiences are, in effect, wiped from (by) the dominant Establishment narrative and are instead relegated to the footnotes. But even here we glean very little, for Yvonne (as a character) is representative rather than authentic, and in any case, some will believe it is impossible for the narrator of the footnotes (i.e. me) to offer a factually correct observation or analysis on characters outside my own community and experiences. After all, while I can be told about, or read up on, genuine experiences from a variety of sources, I still won't truly know what it is like to be Black and female. (Or white and posh, for that matter, as I will only ever be halfway to that one). So, can I genuinely write on these topics? Should I even try? Or, to put it another way, who has the right to write?

Cultural authenticity is a much-debated issue, with copious time, energy and wrath being devoted to the insider/outsider question. Those who hold that everyone should be able to write whatever they want will state that preventing an author from creating a story with particular characters is nothing less than censorship, (you can look up what Kathryn Lasky, Anthony Horowitz, and Lorraine Devon Wilke have all said on the subject, with each one recounting how they were told by anonymous editors and publishers they couldn't/shouldn't write outside their own ethnicity), and would result in men only being allowed to write about other men, women only being allowed to write about other women, and politicians only being allowed to write about other squalid hypocritical criminally-corrupt two-faced tossers. Opposite these writers are those who watch helplessly as their cultures and lives are lost, ignored, or rendered into little more than storybook tourism, a hollowed out, whitewashed act of sanitised literary pornography for armchairs voyeurs, (see Thelma Seto for further particulars), but there are also those (Jacqueline Woodson springs to mind) who believe it is fine for authors to write outside of their own cultural norms *if* they have some genuine knowledge of the people involved, preferably by sharing some real, lived experiences with them. This latter view raises an interesting problem within *Constructing Churchill*, there is no way I'm going to be able to share experiences with people I don't have access to – i.e. the wealthy, powerful Establishment – simply because I can't get anywhere near them; I do not exist in that world, and this is just as the Establishment likes it. This means I can only guess as to the thought processes and assumptions of posh Establishment clones based on the available evidence, which includes research into interviews with the elite, (or those who have experience with them), and extrapolation based on the actions of the Establishment. As such, my characters are little more than one-dimensional archetypes who exist purely to spout pre-determined dogma to the reading public – but then, I think I just accidentally described every English journalist in existence with that sentence, so at least I'm honest in my dishonesty.

Unlike the journalists …

This means that *Constructing Churchill* should be evaluated on a universal level rather than the authentic, as the book is attempting to show how everyone outside the Establishment is being shafted by the status quo, and hence the book's characters are mouthpieces designed to put forward an idea or a point of view that can then be explored, debated, and (if required) challenged. Vansittart, Rogerson and Hutchison-Cockburn (two characters yet to be introduced) all assume theirs is the only valid way of life, and anything different must be the woke lefty immigrant atheist PC Muslim Marxist trans gay agenda at work. And any attempt to tell them anything different is doomed to failure, as they simply won't accept, or even listen to, any other voice or viewpoint. (See Reni Eddo-Lodge for a greater insight into this issue). However, there is a flipside to this argument, as stated by Vivian Yenika-Agbaw, who points out that universal assumptions are usually encoded as white, and so all other lived experiences are relegated or outright dismissed from consideration. (See footnote #83 on Shakespeare being representative of all human experience, and then consider how the dominant Establishment – which moulds society via politics, the media, education, the arts etc – lays down a narrative saying "this is the only way to be").

But we must also consider the issue raised by Rudine Sims Bishop, who points out that cultural authenticity is a difficult term as there is always more than one way to read or interpret a book– an observation which fits very snugly with Roland Barthes' famous essay "Death of the Author", in which he argues we must cast aside the intent of the writer and instead create our own interpretations into the work, as otherwise we end up with just one Establishment-approved explanation which closes down any further thought on the topic.

Oddly, this plurality of the text was seen in my own PhD as one of the external assessors, Yvonne Battle-Felton, stated during the viva that she felt Yvonne is empowered at the end of the novel by her recognition of the corrupt societal system she lives in, which means she is free of orthodoxy and constraint, whereas I saw Yvonne's final end as a crushing blow as she realises how only Establishment players are allowed to achieve anything, and for everyone else life is a disenfranchised struggle in the service of callous capitalism.

This meant the literary world I had created was redrawn by the free-thinking interpretation of the visiting reader, thus proving we do indeed live in a world of multiplicity in which idiosyncratic philosophy assimilates and interprets form and content, and the author's intent is no more valid than the reader's interpretation. And thus I experienced my own literary death in real time.

Which was a little bit disconcerting.

Chapter Three

In which we see a little of Yvonne's character, prompting another extensive footnote on how we are all the products of society, with those at the top being handed the largest plates piled high with the food of opportunity while those at the bottom are lucky to get the crumbs of minimum wage drudgery. Yvonne herself, with her moderately wealthy parents, is closer to the crust than the crumbs, but not by much.

Yvonne, having to be the first into work by an hour to open and prepare the office, had already sorted the post, (including the latest deliveries of several large, heavy boxes of books, all of which had to be opened, catalogued, and distributed to various desks, tables or bathrooms), swept the floor, done the washing up, polished the dark wood table and chairs in the meeting room, cleaned the staff bathroom, (for which she had to provide the cloths, bleach, sprays, and rubber gloves, for Vansittart never thinks of such things), and turned on Vansittart's computer ready for his arrival at whatever o'clock.

And Yvonne did all these jobs because they would facilitate her dream career of becoming an award-winning mega-successful millionaire author, in the pursuit of which she planned to put herself forward for the role of writing the company's new Churchillian biography. This, Yvonne imagined, would not only get her name out there, but it would also clear the way for her to pick and choose her next project, and thus the wealthy career she had mapped out in her mind would be launched.

True, she had never thought about writing a biography before, but Yvonne *believed*. She believed a writer could turn their hand to any genre. She also believed she had the necessary commercial knowledge (derived from her A Level in Business Studies) to carry her plan forward. And she firmly believed in the partnership of meritocracy with hard work, and the inevitable success this would bring forth.

And now the rather grim footnote on the falsity of this position.[22]

---

[22] The idea that hard work will be rewarded is one of the greatest lies circulating in society today. Unfortunately, Yvonne has been spoon-fed this narrative since birth by her parents, (who bought into the fantasy by way of a family loan, and who now look down on those poorer than themselves), her schools, and by wider society hence Yvonne has unconsciously and unquestionably absorbed the myth of the meritocracy. In doing so, she has been rendered into little more than a corporate serf, there to be exploited.

Stunted by her environment and schooling, brainwashed into the values of the status quo, we see how Yvonne's dream of personal success condemns her to work endlessly for illusory capital and then die, a command which diminishes each individual as it gives our obedient, unthinking labour to those in authority.

Yvonne's daydreams do at least serve the vital function of allowing her to temporarily escape (at least mentally) from the tedium of the office chores which have already become her routine. Her favourite scenario focuses upon the rewards of her success, (rather than the contacts needed to attain it), and sees her arriving at myriad film premiers and award shows in a chauffeur-driven Rolls Royce, passing through the adoring crowds, pausing to sign a few autographs, (for Yvonne tells herself she will always make time for her fans), being interviewed on both television and in print, (though not on radio, a dull medium, in Yvonne's view), before attending the after-party clutching an award in one hand and the latest hot footballer/actor/singer in the other.

The author feels he should apologise for this rather brutal analysis of Yvonne's aspirations which (after all) are all socially ordained, with her character and future being moulded decades, if not centuries, before she was even born, and it would be cruel to dismiss Yvonne's dreams or character as being shallow or immature, for she is merely manifesting the values she has absorbed from her home, culture, and the media; that wealth and fame are the only signifiers worth anything, and if you don't have them, you are nothing.

Yvonne will only ever see success in her dreams, so why begrudge her the spurious emotional fulfilment such dreaming brings to her? Especially as she will soon be railroaded onto the next (i.e. only) "acceptable" ambition for a woman, in that she will start to feel the enormous social pressure of finding a man and having his children, with society judging her a personal disaster if she fails in this predetermined directive.

Welcome to reality.

Chapter Four

In which we see a little more of Yvonne's character, and we also meet Rupert Hutchinson-Cockburn, an old Etonian who – unlike Yvonne – will have an incredibly rewarding life as he was born with the hackneyed silver spoon of inherited wealth, privilege, and contacts firmly ensconced within his mouth.[23]

The topic of Vansittart's online meeting for extra funding had dominated office conversation for the past week, and as part of her cunning plan to get the job writing the biography, Yvonne had decided to see what previous material existed on Churchill so she could appear keen, knowledgeable, and enthusiastic in front of the man who

---

[23] Apologies if the reader is getting impatient with the lack of Churchillian detail, but as previously mentioned, this book is *not* a Churchillian biography; rather, it is an examination of the society which enables the construction of Churchillian mythology to rise and then be endlessly replicated. No written work exists in a vacuum, and no biography simply pops into existence; all writers are influenced by the inherent assumptions inherited from their family, class, upbringing, education, newsfeed, politics, etc. Context is everything.
But then, normal, everyday experiences also affect us; rude man in the queue ahead of you? Puts you in a bad mood. Yelled at from across the road? Puts you in a flustered mood. Criticised over something? Puts you in a defensive mood. Even an everyday event like breakfast can affect your outlook for the day; burnt breakfast? Hurried breakfast? Breakfast argument? Breakfast given you the trots? Then you won't be in the most receptive frame of mind when doing your morning's work.

had the power to confer both the biography and paid employment upon her.[24]

Yvonne unpacked several large books onto her desk (some taken from her father's bookcase and some from the local library) which she then carefully arranged for maximum visual effect. Happy with her display of learning, she sat down with a cup of coffee, a drink she didn't care for but she had read many Internet memes on writers running on the bitter stuff and so she drank it accordingly, before selecting a tome at random.

This was Richard Trumper's *Churchill the Brave*,[25] which in the course of the first few pages had Yvonne's mind boggling both at the sheer amount of research Trumper had put into the work (with an entire year being required to collate his interview notes with Churchill's family members) as well as the rich, varied life of Churchill himself. It seemed incredible one man could have done so much; who else could have joined the army, got swiftly promoted to second

---

[24] Vansittart had hinted on Yvonne's first day that employment could be in the offing to the right candidate. But then, he always hinted this with the unpaid volunteers, thus doubling their work rate.
And not one of them had been hired.

[25] Don't bother looking for this; as mentioned in footnote #18, all quotes in this novel are fictional. Admittedly, these fictionalised works are based on factual books, but factual books are (in essence) little more than fictionalised reworkings of factual events. Hence my admitted fictional reworking of fictionalised factual books is designed to get across the fictional nature of these supposedly factual fictionalised books.

lieutenant, and then volunteer for a warzone to prove himself? And then come back, stand for parliament, and be a cabinet minister by thirty-three? And live for years in domestic bliss with his wife, Clementine?

'Wow!' mumbled Yvonne; the man had been a dynamo. Could she achieve even a fraction of what Churchill had? Yvonne believed she could. After all, Churchill had seized events by the neck and had shaken them into a shape which suited him, so why couldn't she do the same?

One reason why appeared at that very moment as the office door opened and Rupert Hutchinson-Cockburn[26] sauntered in.

---

[26] Or "Hutchinson-Coburn" as Yvonne thought it was, for she had only ever heard the name spoken out loud. When she does see it written down, in Chapter Thirteen, she will be unable to repress a snort of laughter at the discrepancy between the written name and the socially correct pronunciation, which will in turn bring down the disapproval of the Establishment (i.e. Vansittart and Hutchinson-Coburn himself) as well as their social sycophants (office drones Felicity and Sarah) thereby reinforcing the philosophy of everyone knowing their place. But I digress; Hutchinson-Cockburn was a fellow volunteer within Clavier and Coldwell, and like Yvonne he was there as his parents knew Vansittart – though unlike Yvonne, this was down to the old boy network rather than retail (see footnote #16) happenstance; Vansittart and Hutchinson-Cockburn's father had been at Eton together.
The disparity between Hutchinson-Cockburn and Yvone's social status was also echoed in the financial, for Hutchinson-Cockburn could afford to work at Clavier and Coldwell indefinitely thanks to his parents' hereditary wealth, hereditary contacts, and his own hereditary trust fund. In contrast, Yvonne's parents had told her she had but six weeks to acquire a paid job within the publishing house before she had to

'Good morning, Rupert,' said Yvonne in surprise, for it was only nine o'clock and Hutchinson-Cockburn usually arrived at around ten, long after the rest of the office staff, a peccadillo which (she had noted) drew no comment from Vansittart – who frequently didn't appear until eleven(ish) in the morning.

'Oh, er, yah, hi,' drawled Hutchinson-Cockburn, realising the office was occupied solely by the Black girl whose name he couldn't recall.

'You're in early.'

'Yah, well, mother said she'd pop me in as she had an early start, and I think she wanted to chat about things,' yawned

---

start searching elsewhere. And both offspring accepted their respective situations without murmur; Hutchinson-Cockburn because incestuous socio-economic nepotism is the fabric of his world, while Yvonne genuinely believes in the meritocracy and her own ability to fly up the ladder of success.

The office keys are a symbolic representation of this reality; Vansittart routinely hands them over to each unpaid volunteer* so they can come in early and scrub and sort the office for the arrival of the main staff, and yet Yvonne's fellow unpaid volunteer, the Old Etonian Oxbridge graduate and inheritor-in-waiting Rupert Hutchinson-Cockburn, is never expected to fulfil the menial duties which form the greater part of Yvonne's working hours. And Hutchinson-Cockburn has never once thought to ask why Yvonne is always in the office so early, or what she does there before his arrival.

*The only time Vansittart hesitated in handing the keys over was with Yvonne. He rationalised this away as being concerns about her age – even though she's not the youngest unpaid volunteer Vansittart has ever exploited.

Just the darkest skinned.

Hutchinson-Cockburn, giving the impression parents were a chore to be endured. He looked at his Black co-worker, wondering if she was going to make him a cup of tea, but she seemed to be more concerned – rather rudely in his opinion – with a large stack of books. 'What are you doing?' he asked, hoping the Black girl would take the hint about stopping whatever she was doing so she could get him a morning beverage.

'Just some research,' replied Yvonne, trying to casually pass off the three teetering book piles as an irrelevance, for she wished to appear cool in front of her near-contemporary.[27]

---

[27] Yvonne's desire to look cool is in fact a manifestation of a much darker psychological issue; deep down, she wants to *be* Hutchinson-Cockburn, for Hutchinson-Cockburn is white, wealthy, and has contacts. His way through life is clear of the hurdles Yvonne has already faced (ethnicity, gender, class, and a lack of considerable inherited wealth) and will continue to face throughout her life, and who wouldn't want to avoid the prejudice, discrimination, and hatred that accompanies your skin colour? After all, over a third of people from an ethnic minority have suffered from some form of racial assault, (verbal or physical, either against them directly or toward their property), and a third (again) have experienced racial discrimination within education and employment.
Black communities also suffer under a huge cultural weight regarding their perceived identities, both as individuals and as a group. Jackie Adedeji, for example, has observed how the crimes of Black individuals are seen/projected as being representative of the entire community, in a way that is rarely (if ever) done with white criminals and their respective societies, and thus individuality is a right denied to every Black individual.

Hutchinson-Cockburn looked suspiciously at the titles closest to him, feeling the Black girl was being less than forthcoming with the truth. The books included *Churchill, Winston Churchill, Winston Spencer Churchill, Churchill's War, Winston Churchill's War,* and *Winston Spencer Churchill's War.* 'Are those books on Churchill?' he demanded.

'Yes; I thought I'd see what was on the market already, given Michael was talking about doing a new biography.'

'Oh, yah, right, I see,' replied Hutchinson-Cockburn, grabbing the book from the Black girl's hands.[28]

But then, as noted in footnote #21, being white is often (i.e. pretty much always) defined as being the norm, and anything else is therefore automatically rendered as different/deviant. Many writers, including Bernardine Evaristo and Divya Kumar, mentioned how as youngsters they hoped and tried to be white, because white was acceptable, beautiful, successful and safe, while being Black … wasn't.
This, then, is why Yvonne wants to be like Hutchinson-Cockburn, though at this stage in her life she would find it difficult to articulate the above so thoroughly. To be white, posh and privileged is to have access not just to opportunities denied to others, but it is also to be accepted without question, without hesitation, and without suspicion. Hutchinson-Cockburn lives in a world designed for him, and others like him.
Yvonne doesn't.

[28] Hutchinson-Cockburn didn't see anything wrong in this; he was simply conforming to the unconscious values instilled in him by his family, class, and education, in which anything he wants is his for the taking, with no real consequences for his actions of any kind. And he isn't even aware there is anything to be aware about, for this is the way the world works – at least, for him and others like him. See also

'Richard Trumper's *Churchill the Brave*,' read Hutchinson-Cockburn before turning to the prologue. 'Ah, an excellent beginning!' he exclaimed, holding the book aloft as though handling a plastic skull in Shakespearean theatre, and declaiming the opening lines. '"This simple book is a biography, but it is a biography of one of our greatest men. As Thomas Carlyle noted, "the earthly pilgrimage of a man..."'

'"The earthly pilgrimage of a *man*"?' echoed Yvonne.

'Well, obviously, back in the day, *man* also encompassed *woman*,' smirked Hutchinson-Cockburn, amused by the idea of a woman doing anything noticeable enough to get into the history books. Not that he considered himself sexist in any way, of course, but it was a simple fact that almost all history was created by men, with women only entering the public sphere through womanly roles such as nursing, as seen with Florence Nightingale. True, there was the honourable exception of the Blessed St Margaret Thatcher, but she *acted* like a man, and in doing so saved the country from the lefties and their demands for better lives for the workers. 'Have you read Carlyle? Fascinating chap.'

'No, he didn't tend to pop up much at Tower Heights Academy,' deadpanned Yvonne.

'Ah, pity, pity,' murmured Hutchinson-Cockburn, who had never heard of Tower Heights and therefore assumed it was

---

Winston Churchill and his dodgy finances in footnote #79 as a further example.

some ghastly failing inner city comprehensive, a hypothesis bolstered by Yvonne's colour and unrefined accent. [29]

---

[29] Both Yvonne and Hutchinson-Cockburn are, of course, formed by their class and upbringing, resulting in two widely differing lives; the Yvonnes of the world must work to survive in a hereditary capitalist society, while the Ruperts need only pretend to work while waiting for the opportunities to be handed to them.

Though as noted above, one thing Yvonne and Hutchinson-Cockburn do have in common is the educational and social conditioning to accept convention rather than to question it.

But that's hereditary capitalism for you.

Chapter Five

In which we are introduced to the other members of the staff including the office manager, Felicity Armitage, who dislikes Yvonne but won't recognise the fact even to herself, (for to do so would call upon her to recognise certain prejudices within her character), Sarah Cooper, a young woman in possession of a sharp business brain but a credulous attitude toward everything else in life, and Helen Hughes, a woman who, upon reaching middle age, has found herself increasingly unable to give a fuck about almost anything except her cat.[30]

---

[30] Helen was one of three editors employed by Vansittart, and the best of the lot, hence she was the only one privileged with a full-time post in the office. She was also shrivelled by decades of dealing with awful manuscripts, appalling ideas, and nonsensical grammatical monstrosities which wandered across the page before running into a different sentence altogether on some other topic littered with superfluous redundant adjectives to definitively manifest superlative literary compositions.

Helen could have been the protagonist of the novel, for unlike Yvonne (who still believes the lies) Helen already knows she has been screwed by society. Unfortunately, the media rarely recognises the existence of middle-aged women, and so she is relegated – literally and literarily – to the sidelines.

Not that Helen exists as a fully drawn-out character anyway; she is instead just a mouthpiece whose entire raison d'etre is to make authorial points for me. Mind you, the cynical could claim that all the characters in this novel are little more than ciphers – but I'd argue any figure written down in a book becomes a cipher, given that 200-odd pages cannot hope to do justice to any human character; you'd

'Morning all,' called Sarah Cooper, the Rights and Contracts Manager for Clavier and Coldwell,[31] as she entered the office. 'Everyone have a good weekend?'

'My cat got scabies,' grunted Helen, entering behind Sarah and making the younger woman jump.

'Oh dear,' said Sarah, her mouth forming an "O" of sympathy and concern.

'And my husband broke his leg,' added Helen as a clear afterthought.

'Oh dear,' repeated Sarah. 'What did you do?'

'Took him to the vets,' replied Helen, slumping down at her desk with a rasping cough.[32]

---

probably need three times as much just to explore one psychological trait.

[31] Sarah was also the entirety of the rights and contracts team for Clavier and Coldwell, having accepted the prestigious title in return for rather lower renumeration than would be expected for such a role, a common business practice in the real world. This suited Vansittart enormously as he was saving money which could then be spent on other important areas of concern. Such as his own salary. And his bonuses. And his expenses.

[32] It was Helen who had the rasping cough rather than the desk – just in case you were wondering. Helen, to complete the thumbnail sketch of her thumbnail character, gave the impression she was surrounded by a haze of cigarette smoke even when she wasn't, an illusion created by her eighty-a-day voice and the permanent acrid miasma of stale smoke which permeated her entire frame. She tended to sit by herself in the office, as even other smokers found her tobacco addiction mildly horrifying.

'And your husband?' asked Sarah.

'What about him?' replied Helen with a look of blank confusion.

'Good morning,' said Felicity Armitage as she walked in, her gaze raking around the area in the hope of finding some job left undone by the Bla – *young* intern who Felicity distrusted *not* because of her colour but because she, Felicity, knew a troublemaker when she saw one.[33]

'Morning,' replied Yvonne in a careful tone of neutrality, knowing exactly what Felicity was doing in her searching

---

[33] In truth, Felicity did have an issue with Yvonne's ethnicity, but she could never admit this even to herself, and hence the explanation for her prejudice appears down here in the subconscious footnotes. Felicity's attitude toward Yvonne were not helped by her intense dislike of all the recent female interns used by the company, as she felt increasingly threatened by their youth and determination to succeed, and hence she views all other women in the office as potential rivals rather than as friends, colleagues, or support.

In this, Felicity was forgetting what she had been like at Yvonne's age, and she was also overlooking how each new generation of fresh hopefuls were willing to work harder, longer, and for less, in the desperate hope of getting ahead. Felicity's own drive and ambition to reach an eminent position had been derailed by marriage, children, and a husband who proudly supported his wife's career while assuming Felicity would also provide the traditional wifely duties of childcare, home care, and husband care.

Unfortunately, Felicity has imbibed deeply at the same well of gender traditionalism, and hence she finds herself being debilitated by years of performing the "double shift", leaving no space for personal reflection or growth.

Which is probably just as society wants it.

glance around the office. Yvonne also knew Felicity, having found no job to complain about, would then check the old Oxo tin on the shelf to ensure no money was missing from the kitty, after which she would tally the amount of tea, coffee, milk, and sugar against yesterday's quantities.[34]

Having verified the victuals, Felicity hung her jacket on the coat rack and sat down at her desk to check the letters deposited there by Yvonne, slitting through them quickly with a knife taken from her drawer. It was the third letter which caused a smirk of satisfaction to spread over her lips. 'I see we've had an invoice returned,' she exclaimed in a loud voice, drawing the attention of the office. 'It seems it wasn't filled in correctly. It's an order for the stationery cupboard.' Her gaze drifted around the office, as though she had no idea who had filled in the green chit. 'Er, who last put an order in? It's for some new reams of printing paper.'

You know who it was, you ancient crone, thought Yvonne, though she carefully kept her reply in its accustomed neutral tone. 'That was probably me.'

'Ah, I see,' replied Felicity, gazing down at the order as though she had expected nothing less of the Bla—*youngest* member of the staff. 'Well, I'm afraid, my dear, you have made a mistake in this; it's been sent back by the stationers.'

---

[34] "Racial microaggressions" are not words which appear in Felicity's vocabulary, alas.

'Really?' answered Yvonne, the neutrality in her tone breaking slightly. 'I filled it in the same way as all the previous slips.'

Felicity's upper lip trembled at the counterattack. 'Not quite, I fear, otherwise it wouldn't have been sent back, would it?'

Yvonne rose quietly before moving over to Felicity's desk, noting the tremor on the manager's face who clearly feared the Black woman was about to become violent. 'And where exactly is the mistake?'

'It, um, just here,' mumbled Felicity, cowed by the skin colour now standing in perilously close proximity.

Yvonne stepped to the stationery cupboard[35] and pulled out the file containing the relevant invoices before returning to Felicity's desk, opening the folder, and extracting a handful of carbon copies marked *Cartwright's Stationary Supplies*. 'That means this one hasn't been filled in correctly either,' said Yvonne, placing the relevant paperwork down. 'And neither has this one. Or this. Or this. Oh, and here's another. And all filled in the same way. The way I copied.'

---

[35] Located in Felicity's self-imposed power zone and containing the precious staples, staple gun, paper, paper clips, rubber bands, and all other symbols of Felicity's authority. She exercised this authority by grudgingly doling out each item in a manner which suggested she was undertaking a Herculean task for which she expected to receive no thanks whatsoever, allowing her to add a soupçon of martyrdom to the performance. Yvonne's blatant invasion of Felicity's cupboard exacerbated the older woman's feelings of white fragility tenfold.

'Ah, yes, well, I think more training is needed,' blustered Felicity.

'I've never had *any* training,' retorted Yvonne.[36] 'That's why I had to copy from the other forms. Has Cartwright's been in touch before about any orders? Let's see, the last one was done by Rupert.'

'Oh, yah, right,' drawled Rupert, glancing up from the Trumper biography he was now clearly posing over, with one hand resting contemplatively at his temples while the other held the book for all to see. 'I did have a phone call from Cartwright after I did an invoice to them.' He shrugged in genuine unconcern, for any mistakes he made were natural, trivial, and unremarkable.[37]

'And has anyone else had similar phone calls after sending off an order?' queried Yvonne, looking at the other two women; Sarah nodded, a smile of embarrassment spreading over her face, while Helen tried to reply,

---

[36] Had it been Vansittart claiming she had made the mistake, Yvonne would have been far more deferential – and she might even have taken the blame for something she hadn't done, conditioned as she was to be docile and compliant when dealing with the elite. And Vansittart was the English elite personified in his class, wealth, sex, and race – and also in being her employer. This, of course, is an important theme of this novel, hence the anachronistic presence of carbon copies which allows the scene to unfold in a way it probably never would if everyone was simply using the Internet to order the supplies.

[37] Hutchinson-Cockburn's class and background did not permit such things as embarrassment or imposter syndrome; see the research by Jerrim, et al, 2019.

developed instead another rasping cough, and cheerfully held up two thumbs of acknowledgement. 'There we go. They must have decided to do it by paper rather than phone, this time,' concluded Yvonne.

'Yes, well, clearly more training for everyone in basic office management,' muttered Felicity, looking in disfavour at the angry and opinionated Bla – *young* woman whom Felicity had unerringly identified as a potential troublemaker on the very first day they had met. Her eyes fell on the large pile of books on Yvonne's desk, prompting suspicion as to how one so Bla – one so *young* could have gathered so many artefacts of learning together. 'Are those company books?' she demanded, her eyes flying around the shelving in the room, checking for tell-tale gaps of guilt between volumes.

'No; I brought them in,' replied Yvonne, her voice hardening slightly at the implication in Felicity's expression before swallowing down her irritation, partly because she needed the work experience and partly because of her inculcated deference to authority.

'What have you brought them in for, Yvonne?' asked Helen.

'I just wanted to see what was out there,' replied Yvonne, glossing over her hopes of impressing Vansittart for fear of being ridiculed by office society.

'This is excellent stuff, you know; listen to this!' interrupted Hutchinson-Cockburn, eager to put himself at the centre of attention where it so rightfully belonged, for he had the qualities (breeding and schooling) to lead while others followed.[38]

'Listen to what?' asked Sarah.

'*Churchill the Brave*, by Richard Trumper,' muttered Yvonne in irritation at having her book (and thunder) appropriated by Hutchinson-Cockburn.

'Oh, gawd, no,' sniggered Helen. 'I've had enough of him in this job.'

Hutchinson-Cockburn stared, but being unable to comprehend the idea of anyone being uninterested in a subject he was holding forth upon, he filtered Helen's comment out of existence and returned to the biography, ready to selflessly inform, educate and to entertain the gaggle of females gazing at him. 'This is top-notch stuff; Listen! "To do full justice to a great man, we need first to examine his era."'

'No, really?' rasped Helen in mock amazement, something Hutchinson-Cockburn missed as he was too absorbed in finding the next suitable section for his one-man dramatic recital.

'"Churchill was the grandson of a duke,"' began Hutchinson-Cockburn with the solemn dignity needed when reading about Churchill before being interrupted.

'Yes; Churchill was born into wealth and privilege,' said Helen in a scathing tone, much to Yvonne's discomfort, for

---

[38] A common enough view, it seems, amongst Oxford Tories. See Kuper, S, 2019.

the younger woman was still firmly bound upon the altar of Churchillian worship. 'I wonder how that affected his life? You know, having access to all the opportunities denied to the lower orders?'[39]

'"Winston was a rebel at school …"' continued Hutchinson-Cockburn before being stopped again.

'Hang on; when did he suddenly become "Winston" in this biography?' grumbled Helen, her editor's senses tingling.

'Well, it was his name,' sighed Hutchinson-Cockburn at the rude interruption to both Churchill and himself.

'Shouldn't a biographer be impartial?' queried Helen, sarcastically. 'I mean, if Trumper is going round calling his subject by the familiar name of "Winston", then it seems there's no impartiality at all.'

'Ah, well, no, you see,' replied Hutchinson-Cockburn, speaking with considerable authority on a subject about which he knew nothing.[40] 'The biographer will have a relationship with his subject, and it's quite in keeping when talking about such a great man as Churchill that occasionally, you know, on and off, you may well slip and call him by his first name, in a familiar gesture of respect, because, you feel you know the person well from your

---

[39] An essential aspect of this novel; Churchill was allowed – and enabled – to be Churchill by both his privilege and his peers. See also chapter thirteen, and most of the rest of the book.

[40] Something students learn at Oxford, apparently. Again, see Kuper, S, 2019.

research. *Abbati, medico, patrono que intima pande,*' he added, rather grandly.[41]

'"Conceal not the truth from thy physician and lawyer?"' replied Helen, after taking a moment to mentally translate the words. 'What's that got to do with anything?'

'"Winston was a rebel at school,"' repeated Hutchinson-Cockburn, rather heavily, demonstrating he was not to be interrupted by any prattling objections by anyone, but especially by a woman unexpectedly revealed to be almost his equal in intelligence, '"for which reason he found himself at Sandhurst."'

'Sandhurst?' mumbled Yvonne, almost intimidated beyond speech by Hutchinson-Cockburn's accent, familiarity with Latin, and social breeding.[42]

---

[41] Latin is a useful way of silencing both the plebs and awkward questions. It is therefore used quite a lot by certain types of blue-blooded parasites. See Bull, 2017, and Simpson, 2023, for more.

[42] It's interesting Yvonne should feel this yet not be able to analyse where the reaction originated – i.e. a lifetime of sociological brainwashing imposed from the cradle onward, stamping a code of deference and diffidence on the lower orders in which they know their place: "We never ask for nuffink, guvnor, because although we're poor we're proud, got blimey, stone the crows, I saw the king once he was a luvvery man, waved at us and everyfink he did as he went past in 'is 'orse an' carriage, gor blimey apples and pears shine your shoes, sir?" You see why the ruling elite like to emphasise tradition (and hence traditional beliefs and behaviours) as being so important in everyone's lives?

'Where posh people learn how to give orders in the military,' explained Helen. 'As opposed to Eton and Oxbridge, where posh people learn how to give orders in society.'

'Sandhurst is simply a military academy for officers,' replied Hutchinson-Cockburn, glaring at Yvonne as he was too nervous to direct the expression toward Helen.

'Oh, right,' mumbled Yvonne, her face hot with embarrassment. 'I didn't know.'

Hutchinson-Cockburn smirked at Yvonne's admission of ignorance, knowing he could teach her a thing or two on such matters. And in other areas besides. His eyes roved over her dark skin as he contemplated the tricks she could perform in bed. Because, you know, he'd heard stories ...[43]

---

[43] A prime example of race fetishization. And why does race fetishization still exist today? Because it's part of the Establishment and so the media promotes it, thus making its willing readers and viewers (of all classes) think and react in established, white, heteronormative ways. And this is just one example of media orthodoxy; now expand the basic methodology toward class, wealth, immigration etc, and see what sort of society you get. Hint; it's probably the one you live in. See also footnote #85 on the Jezebel for more.

Chapter Five (a)[44]

With footnotes galore, as there is a fair bit to unpick here …

'To continue,' declaimed Hutchinson-Cockburn, shifting back from personal priapic speculation to the public oratorical stance taught by the Oxford debating clubs he had attended during his undergraduate years. '"In 1895, Young Winston was commissioned for the Fourth Hussars."'

'He got a commission?' squeaked Sarah, admiringly.

'The wealthy just bought them, in those days,' said Helen, checking her phone for any message from the vet concerning her cat, but the only unread text came from her husband, which she dismissed with a grunt. 'Yet more jobs for the boys. Or commissions for the boys, in this case. No special ability required.'

---

[44] Having moved yet more material around via cut and paste, I couldn't be bothered to renumber every sodding chapter again, hence the alphabetical labelling. Plus, after twenty-odd years of trying to make it as an author with nothing to show except a handful of published short stories barely read by anyone, innumerable digitally published novels and novellas ditto, two traditionally published novels which faired even worse, and triple figure rejections, I've now lost all enthusiasm for the PhD project and any form of creative writing.

'This is Winston Churchill you're talking about,' sniffed Felicity, using the name as both rebuke and a demand for greater respect.[45]

'And he was a self-educated man,' interrupted Hutchinson-Cockburn. 'Listen to this! "Whilst in India, he read widely of all the great Western philosophers, as well as immersing himself in innumerable accounts of parliamentary debates."'

'There, you see?' demanded Felicity in acidic triumph.

'See what?' rasped Helen in exasperation. 'You mean the incredible snobbery and classism on display?'

'But his learning!' insisted Felicity, though with a less strident tone than she used against Yvonne, for Helen's position commanded respect, as did her learning, experience, and no-nonsense attitude.

'Churchill was the elitist son of an elitist aristocrat, educated in the elitist way in various elitist establishments,' replied Helen. 'His supposed self-learning was him continuing in his own time what his school had started

---

[45] Please note the significance of this.[*] The staff at Clavier and Coldwell represent a macrocosm of society, meaning their comments and beliefs can be mapped outward onto the wider community. Felicity's attempt to use the name "Churchill" as a way of maintaining order and suppressing alternative views in the office is *exactly* the same methodology employed by the Establishment (via the media, education etc) to suppress the voices of anyone considered a danger to their system of insular privilege.

[*] If you feel the author blatantly pointing out what he's doing lacks nuance or sophistication, then please consider what a meta-novel is.

beforehand. What would be surprising is if he picked up books like *The Communist Manifesto* for any reason other than his own benefit. And he wanted a career in parliament – just like his father – so of course he read up on parliamentary matters.'

'That's a shocking thing to say,' muttered Felicity, shifting uneasily in her seat. She would have said more but her stomach was beginning to curdle, and she rather suspected the milk on her breakfast cereal had been on the turn. And being shouted at by her teenage son had unsettled her, as had her husband's implied criticism of her work outfit. She glared at an email containing an unsolicited romance submission and brusquely rejected it with a copy and paste message. She wasn't a fan of the romance genre at the best of times, and this morning was not the best of times, digestively speaking.[46]

'You're saying Churchill was formed by his background?' asked Yvonne, slowly, as a fresh way of contemplating the world began flowering in her mind.

'Yup,' nodded Helen. 'And the warping of any individual into a particular set of ideologies should be a matter for deep discussion and analysis, but instead it just becomes an unquestioning acceptance of the status quo.'

---

[46] This is known as Chekhov's gag, (after Chekhov's gun), in which a joke you thought was done reappears later in the story. It therefore has nothing to do with the character from *Star Trek*, but instead draws on the oft-repeated advice from writer Anton Chekhov.

'"Winston also discovered within himself a felicity for words,"' continued Hutchinson-Cockburn, ignoring Helen's points to instead wonder at the sheer rudeness of those interrupting him, '"and he was soon in demand as a writer of books and articles."'

'Because everyone just stumbles over the fact they can make money from writing,' sniggered Helen. 'I mean, it's not like anyone common has to keep on submitting and being rejected time and again – oh, wait, it is *exactly* like that. But not for old Winston. Because he had contacts.'

'He had talent!' snapped Hutchinson-Cockburn.

'He had connections and time to write,' retorted Helen. 'How many rejections did we send out last week?'

'Um, I don't know,' replied Yvonne, feeling a little apprehensive at Helen's ongoing blasphemy against the Great Man, and hence demonstrating how effectively the worm of servility was munching through the apple of her existence.

'Fifty-six. And how many of those will ever get anywhere with another publisher? Probably none. Regardless of talent. You need connections in this business.'

Hutchinson-Cockburn's lips thinned at the socialist criticism of the Hero of the Country, but rather than risk engaging Helen in debate he instead raised his voice and continued to read from the script. '"It was at this time Winston decided he would enter parliament."'

'Yes, because anyone can suddenly decide to enter parliament,' gurgled Helen. 'Well, you do if you're rich and already part of the social elite. Everyone else, however, can take a running jump. I wonder if that crucial aspect of English society gets a mention?'

'Surely not?' protested Sarah, her eyes widening, for though she carried a sophisticated and devious set of values into any argument concerning contracts with authors and agents,[47] she was extremely gullible in many other areas of life. 'Surely Churchill must have been special, to decide to go into politics and to succeed?'

'He was just following in daddy's footsteps,' replied Helen. 'Do you think *you* could just walk into a newspaper or magazine and get commissioned, and then walk into a parliamentary seat without any social contacts? And without pay? Members of Parliament didn't get paid back in those days, making it a sport only for the wealthy. And it still is today, even though the parasites now pay themselves a massive wage to screw us all over.'

'Yes, I mean, no, but Churchill was different, wasn't he?' replied Sarah.

'He certainly was,' said Hutchinson-Cockburn, indignantly. 'Listen to this! "Churchill's talent was recognised straight away and he found himself the president of the Board of Trade, wherein he launched a series of measures to help the

---

[47] Sarah's way with a contract is just another manifestation of capitalist dogma (that of screwing people legally as well as financially, morally etc) and is hardly admirable.

working man – all to be paid for by the wealthy in the form
of higher taxation." What do you think about that, eh?'[48]

---

[48] The answer here is "not much." It's instructive to consider Churchill's
attitudes as reported by his contemporary, Virginia Cowles, who
published her biography on him (*Winston Churchill: the Era and the
Man*) in 1953, back when class-hatred could be presented far more
explicitly than any journalist or politician would dare do today. Both
she and Churchill thoroughly disapproved of the working man
demanding greater equality, taking instead the view that the poor
should make their own way up the ladder before being given any social
or financial benefits.

In contrast, she thoroughly approved of Churchill gaining access to
power simply because of his birth. (For Cowles and Churchill alike,
breeding was on an equal footing with the laws of physics, with both
being built into the very fabric of the universe). The arrogance,
unfairness, and malicious snobbery emanating from Churchill and
Cowles drips off the page. And this, alas, has changed very little in
recent times, with various populist Establishment politicians calling
blue collar workers feckless criminal drunks, while Northerners were
labelled dirty and toothless, and those outside the privately educated
elite were described as potted plants.

Perhaps the best way of summing up this footnote is to point out that
although Churchill campaigned in his earlier days for greater rights for
the workers, he never once fought to change the Establishment itself in
any fundamental way. And this, really, is the cornerstone of this book;
politicians and journalists may publicly squawk about equality for all,
but they are all owned, body and soul, by capitalist/Establishment
dogma, meaning none of them will ever make any genuine attempt to
offer an alternative to those who don't want to be corporate serfs for
all their days.

And it probably wouldn't even occur to them to try.

Chapter Five (b)

With ever increasing footnotes, as there is yet more to analyse in this chapter...

For an answer, Helen delved into Yvonne's stack,[49] withdrew Maurice McGrory's *Churchill Uncovered,* and flicked it open with one practiced, nicotine-stained finger. 'It's in here somewhere ... oh yes, here we are: "Churchill had little interest in people's inalienable rights. Instead, he saw his role as a form of paternal patriarch graciously bestowing favours". What do *you* think of that?'[50]

---

[49] Not a euphemism. This isn't a *Carry On* film.

[50] Again, the quoted text doesn't exist, though it has been adapted from a genuine Churchillian biography. But while we're looking at Churchill's attitudes toward the workers, consider this; during the General Strike of 1926, Churchill created a new paper (the British Gazette) for propaganda purposes, and used it to label the workers as the enemy while demanding their unconditional surrender.
The workers arraigned by Churchill? Coal miners, who were seeing their wages decrease while their hours were lengthened, and all for a job both dangerous and filthy. It seems Churchill failed to see, or failed to care, that he was dealing with his fellow men; men who were suffering under appalling living and working conditions.
But then, it seems to be entirely in keeping that Churchill (as the Establishment) viewed the workers as something expendable, and less than human. A resource to be used and abused. Something that could (and should) be policed, brutalised, and shot at.
No wonder the workers lost.

'And what exactly is wrong?' demanded Hutchinson-Cockburn.

'What's wrong with a patronising elitist man conferring basic human rights on the population as though he's personally doing them a favour?' asked Helen rhetorically as she spun the volume back onto Yvonne's small desk, almost dislodging the three piles of books on top.

'How did you know about that quote?' asked Yvonne.[51]

'I've been in this ghastly business for over twenty years, and I've worked on over a dozen Churchill biographies,' replied Helen, puffing on a well-chewed pencil in the absence of any real cigarettes. 'You soon get to know the game, believe me. It's played by the same people, in the same way, and with the same results.'

'This is history!' exclaimed Hutchinson-Cockburn in outrage at the Cultural Marxist agenda[52] being forced on

---

[51] What actually happened here is that Yvonne yelped in alarm at seeing the ordered piles of the Establishment being scattered by independent thought, and unconsciously flung herself across the books to keep them safe, before asking of Helen; 'How did you know about that quote?' Note the discrepancy between what the Establishment narrative on the page is telling you and what's happening down here in the footnotes. And then think about how this applies to the media in the real world.

[52] Cultural Marxism is a handy catchall term of abuse for those on the political right against anything they don't like, including (but not limited to) equal rights, egalitarianism, LGBQT issues and so on. Its roots lie in the Nazi belief in Cultural Bolshevism, and as such, the stench of anti-Semitism is never far away from the term.

him. He swiftly plunged back into the Trumper biography, as much for the sense of stability it gave him as for any facts therein. '"It is today held to be true by military analysts that Churchill's Dardanelles strategy might have ended the war early, had it worked". See? Military analysts agree!'

'No, really?' sneered Helen. 'A military strategy could have defeated the enemy if only it had worked? Amazing analysis! It's like saying I would have been a great footballer if only I could pass, dribble, and score at the highest level.'

'But it was all down to external factors beyond Churchill's control,' blustered Hutchinson-Cockburn. 'It was all down to "weak military types" – but it was Churchill who paid the price. Listen! Churchill "had to take the blame as he was so closely identified with the operation." He took the blame![53] His career was derailed, and everyone thought it was the end of him!'[54]

'It was certainly the end of the two hundred and fifty thousand Allied soldiers killed in the campaign,' rasped Helen. 'A quarter of a million slaughtered men, their hopes

---

[53] In fact, Churchill tried to shift the blame to the First Sea Lord, John Fisher. Yvonne had this information at her fingertips in one of her books but social conformity, coupled with the need to ingratiate herself with authority, kept her quietly compliant.

[54] It's certainly difficult to imagine how a commoner would have been able to survive such a disaster, but this wasn't an issue for Churchill, a card-carrying member of the wealthy-titled-white-male-Establishment-elite. It's almost as though the law and/or consequences exist only for the poor, and not for anyone else ...

and dreams torn apart by Churchill's political decisions. But yes, you worry about the effect on his career; that's the real tragedy here, isn't it?'

'And look at how patriotically he reacted,' replied Hutchinson-Cockburn, again ignoring the inconvenient point. 'Joining the army and going to France to defend his country!'

'Churchill already knew he'd need a way out of the political disaster – that's the political disaster, not the humanitarian disaster – and he contacted an old friend, Sir John French, who obtained him a command in the army,' said Helen. 'And note he didn't go out as a regular Tommy; he made damn sure his privileges were still working for him.'

'Nonetheless, he did it,' snapped Hutchinson-Cockburn. 'He went out and served on the front and you can't deny his bravery; "Churchill joined his men in the trenches." There, see! He was in the thick of it!'

'He was posted from his first relatively quiet command to a second quiet command South of Ypres,' said Helen with a deep sigh of exasperation. 'But in any case, Churchill was barely there as he kept popping back to London to revive his political career. Eventually, his corps commander refused him any further leave. And then a few months later, Churchill was given the opportunity to resign his command and return to civilian life, on the proviso he never again applied for a commission. Which he did, returning to London to start again in politics. Hardly the same experience as the common soldiers in the trenches, was it?'

'But Trumper makes it seem like Churchill was out there for ages,' said Yvonne in shock. 'Are you saying the book isn't true?'

'I'm saying it's nothing but a series of broad-brush statements which assumes the reader will be compliant enough to accept rather than to question.'

'This is scholarship!' protested Hutchinson-Cockburn.

'But Helen's just told us things which aren't in the Trumper book!' exclaimed Yvonne. 'I mean; can we believe him if he misses out all that?'

'I'm sure it's the truth,' snorted Felicity. 'It wouldn't be published, otherwise.'

'Stating Churchill went out to the front is true,' replied Helen, 'but it isn't honest or accurate. It's omitting the full details.'[55]

'But his bravery!' insisted Hutchinson-Cockburn.

'Churchill thought he was anointed by Destiny to do great things, so running off to battle when you honestly think you have divine protection is not bravery; its narcissism verging on mental illness. But that's the posh wealthy bastard classes for you.'[56]

---

[55] Indeed. And the entire point of this novel is to plead for honesty and integrity in all forms of media, for without honesty and integrity, society will never be able to understand itself and thus grow into something better. Idolising Churchill, and turning him into something he never was, is actively harmful and dishonest. And yet the Establishment does it. Repeatedly.

[56] In case the reader is wondering at the sarcastic humour coming through, I would like to point out that when you are born with nothing

and have no real opportunities, then humour is all you have left. You can either laugh, or you can go under. They may have taken our freedom and chances, but they'll never take our sense of humour! Except if the wealthy elite do see us laughing, they'll use this as a justification for pouring more economic scorn and cultural misery upon us in the belief we can't be having it too bad if we're going around sniggering at everything. So, in fact, they win again.

Which is the entire point of this novel.

But to resume; the purpose of this book's heavy-handed humour is purely satirical, for satire is (technically) meant to affect some sort of reform on society. Viewed in this light, the reader may immediately think of Charles Dickens, who frequently turned to satire to highlight injustice. *Bleak House*, for example, focuses on how those who have power are entirely separated from the cares and concerns of everyday people struggling to survive. (Though this author believes our own ruling elite is not merely separate, but is in fact actively cruel in its attitudes toward the most vulnerable in society).

However, it should also be noted that Dickens was a massive racist twat. He defended the conduct of John Eyre, the Governor of Jamaica, who ground the (Black) poor even further into poverty via legal brutality and oppression, prompting an uprising, which resulted in Eyre killing over 400 Black people, flogging 600, and burning down 1000 houses. And *Bleak House* features Mrs Jellby, a woman who works tirelessly for Africa while being oblivious to problems in her own country – a favoured trope of the far right, who like to bang on about how foreign aid should be scrapped as "we need to look after our own first" while (of course) doing absolutely fuck all about looking after anyone except themselves. So, while Dickens did agitate for social reform, it was only on behalf of those he saw as the deserving poor. If Dickens were alive today, he'd be writing for the Daily Crier.

Turning to modern satirists, one of the most successful must be Terry Pratchett, whose Discworld series explored (amongst many other things) issues concerning gender conformity and trans rights, albeit filtered through the prism of the Discworld's dwarf community. The dwarves are initially presented as standard fantasy fare; shorter than humans, bearded, with iron helmets, large axes, bad tempers, and all identify as male. However, as more dwarves move into the city, new ways of living/existing are revealed to those dissatisfied with their lives, as seen in the character Cheery Littlebottom, introduced in *Feet of Clay*, who "comes out" as a woman.

The reaction from the dwarf community – horror and disgust – demonstrates the folly and hubris of human society, though humour is never far away as one dwarf, once the dominant censorious social group has moved away, expresses his(?) liking of Cheery's ankles, while another asks shyly if she(?) can try Cheery's lipstick. Pratchett therefore uses Cheery's journey to demonstrate how bigotry affects everyone in society by limiting choices, awareness, empathy, and ultimately personal freedom.

Gentle chiding is hence used to make humans more humane, which links directly to the satirical intent of the ancient Roman poet Horace, who saw the exemplary satirist as a man upset about folly, but who laughs rather than rages. Pratchett allows his laudable characters (Cheery, Vimes, Magrat) to grow and mature, unlike the small-minded (such as Lord Rust) who are forever trapped in their small, insular bigotry.

In contrast to Pratchett's progressive humanism, however, is Evelyn Waugh's sneering Elitism. And racism. Huge amounts of racism. A perfect example can be seen in *Scoop*, (1938), in which a mis-identified journalist, William Boot, must visit the fictional Ishmaelian embassy for a visa to visit the African country. The unnamed Ishmaelian ambassador is portrayed as an inherently mendacious character who literally foams at the mouth as he appropriates the work and achievements of others on behalf of Black people – presumably because he (and every other Black person) has no genuine accomplishment of their own to brag about.

But then, in Waugh's world, Black is synonymous with savagery; the Ishmaelians as a people are presented as naturally cannibalistic, and too lazy (or stupid) to better their society, while the country itself lacks any coded descriptor of civilisation. And the final sovereign nail hammered into the coffin of Establishment superiority/hatred comes with the revelation that the country is a republic – a further hint of the degeneracy of the place as it could have chosen to be a 'proper' monarchy, with a legitimacy derived (as with all monarchies) from its own existence.

Waugh, then, appears fundamentally opposed to any idea of Black people being worthy of respect, and they are encoded from first to last as untrustworthy, inferior, and dangerous, unlike the white English who are merely untrustworthy in journalism and genially incompetent elsewhere. The blunt racist humour employed against Black people is in sharp contrast to Waugh's light, ironic detachment toward his bumbling white characters such as the press baron Lord Cropper, who believes himself to be a visionary when he is but a fool, or Lord Cropper's editor, who selects the wrong William Boot from the staff list to be a war correspondent, while the war correspondents themselves are shown to be amusingly fraudulent in their reporting.

At no point does Waugh seriously challenge these characters, or by extension the Establishment and its systems; instead, he merely teases the world that created him, with incompetence, corruption, and dishonesty all ultimately passed off as being little more than peccadilloes, and so the Establishment is preserved, unharmed and unchanged by the book's end.

This may explain why Waugh remains perennially popular with the elite, for he posits human nature will never change, which logically dictates human society will likewise never change, leading to the comforting conclusion (at least for the Establishment) that their lives and privilege will remain unaltered forever.

We shall finish this footnote on literary satire with a real-world occurrence of the same; a cultural commentator once claimed Waugh himself is the true victim – not of his insular, prejudiced upbringing or his own insular, prejudiced character, but of Woke society. Luxuriating in his role of Establishment victimhood, the commentator went on to bemoan the "fact" that Waugh's social pedigree would prevent him being published today – though how the critic came to this conclusion, given the actual statistics on the publishing industry show 94% of UK

---

authors are white, while the gatekeepers of the creative industries are predominantly white middle class and higher, was never explained.
And yet the point was made in all seriousness.
And was probably agreed with by most of his slack-jawed readers ...

Chapter Five (c)

And a slight easing of the footnotes. Almost.

Hutchinson-Cockburn placed the book back onto Yvonne's desk[57] with a snort of well-bred disdain, sparing him the need to articulate a proper response, before sulkily sitting down at his desk and burying himself in his blank computer screen, which he hastily turned on as Vansittart breezed into the office.

Vansittart checked his watch as he entered, seeing he was right on time for his early morning 11 o'clock (ish) start.[58] His plan was to check his emails and post, browse a spreadsheet or two, and then head off to lunch with an agent who was pitching some new comedy writer as the next PG Wodehouse. Vansittart wasn't really in the market for humour, but neither was he averse to spending a few

---

[57] Compare this carefully controlled action with Helen's almost identical move a while ago; Hutchinson-Cockburn's attitudes preserve the Establishment piles on Yvonne's desk, while Helen's learning threatens to scatter them, with only Yvonne's servile reaction saving the whole lot from toppling over. Symbolism, people!

[58] This shows the reader a solid hour has passed by during the above discussion. However, it should be observed that time in fiction can be a problematic area; would the events depicted really have taken an hour?

hours at the Chummo Club before returning home. Especially as the agent would be paying.

'Good morning, Michael,' purred Felicity. 'How was the meeting?' She didn't ask how the meeting had gone as this could imply doubt on Vansittart's ability to handle the occasion; instead, Felicity let the unspoken assumptions of Vansittart's capability twine through her opening question like a cat's tail winding around a pair of human legs.

'Very good indeed,' beamed Vansittart, cheerfully oblivious to Felicity's coded message. 'I think we ought to get the submission guidelines out today for the biography, to show we're on the ball.' His eyes fell on the pile of biographies on Yvonne's desk. 'Good lord; what have you got there?'

'We've been looking at what's already on the market,' replied Hutchinson-Cockburn before Yvonne could even open her mouth.

'Excellent!' beamed Vansittart at Hutchinson-Cockburn. 'What have you started with?'

'Trumper's *Churchill the Brave.*'

'Hm; not sure I recall it,' said Vansittart, though he carried no doubt the book would be a splendid paean to the Great Man.

'A splendid work,' simpered Hutchinson-Cockburn, echoing Vansittart's thoughts.

Jesus wept! thought Yvonne, annoyed at both Hutchinson-Cockburn for taking credit which wasn't his, and at

Vansittart for accepting Hutchinson-Cockburn's annexing of her books and research.[59]

'Jesus wept!' exclaimed Yvonne out loud as she flipped through a few pages of the Trumper biography and saw a truly upsetting comment.

'What's up?' asked Helen,

'"Churchill considered black people to be a secondary race."' Yvonne stared round the office and was met by sympathy from Helen, bewilderment from Sarah, and carefully posed neutral expressions from her remaining three colleagues.

'It was the era,' muttered Hutchinson-Cockburn. 'You can't judge Churchill by modern standards. You have to look at the society he was in at the time.'[60]

---

[59] In Vansittart's world, the mound of books could only be related to the Oxbridge educated Hutchinson-Cockburn – even though they are clearly on Yvone's desk. See also footnote #28 on Hutchinson-Cockburn's Establishment assumptions.

[60] Michel de Montaigne, in his essays printed from 1580 to 1595, pointed out the descriptors of cannibals and barbarians by supposedly civilised people is little more than cultural superiority coupled with ignorance, and "we" are no better – and indeed may be rather worse – than "them".
Samuel Sewall was busy decrying slavery in 1700.
And the UK Communist Party had an anti-racist agenda in the 1920s. These examples do seem to knock a bit of a hole in the "you can't judge Churchill by today's standards" argument; antiracism didn't pop into existence last Wednesday. But also, if Churchill was such a Great Man, why was he a scuzzy racist at all? Surely Great Men should be able to see through the veil of standardised cultural assumptions and behold

'I notice Trumper doesn't judge him at all,' replied Yvonne, her anger momentarily lifting the brain fog of deference and giving her the bravery to speak. 'He seems to pass it off as a minor issue, scarcely worth mentioning.'

'Maybe Trumper is rather too forgiving of Churchill's racism,' interrupted Vansittart, deciding his kind yet firm opinion was needed to reassure[61] Yvonne. 'But let's look at the publication date. It's probably from the fifties, before everyone got so sensitive.'

'It was published in 1985,' deadpanned Yvonne, noting the "sensitive" comment.

'Ah, yes, well,' squirmed Vansittart. 'Still; things are different now. And the art of the biography has moved on. The readers can make up their own minds.'

'And this is serious scholarship,' interrupted Hutchinson-Cockburn, disliking the amount of attention the Bla – the fema – the *other* person was getting from Vansittart.

'Surely any genuine scholarship involves sifting material to try and find the truth rather than accepting the standard narrative of the status quo and then obediently writing it up?' pointed out Helen.

'An excellent point; we must make sure our biography will be innovative, and will stand out from the madding crowd,' announced Vansittart, throwing in the literary reference

the truth beyond? How therefore could he get this so wrong? Could it be he was just a bog-standard man, riddled with all the flaws of his era?

[61] By which Vansittart really meant "silence".

with ease. He had originally started dropping such allusions to impress people with his learning, but now, thirty years later, it was just habit.

'And what exactly should we put in the submission call?' asked Helen.

'Oh, just put the usual stuff up,' replied Vansittart with an airy wave of the hand as he walked through to his own office. 'You know the drill.'

Chapter Six

The call to publishing!

And a footnote deconstructing the call.

Clavier and Coldwell are delighted to put out a call for a new and vibrant biography on the life of our greatest ever leader – Winston Churchill!

For all non-fiction, please send:

- *A synopsis (no more than one page) telling us why your book is different to all the rest, complete with the unique selling point. Please use bullet points rather than prose for this.*
- *The word count and delivery date.*
- *Your relevant qualifications.*
- *The most recently published books you have read on the topic, (please give all details including author, date, publisher, sales figures etc), and tell us how your manuscript fits within these latest releases and how you will build upon the research and arguments made by your peers.*
- *The expected readership demographic.*
- *Your previously published books and articles on the topic.*
- *Your social media presence and the number of people following you.*

- *Any organisations where your book can be advertised, with costings.*
- *The first three chapters, fully edited and ready for publication, with referencing.*

To improve your chances of success, we strongly advise you to obtain some of our previous titles so you can see the type of work we publish – and the quality we strive for. And before submission, please consider:

How familiar are you with our publishing list, and how confident do you feel about your work fitting our requirements?

How confident are you in working with us to make your book a success?

Do you have the time to promote your work thoroughly and widely?

Are you prepared to work with us and our partners in the trade to promote the book to the public?[62]

---

[62] The above is an amalgamation of varying submission calls from genuine publishers. Depressingly elitist, isn't it? After all, which demographic is the most likely to have time to write? Who has the time to research? Who has the spare money to purchase several previous titles? Who has the time and money to promote their books by traveling from one venue to another, staying over at innumerable hotels as and when required, as well as posting online at any given time of the day? The answer? Mostly the privileged.
Welcome to the corporate world of publishing.
Enjoy trying to get in without wealth or contacts.

Chapter Seven

Social media reacts to the new call for submissions.

63

Mahad Korhonen: That's all we need; yet another biography about a racist warmonger.

Hatim Sethwi: Yeah. Shelves are already full of Churchill. What else is there to say about him??

Mahad Korhonen: Maybe the truth about his racism?

Rich The Smith: LOL! That would be a surprise.

Gabrielleinspires: Why can't we have more books on people like Rosa Parks?

Thedoctorsdog: I like the bit about "our greatest ever leader" and "how your manuscript fits within these latest releases". Shows they've already made their minds up!

Rich The Smith: Rosa really inspires people!

Washingline387: Yeah, nothing like a call for new books which are just like all the other old books, is there?

Gabrielleinspires: Bet some rich white guy gets the job and

---

63 If you think the footnote number for this footnote is placed in an unusual position on the main page above, you would be correct. But then, the whole point of this book is that it's a constructed facade which invites the reader to consider the fact the book is a constructed facade, and to further consider how all other books, fiction and non-fiction alike, are also constructed facades. So please apply this awareness of fakery to all media relating to Churchill.
And any other subject, for that matter.

gives us another whitewash.[64]

Patriotman: Cant beleive im reading this lefty hate on our greatest prim minster.

Leftybaiter: Yeah, we'd all be speaking German now if not for Winston!

Mahad Korhonen: "Greatest Prime Minister?" Then why did the public vote him out straight after the war?

Leftybaiter: And then voted him straight back in again after! That don't fit your narrative does it?

Mahad Korhonen: Voted in by the first past the post system. Labour increased its voting share but lost in a corrupt electoral system.

MaureenFreebody: Churchill voted against the NHS several times. He hated the idea.

Taratime: Really? I didn't know that about him!

Rich The Smith: We just keep on being told how great he was and how he won the war! Nothing else matters to the Right.

RobynwithaY: I think the Russians and Americans would disagree with Churchill winning the war!

Patriotman The Russians are commies!

RobynwithaY: What's that got to do with anything?

Mahad Korhonen: It's just whataboutery.

MaureenFreebody: Churchill thought the NHS was a "first step to turn Britain into a National Socialist economy." He

---

[64] A reasonable suspicion, which turns out to be 100% correct.

honestly viewed the NHS – the actual NHS – as a precursor to Nazism!

Britbadboy1939: So much for the tolerant left!

Englandalways: He saved us from the fascists!

Mahad Korhonen: And never forget he was instrumental in the murder of millions of Bengals, and he hated the Arabs as well.

Gabrielleinspires: Churchill hated anyone who was dark skinned.

AttackHelicopter279: No one is saying Churchill was perfect, but he saved us from the Nazis. He was an inspiration.

Mahad Korhonen: Churchill had no problem with fascism. He only eventually fought Germany when they threatened Brit interests. Morality had nothing to do with his decisions.

Africangirl: And even now we still have to explain how Churchill was an imperialist who hated foreigners.

Ukisbest: we had a empire until you lefty scum bought it down!

Britbadboy1939: The left are the new nazis now!

Englandalways: Yeah, it was the National SOCIALIST movement!

Britbadboy1939: Immigratns are cancer!

Cornwallenglander: He stood up to the fascists and nazis!!![65]

---

[65] Even this simple belief – Churchill was anti-fascist and anti-Nazi – is not as simple as popular perception would have it, as traitors and Nazi collaborators from Churchill's own class often faced no real punishment for their behaviour, as detailed in Tim Tate's excellent

Truepatriot: Wed all be speaking German if it wasnt for him!

Georgepatriot: Wed all be speaking German if it wasnt for him!

Englishpatriot: Wed all be speaking German if it wasnt for him!

Redwhitebluepatriot: Wed all be speaking German if it wasnt for him!

---

book *Hitler's British Traitors*, (from which this section is drawn). William Forbes-Sempill, for example, a member of the House of Lords, spied on behalf of Japan from the 1920s right up to the Second World War. Churchill sprang into action and sacked him. To which Forbes-Sempill protested. Churchill sprang into action and backtracked, suggesting he only ever meant Forbes-Sempill should be given another role elsewhere in the Admiralty. Eventually, Forbes-Sempill faced the ultimate sanction for any posh titled bloke who has undoubtedly committed treason; he was told to resign or be sacked. He resigned. And lived the rest of his life a free man.

Similarly, Hastings William Sackville Russell, (or Lord Tavistock, to give him his title), was a known anti-Semite, a patron of British Nazi groups, and an open admirer of Hitler. He travelled to Dublin to illegally negotiate terms between Britain and Nazi Germany. Despite this, Tavistock faced no prosecution.

This, then, blows away the idea Churchill was heroically committed against Nazism in all its forms, simply because he did nothing significant about the posh white English Nazi sympathisers in his own party. Unlike working-class Nazi sympathisers, who were routinely imprisoned or executed.

Establishment corruption at its finest.

Chapter Eight

The writers start to write. In doing so, they share a purpose (writing a biography) though not necessarily a vision (as all approach the work with differing motivations), and their success (or lack thereof) will also be different in each case, for those born into privilege are already half-way round the track before the starting pistol is even fired.

Please note this chapter is devoted to telling rather than showing, done purely to annoy the "show don't tell" brigade, thus allowing the snarky prole novelist a chance to write on the main page for a while, rather than being marginalised within the chapter headings and footnotes.

Though the footnotes do continue, for the author finds it difficult to break the chains of his own literary deference. And it's not like I can fit all the snark onto the main page, you know …

And so, as the minimal plot rolls forward, we can be introduced to our next literary and sociological construct as he becomes aware of Vansittart's call for "a dynamic and ground-breaking fresh interpretation" of Churchill. And where better to start than with a man who already holds the golden keys of success simply because of his birth?

Meet Terrance Rogerson, though first we shall meet his parents, to show his impeccable breeding. Rogerson senior attended Oxbridge as a matter of course, worked for a short term as a barrister in the family law firm, and then moved seamlessly into politics. Once ensconced in his safe Labour seat in the early 2000s, Rogerson senior was barely indistinguishable from any other wealthy Labour (or Conservative) politician in that his every thought and vote while in parliament was guided toward making sure a genuine meritocratic society never had any chance of materialising. For this he was rewarded with several consultancy jobs and a life peerage on his retirement from public life, while also enjoying a thoroughly undeserved reputation in the media as a man of principle.

Rogerson's mother, meanwhile, made her reputation in the approved manner of the upper classes; by being posh, pretty, and pliable. The most significant act in her life was birthing – a year apart – two sons, (one heir and one spare, both promptly passed on to the nanny), and having served her purpose the unnamed Mrs Rogerson can be dismissed from this account as readily as she has been in real life.[66]

Rogerson himself, like his father, takes his privilege for granted. He attended Eton, (naturally), where he failed to get the grades required to enter Oxbridge, but his father had a discreet word and Rogerson's place was assured – though in a determined effort to prove he was his own man,

---

[66] If this seems a harsh dismissal of Mrs Rogerson's character, do bear in mind this is how Rogerson himself views his mother. And how Rogerson's younger brother views his mother. And how Rogerson's father views Rogerson's mother. And how Rogerson's father's mistress views Rogerson's mother. And how Rogerson's father's secretary views Rogerson's mother. And even how Rogerson's mother views his mother, thanks to social conditioning.

Rogerson joined the Conservative Party rather than Labour. In terms of ideology, either would have done, but statistically the Conservatives have been in power far more often than Labour, making them the only logical choice for a man of Rogerson's limitless ambition and minuscule ability.

Although Rogerson has yet to publicly start his political career, this is privately already in hand as he is merely waiting for a safe seat to be made available for him. In the meantime, he has made himself useful to the Establishment by editing many newspapers and magazines on the political right, (all utilising the same trick of claiming to be at the centre of political ideology), in which he routinely copy and pastes his politics from disaster capitalism, his populism from the Murdoch press, and his jokes from the 1970s, thereby presenting himself as an anti-establishment non-PC bloke you can trust.

Astonishingly, Rogerson genuinely believes he is an original creation; never once does he suspect he is the construct of a class whose members spend more hours at play than work, busying themselves only when giving and receiving nepotistic favours, marrying into identikit families, dutifully getting the wife pregnant, then knocking up the au pair, the secretary, and the mistress before trading yet more favours while also impregnating the new secretary, the divorce lawyer, the replacement wife, the next mistress and the new au pair. And thus are the

Rogerson's of this world replicated down the generations.[67]

Picture Rogerson, then, in his office at the Daily Crier Magazine, a self-styled "modest operation which seeks to comment judiciously and fairly upon all British life and society,"[68] which was founded in 1863 and which currently inhabits a modest three-storey Grade II Georgian townhouse of 5 bedrooms, 3 bathrooms supplemented by 4 shower rooms, dining room, study, drawing room, kitchen and utility room, all overlooking St James' Park, London, and rented for the modest fee of £40,000 per month.[69]

---

[67] If one were to be cynical about the English social elite, one could wonder how any of the insular buggers living in their small cloud of privileged complacency can ever hope to serve the entire country rather than just their own interests.
Which probably explains why they don't.

[68] In reality, the Daily Crier is a right-wing rag owned by a billionaire nepo baby/trustafarian, and it exists to protect the status quo by creating hatred and thus division within society. If anyone goes "full Daily Crier", it means they are raging against the notion of genuine equality for all, though their words are usually carefully encoded under the standard dog whistles of "We have legitimate concerns" or "you can't say anything now" or "feminism has gone too far" or "inner city youth" etc.
The magazine is, of course, representative of any UK media outlet owned by, and working on behalf of, the wealthy Establishment, ensuring nothing ever changes by inflaming their readers into a catharsis of spurious morality aimed at the woke lefty immigrant atheist PC Muslim Marxist trans gay agenda.

[69] This figure derives from the actual rental on a five-bedroom house in Westminster, London, as of 2021.

More importantly for Rogerson, however, the house is located geographically and spiritually in the centre of the known universe, for as described by the letting agency, Knight, Knight & Knight Holdings, the house "sits most attractively in the heart of London, abutted by Knightsbridge, Mayfair and Belgravia, and the area is known to those who matter as having sheltered innumerable men of power and women of grace, including royalty, the aristocracy, prime ministers, politicians and businessmen."

It is the political angle which interests Rogerson, and it was to attain high office that he embarked on his career in journalism – though Public Relations would be a truer description of his profession as he hides, excuses, and deflects from Establishment greed and corruption on a daily basis.[70] His work rate only really picks up, however, when he turns to self-promotion, and hardly a week goes by without a TV or radio appearance, as well as several photo opportunities held in the offices of the Daily Crier so the

---

[70] By 2019, six billionaires owned pretty much all the UK national newspapers. By a massive coincidence, the newspapers owned by the wealthy elite all supported the Conservatives. By another massive coincidence, the Conservatives gave massive tax concessions to the wealthy elite who owned pretty much all the UK national newspapers. By a massive coincidence, the newspapers owned by the wealthy elite all supported the Conservatives. By another massive coincidence, the Conservatives gave massive tax concessions to the wealthy elite ... repeat ad infinitum.

people can see his casual yet determined aura.[71]

The office is particularly suited to transmitting a sense of power and authority, consisting as it does of antique fixtures and fittings which denotes (according to the *Crier's* website, and quoted thereafter by innumerable other media outlets doing a lazy and unverified copy-and-paste) "a sense of nineteenth century stability and Victorian rectitude." The wood is highly polished on the chairs, the shelves, and the desk Rogerson uses on the few occasions he's in each week, carefully buried under artfully arranged paperwork and books selected for the public view.

The books Rogerson really refers to when in the office, such as the small dictionary, thesaurus, and the latest copy of the *Easy Guide to the Internet and Microsoft Office*, are carefully hidden in one of the desk drawers, along with a few spare fountain pens, bottles of scotch, cocaine, and a few sealed boxes of expired condoms, explaining his many (publicly unacknowledged) children arising from his affairs.

Rogerson himself fits in well with the general air of untidiness and learning, for he has paid a lifestyle coach to select his look of carefully constructed shabbiness, giving the impression he is the man in the street – assuming the man in the street can pay thousands to a life coach – and thousands more for the best suits, shirts, and shoes, as well

---

[71] The reader may be wondering about the sudden lurch into the present tense; don't forget this is a work of serious literary fiction, where such things are allowed. Also, Rogerson is (among other things) a pretentious twat.

as hundreds for the carefully tousled hairstyle. Rogerson can afford these items thanks to his family wealth and the substantial wages he draws from the magazine, though he is always meticulous in claiming his "image money" back on expenses.

He is far less meticulous in his articles and opinions, at least as far as the facts are concerned, and he uses his position at the magazine either shamelessly (according to his critics) or else brilliantly (to those who hope to receive favour from him) to promote himself in the public eye, and upon seeing the call from Clavier and Coldwell for the new biography on Churchill, Rogerson knows his time has come.

This is his break into the mainstream, for while Rogerson's name is known amongst those who matter, he is still only a peripheral figure on the part of the hoi polloi who vaguely know him as "that bloke on the telly who tells it like it is", and unfortunately (for him) Rogerson needs several more members of the great unwashed to further his ambitions by voting for him when a safe political seat becomes available.

And Rogerson knows the people should vote for him, for his needs – naturally enough – align with the needs of the country, and what the country needs is Rogerson in politics and, in due course, Rogerson in Number Ten, Downing Street. This is Rogerson's destiny, for Rogerson, like most of his peers, is a firm believer in the Great Man theory of history.

And what better way to manifest his destiny than by championing the other true hero of the country, Winston Churchill? True, he doesn't know enough about Churchill to fill an entire book, but a little research will soon put that right. And after all, Rogerson does feel a profound and genuine connection to Britain's greatest man; both were men of Destiny, born to Greatness, and Destined to lead by their Greatness to Great and Destined things.[72]

Excited by the self-comparison, supreme in his confidence that he merely has to dash off the tome and reap the rewards, Rogerson reaches into his lowest drawer and pulls out the Knowle Notepad bought for him one Christmas by his second – no, his third – wife, which he has stashed away ready for a suitable project. And what could be more suitable than this, a biography of the Greatest Man in British History, and the tale of how England[73] stood alone against the Nazi menace and no, wait, it was his mistress who had given him the notebook, shortly before she became his third wife. Now his soon-to-be ex-wife. He should have known she wasn't quite top-drawer when she presented him with the Knowle rather than a Phillips notepad, even though he'd directed several thousand

---

[72] The reader may have noticed that for Rogerson, the whole point of the biography is to create a Rogerson-shaped space so he can manifest himself into the public consciousness. He has absolutely no time for the theory that the art lies in hiding the art.

[73] Today, some still consider "England" and "English" as being synonymous with "Britain" and "British". Please note that when I refer to England, (usually down here in the footnotes), I am being specific in the geographical, cultural, or political sense. Unlike certain characters within the novel.

pounds of the magazine's money her way when she'd been acting as his "researcher" – a pattern he will repeat with taxpayer money and a fresh series of mistresses once he reaches public office.

Unscrewing the top from his fountain pen, Rogerson jots down a few practice sentences, to get the creative juices flowing.

Churchill was exactly what England needed; a hero, a man of honour, a man committed to standing against the Nazi jackboot.

Rogerson smirks, knowing this is the stuff to give them. But, of course, a real genius is one who can see the other side, one who is aware of all issues, and Rogerson knows he needs to pay a little lip-service to the moaning lefties who insist on calling Churchill a racist just because he said a few perfectly reasonable things about the darkies. But for now, he'll press on with Churchill's finest hour, teasing out the self-same qualities that he, Rogerson, possesses, so the future readers will see the similarities between himself and Churchill and draw their own conclusions.

It is no coincidence these elements of his character would prove to be the lynchpin of his victories over not only the Nazis, but of history itself, for just as England was threatened by Germany in the 1940s, it was Churchill himself who said we must fight against all history and those who consider oppressing us from abroad and on the beaches …

Rogerson pauses, feeling he has lost the sentence. He scribbles out the last few words and tries again.

For when England was threatened by a nationalistic tyrant who would happily sacrifice millions to see his vision of an Aryan future come through the ranks to take on the enemy, it took one of their own to ...

Damn, lost the sentence again! Rogerson frowns at the words. He'd have to rework the last bit, as he's made Churchill sound the same as Hitler. Preposterous thought! And he'd better change "England" to "Britain", in case the lefties start moaning again.

Of course, the issue with his false starts, as Rogerson knows, is he's always better at talking than writing, for it is a pleasure for anyone to listen to his smooth words pouring forth, entertaining and enrapturing his audience. But these first few attempts to write have revealed a definite snag; during his journalistic career, Rogerson has only ever written in glorified soundbites, and he often (always) relies on his staff to "prepare" his articles for publication by dropping in extra words, sentences, paragraphs, or even complete pages, as and when needed. Meaning anything longer, such as a book, could prove a stretch ...

The solution is clear; Rogerson will dictate the work as he did with his own novel of some two years ago, *And There She Rides a Revenant,* a searing insight into modern human relationships and the unfair advantages held by women over men in society.[74] The novel was published by Clavier

---

[74] The innumerable criticisms of *And There She Rides a Revenant'*s inaccuracy and sexism were merely blunt facts which bounced off the impenetrable armour of Rogerson's socially constructed superiority.

and Coldwell, so this will give him an excuse to pop round and tackle Michael Vansittart about his (Rogerson's) disappointing sales, and find out further particulars of the Churchill biography.

Rogerson nods in modest wonder at his own genius – but then, he knows he is at his best when allowing his amazing free-flowing mind to rove over the issues at hand, improvising and elucidating toward a solution. And afterward he can give it to his secretary (that is, he can give the biography to his secretary, for Rogerson's amazing free-flowing mind has now jumped back to the upcoming Churchillian account which is his by right) to transcribe and to fact check, as she has done on many other occasions when he'd been too busy to pop into the office and type anything up. Which was uncannily how Churchill himself worked,[75] and Rogerson is acutely aware of yet another remarkable resemblance betwixt himself and England's other Greatest Man.

Yes, Lynne will sort out that end of the affair. She is technically on maternity leave, but Rogerson knows she will be pleased to do the work for him. Although – and a chill goes down his spine at the very thought – she may want to

---

[75] Churchill made use of battalions of poorly-paid researchers and assistants when writing – though it seems Churchill didn't actually 'write' at all; instead, he either got his assistants to do the research, after which he dictated their own notes back at them and they transcribed his words ready for publication, or else he simply got a ghost writer in, as happened with the final essay of the single-volume edition of his war memoirs. See Browne, 1995, and Toye, 2011.

talk about the pregnancy. Again. And what he's going to do about it. So perhaps he'd better get Grenville in the office to do it. Bright lad, Grenville, if not quite top-drawer material, for he only went to Harrow.

Not that it matters, at this stage. Find out the money being offered first, then deliver and bask in the inevitable glory. Unless the money isn't up to much, but he can always sell the book to a better, bigger publisher; he knows most of the corporate publishers for they are all part of the same social circle. Being accepted is not – and never will be – an issue.

Rogerson knows he deserves an early lunch at the Chummo Club for his morning's hard work. Humming the "Matter Patter" from Gilbert and Sullivan, he strolls from the office, leaving the rest of the day's edition to his assistants.[76]

---

[76] The reader may have noticed that Rogerson, Vansittart, Featherstonehaugh and Hutchinson-Cockburn are essentially the same character type as all have been moulded by their identical environments into near identical people, who honestly believe themselves to be unique and original rather than starch-filled dumplings squatting in Establishment gravy.
This is why Rogerson genuinely thinks his plan of gaining popularity by writing a Churchillian biography is both unique and individual despite knowing the Great and Beloved Party Leader of the Nation Anointed by Brexit All Profit Be Upon Him* (aka Boris Johnson) *did exactly the same thing only a few years beforehand*. This is how clichéd Rogerson is, following someone else's footsteps while thinking he is blazing a trail.
*Sarcasm.

Chapter Nine

In which the snarky narrator of the footnotes extends his chance to appear on the main Establishment page and immediately renders the entire story as a populist superhero comic rather than as a highbrow literary art form.

His justification for this is that Chapter Eight was constructed entirely from the omniscient narrator's point of view[77] with no action of any kind, thus committing the cardinal sin of "telling" rather than "showing". Meaning we now get the chapter again, but this time with added spandex. And violence.

Specifically, we see the muscular costumed superhero Zatman!™ taking on his arch-nemesis, the 1%er!™ (All rights reserved). Zatman™ and all related characters and distinctive likenesses and related indicia are trademarks of Kidtastix™ Comix™ Ink™™

Page 1 panel 1
A FULL WHITE MOON SHINES DOWN ON OLD LONDON TOWN. THE BUILDINGS ARE IN DARKNESS, LITTLE MORE THAN SILHOUETTES. WHITE SNOW LIES ON THE GROUND.
Caption: Night! The city sleeps, but it doesn't rest.
Page 1 panel 2

---

[77] And dear God, do some editors and reviewers hate the omniscient third. "How can anyone possibly know that?" they demand. "It's head-hopping!" they state, unable to comprehend how third person omniscient actually works.

WE PULL BACK ON THE VIEW AND SEE THE ZATMOBILE MOVING THROUGH THE SNOW.

Caption: This city never rests – can never rest – because it has too many secrets.

Page 1 panel 3

FOLLOW THE ZATMOBILE AS IT DRIVES THROUGH THE EMPTY GOTHIC STREETS.

Caption: This city has too many sins to ever rest easily. Believe me. I know. I've not just seen the darkness beneath the light …

Page 1 panel 4,5 and 6 run together

ZATMAN LEAPS UP FROM THE ZATMOBILE, SPREADING HIS ZATWINGS LIKE A DEMON.

Caption: I <u>am</u> the darkness beneath the light.

Page 1 panel 7

ZATMAN RISES ON HIS ZATROPE TO THE HIGHEST BALCONY OF THE OFFICES OF THE DAILY CRIER MAGAZINE.

Caption: Where there is darkness, there I am.

Page 1 panel 8

ZATMAN OPENS THE FRENCH WINDOWS ON THE BALCONY USING HIS ZATPICK.

Caption: Where light is needed, I bring it.

Page 1 panel 9

CLOSE UP OF ZATMAN'S HORRIFIED FACE AS HE SEES SOMETHING.

Caption: But sometimes the light isn't enough. The light can be dimmed … by utter darkness.

Page 2, complete spread:

WE SEE TERRANCE ROGERSON IS WAITING IN HIS BLUE

ROMPER SUIT WITH LASER ATTACHMENTS, GIGGLING INSANELY, THE OFFICE IN DARKNESS AROUND HIM, NOTHING VISIBLE AS WE FOCUS ON THE VILLAIN. BENEATH ROGERSON, IN AN EXCITING FONT WITH BLOOD DRIPPING FROM IT, WE HAVE THE TITLE:

The 1%er Returns!

Rogerson: Expecting someone else, Zatman?

Page 3 panel 1

CLOSE UP OF ZATMAN AS HE STEPS INTO THE DARK OFFICE.

Zatman: So, 1%er, you survived the fall from Tower Bridge?

Page 3 panel 2

SWITCH BACK TO ROGERSON, CLOSE UP, HIS MAD EYES GLEAMING IN THE DARK, NOT MUCH ELSE VISIBLE.

Rogerson: Of course! It would take more than a 500-foot plunge into an icy river as my Doom Missile rebounds with a ten-kiloton explosion to stop me! Not when I have so many consultancies on the go, media appearances to make, and jobs to give away to my peers who have donated time, money, and influence to my political aspirations!

Page 3 panel 3

SWITCH TO CLOSE UP OF ZATMAN'S EYES AS THEY NARROW EVEN FURTHER IN REALISATION (BUT DON'T MAKE HIM SQUINT; THAT WOULD LOOK TERRIBLE).

Zatman: So, that's your evil plot? To continue living off your inherited wealth while accumulating yet more wealth until you have all the wealth?

Page 3 panel 4

CLOSE UP OF ROGERSON'S SURPRISED EYES, A HINT OF SWEAT ON HIS BROW.

Rogerson: Damn you, Zatman, how did you discover my evil plot?

Page 3 panel 5

CLOSE UP OF ZATMAN'S COOL, KNOWING LOOK.

Zatman: I know you, 1%er. God damn you to hell, after so many years locked in battle, I know you well. Besides, it's the same plot you used last week. And the week before. And the month before that. Seven times. And your father used it before you. As did *his* father, and his father's father before him.

Page 3 panel 6

BACK TO THE FACE OF ROGERSON, AN INSANE GRIN BREAKING OUT.

You know too much, Zatman. Your knowledge is a burden unto others – and to me. Allow me to relieve you of my burden! To me, my mooks!

Page 3 panel 7

5 MOOKS, DRESSED LIKE STEREOTYPICAL 1930S ROUGH GOONS, RUSH FORWARD. THEY FIRE THEIR GUNS AT ZATMAN, WHO FLINGS UP HIS ARMS IN A DEFENSIVE ZATMAN POSTURE.

Page 3 Panel 8

CLOSE UP OF MOOKS 1 AND 2 AS THEY REACT.

Mook 1: Gulp! Our bullets are bouncing off his Zatarmour!

Mook 2: Argh! I've slipped on his skilfully thrown Zatmat!

Page 3 panel 9

ZATMAN STRIKES A DRAMATIC POSE.

Zatman: My Zatclaws will make short work of these goons!

Page 4 panel 1

CLOSE UP ON THE 1%ER.

Rogerson: Curses! He's taken out my goons! I'd better summon all my forces. After all, they've never failed me yet!

Page 4 panel 2

THE 1%ER SPEAKS INTO HIS GOLD-PLATED RADIO:

Rogerson: Mainstream Media! Cronyism! Tax Avoidance! Flag Shagger! Get out here and kill Zatman! And don't bother using comic book panels anymore; it's a convention we don't need to follow, like morality and paying taxes. Because we're rich! We're different to the common herd! We're special and favoured by God! We're white English toffs![78]

FOUR NEW GOONS RUSH FORWARD, THE FIRST THREE - MAINSTREAM MEDIA, CRONYISM AND TAX AVOIDANCE - ARE ALL IN SUITS, WHILE FLAG SHAGGER IS IN JEANS AND A UNION JACK T-SHIRT. HE IS ON A LEAD HELD BY MAINSTREAM MEDIA.

Flag Shagger: 'Ere, what's going on?

---

[78] Varying Conservative politicians in Boris Johnson's government broke lobbying rules, broke covid restrictions, employed their own family to work for them (after complaining about nepotism elsewhere), broke the law by approving a Tory doners £1bn luxury housing development, (which the government's own planning inspector was against) and one extended their family home despite this apparently being against the local council's policy, and *then* there's the controversy over NHS contracts (see footnote #9)

And all this was probably just on a Tuesday ...

Tax Avoidance: Zatman wants to raise taxes on the wealthy – and this is a bad thing![79]

Flag Shagger: I'm too fick to realise raising the taxes on the wealthy to pay for vital services is actually a good thing,[80] so I'm gonna hate him for his tax plans!

Tax Avoidance: We must encourage entrepreneurs, because they are the wealth generators of the country!

Flag Shagger: You what?

Mainstream Media: He means wealth will trickle down to you. But Zatman wants to stop it because he's a lefty

---

[79] A longstanding belief amongst the wealthy and their sycophants. Oddly, the wealthy aristocratic politician, the Right Enriched Winston Churchill, was also against wealth taxes. A staggering coincidence. Mind you, Churchill, employed his own lucrative and morally corrupt tax evasion scheme while in power. Finding money was short, (despite living the high life throughout his days), Churchill asked the Inland Revenue for advice. The advice was not, as you might expect, "pay your damn taxes like everyone else." Rather, the chairman suggested a Splendid Wheeze in which Churchill could retire from writing so any unpaid fees could then be collected as untaxed capital receipts. Churchill, however, still couldn't make do on his Cabinet minister's salary (which in today's money would be about a quarter of a million pounds) and so he needed to start writing again. The chairman of the Inland Revenue was again consulted, and he came up with a Splendid Wheeze Part II ... which was to let Churchill earn what he wanted, with no questions asked and no taxes taken.
A raging cynic might just suggest there is one law for the poor and no sodding law at all for the elite ...

[80] The University of Greenwich estimated a new tax on just the top 1% could raise anywhere between £70-130bn.

allowing immigrants into the country!

Flag Shagger: Bastard!

Mainstream Media: Zatman is anti-Semitic!

Flag Shagger: Great, bloody Jews, they control everything!

Mainstream Media: How many more times? Not Jews, you moron, Lizards! We now say Space Lizards!

Flag Shagger: Oh, yeah, right. Same thing, though, innit?[81]

Mainstream Media: Yes, but we accuse others of being that which we are, to manipulate thick gullible arseholes like you.

Flag Shagger: I love you, sir.

Zatman: I'm taking you all in, to answer for your crimes!

Cronyism: What crimes? All procedures were carried out in accordance with the laws we laid out beforehand. We have done nothing wrong, as any investigation will show.

Flag Shagger: You hear that? He's done nothing wrong, so leave him alone!

Mainstream Media: He's a socialist!

Flag Shagger: Well, I dunno what that means, but as you're always telling me it's wrong, I hate him for it anyway.

Mainstream Media: Zatman is a Muslim immigrant woke lefty Muslim immigrant atheist PC Muslim immigrant Marxist trans gay Muslim immigrant Muslim!

---

[81] The "Giant Space Lizard" conspiracy theory has been criticised for being a virtual rerun of previous anti-Semitic conspiracy theories, with the all-powerful world-destroying Jewish cabals/Illuminati/secret bankers now being replaced by lizards. See also footnote #52 on Cultural Marxism.

Flag Shagger (HIS FOREHEAD PULSING ANGRILY): I hate him! Aaarrggghhhhhhhh!

ZATMAN IS DIMINISHED BY MAINSTREAM MEDIA'S ATTACKS AND FADES AWAY TO NOTHING.

Rogerson: Excellent! That deals with him. Flag Shagger?

Flag Shagger: Yeah?

Rogerson: Get back on your knees where you belong.

Flag Shagger: Yes sir, right away sir. I'm an individual, I am. No one tells me what to do or what to believe. I'm on my knees now, sir.[82]

Mainstream Media: Good! Tomorrow, we want you to hate on Doctor Binita Khatri.

Flag Shagger: I hate her! Why do I hate her?

Mainstream Media: She's a woman of intelligence and

---

[82] It was mentioned earlier how Vansittart and his ilk never question their assumptions or good fortune in being born wealthy; it's far more difficult, however, to understand why those born with nothing should likewise never question the massive imbalances in society and instead simply accept being railroaded onto society's pre-laid tracks of unending underpaid underclass misery.

The best answer this novel can offer is deference to authority, coupled with the effectiveness of mass media manipulation and sociological conformity, all of which deflects blame from where it belongs (a corrupt and incompetent ruling elite) onto the far more innocent targets of immigrants, socialists, feminists, gays, young people, transsexuals, the EU, Black people, Muslims, Pakistanis etc. Which suggests that ignorance, stupidity and bigotry all play a part in keeping society as it is, which would certainly explain the unthinking acceptance of the status quo by Flag Shagger.

See also Chapter Thirteen.

colour who calls out the racism we perpetuate. So, we're running a hate campaign against her, but we can't do it without you.

Flag Shagger: What a bitch! She needs to be raped! I'll fucking have her tomorrow, I'll get the lads onto it, you'll see. The whore needs to go back where she comes from! After being raped and watching her family be killed!

Mainstream Media: That's my boy. Now get sucking down there …

MOMENTARY AWARENESS MAN SPRINGS INTO THE FRAME, LEGS AKIMBO, HANDS ON HIPS.

Momentary Awareness Man: Not so fast, you foul fiends!

Rogerson: Gasp! Momentary Awareness Man!

Momentary Awareness Man: Yes, it is I, Momentary Awareness Man, here to give a moment of awareness to your man, Flag Shagger.

MOMENTARY AWARENESS MAN RAISES HIS MOMENTARY AWARENESS RAYGUN AND SHOOTS FLAG SHAGGER WITH IT, THUS GIVING HIM A MOMENT OF SELF AWARENESS.

PANEL 1, FLAG SHAGGER, ENVELOPED BY SELF-AWARENESS, LOOKS UP IN SUPPLICATION AT ROGERSON.

Flag Shagger: Mm, slurp slurp, Establishment dick, I've been conditioned into eating it and now I believe in it totally slurp because I have nothing else and never will slurp and I've been conditioned so thoroughly I even think I have a *choice* in being down here on my knees sucking Establishment dick slurp slurp!

PANEL 2, TEARS ARE NOW FORMING IN FLAG SHAGGER'S EYES.

119

Flag Shagger: I really am just a whining welp of the Establishment slurp keeping the status quo in place by my unthinking slurp deference and obedience to all their slurp pronouncements through the mainstream slurp media, education slurp, and every other manifestation of the oligarchical slurp society in which we are born, raised, and die without ever slurp having a chance to become something better, something slurp more slurp.

PANEL 3, THE SELF-AWARENESS FIELD FADES.

Flag Shagger: At least it's not woke lefty immigrant atheist PC Muslim Marxist trans gay dick! Mm, slurp, good English sausage, slurp, I love my country, we'd all be speaking German if it weren't for Winston, bring back Thatcher, bloody woke snowflakes, no sense of humour, you can't say anything now SLURP SLURP SLURP!!!

Caption: Next week: expect the unexpected as the 1% unexpectedly returns! And join us the week after as the 1% unexpectedly returns ... again! And the week after that when we discover the 1% never left! They were always here, running things for their own expediency![83]

---

[83] The prime purpose of this novel is to examine how society perpetuates itself via the codification of its own history, and the affect this has on wider society. To do this, the book focuses (in part) on Churchillian mythology, with questions being raised on who creates - and therefore holds the power – of the Churchillian narrative. Here, however, in a ridiculously long footnote, we shall expand beyond the figure of Churchill to focus on the nature of our mythical heroes and narrative control. And we begin with a comic book character.
The above chapter should have featured Batman, but I was worried DC/Warner Brothers would sue my arse off if I used the actual

superhero identity, even if it was done satirically. Hence the cunning creation of a new costumed superhero clearly modelled on another costumed superhero – standard practice, it appears, in comic book history, wherein any popular character could spawn several imitators – some of which went on to enjoy longer careers than the original. (A few examples include Deadpool "resembling" Deathstroke, Doctor Strange taking "inspiration" from Doctor Fate, while Batman himself "borrowed" heavily from Zorro and the Shadow.

The desire for heroes is seemingly inbuilt into our collective psyche, (or maybe it has been inbuilt by sociological conditioning?), and English society has obligingly moulded several mythic heroes (of differing types) for public consumption: King Arthur, who fought the Saxons. Beowulf, who fought the monstrous Grendel. Shakespeare; the greatest playwright ever. Sherlock Holmes; the world's greatest detective. Churchill, who saved us from the Nazis. James Bond, who saves the world from super villains. Doctor Who, who saves the Earth from alien monsters.

These, then, are our heroes, our personal identifiers, our cultural landmarks who anchor us to a shared heritage and consciousness. But in this we see a problem with our national mythic heroes, for they all seem to be looking inward rather than outward, and backward rather than forward – unless the future can be as much like the past as possible. King Arthur? The *once* and *future* King, ready to lead us forward to earlier times, wherein the status quo is preserved. Beowulf? Preserves the status quo from an external threat. Shakespeare? Preserves the status quo in his plays. Sherlock Holmes? Preserves the status quo at the resolution of each criminal case. James Bond? Preserves the status quo against sinister foreign/scarred/sexually divergent Neo-Nazis. Doctor Who? Preserves the English-speaking universal status quo from Space Nazis while ignoring any home-grown corrupt regime on contemporary planet Earth. All are bound by the same ideal; protecting the existing social order from any "external" (i.e. different) threat. They win when society is put back the way it was, with the ruling elite safely at the top and everyone else below. And it was ever thus.

121

King Arthur, for example, has long been used by the elite to mould public opinion. The ninth century text the *Historia Brittonum*, usually attributed to a Welsh monk, Nennius, presented Arthur as a real historical figure – albeit in the form of a war leader rather than a king. Nennius, however, was writing at a time of political inter-church wrangling between Rome and Britain, prompting him to portray the Britons as modern-day Israelites with a shared Roman/Celtic heritage, presumably to help smooth over any theological/political cracks in church unity, leaving the *Historia Brittonum* as a very early example of Arthurian propaganda.

Geoffrey of Monmouth is the next figure of note for his *History of the Kings of Britain*, which featured new Arthurian elements such as Merlin, (adapted from the Welsh *Myrddin*), as well as Arthur being taken to Avalon after his final battle. What Geoffrey also did, (apart from making his *Kings …* look like a researched, historical document), was to recast Arthur from a war leader who successfully repelled post Roman invasions into a one-man empire-building unification machine – and subsequent kings found old tales of Arthur invading other countries to be valuable propaganda (and legitimisation) for their own dreams of overseas conquest.

This was a trend followed by Henry VIII, who went as far as to paint the Winchester Round Table (dated to the time of Edward 1st, though its provenance remains unknown) with the legendary Arthurian Knights gathered around the Tudor rose – the rose being Henry's signature calling card to remind everyone of his presence and royal legitimacy, hence the repeated appearance of the emblem in so many churches during his reign. But then, Henry VIII is perhaps the prime example of modern nation building; by making the king (i.e. himself) the head of the Church of England, he gained access to the power of the pulpit preachers across the land, (an early form of mass media propaganda), who from that moment on would all be preaching from the Tudor hymn book, ensuring everyone would then think and believe in the approved Tudor manner.

But then, religion has always given authority, legitimacy, and a justification to the powerful to do anything they want, for there is no deed so evil it cannot be condoned, excused, and sanctified by religion. One such example can be seen when Pope Innocent III sent his Crusaders in 1209 to Beziers, where the Christian Cathars had rejected certain aspects of Christianity – including the authority of the Pope. Simon de Montford was promised the land of all the heretics he killed, and he and his crusaders set to with a will and practically slaughtered the entire town – an estimated 20,000 people.

But we must return to the mythical figures and narrative control mentioned at the start of this footnote, for it is now time to focus on the Mythic Forging of England's Greatest Writer.

And forging is the word ...

(ii)

William Shakespeare! Actor. Playwright. Propaganda tool. And Establishment capitalist, given his primary interest was not writing but rather buying, hoarding, and selling food, which gave him the means (even after being fined for the hoarding) to buy up land and become a wealthy figure in his place of birth. And like Churchill, Shakespeare was an Establishment tax-dodger, frequently moving house while in London so the taxman couldn't find him. (Which, incidentally, leads to the conclusion that tax evasion is an essential part of National Mythology. Did King Arthur have a corrupt tax scheme signed off by the very people who were supposed to be upholding the system? Or did he just employ a financial hedge wizard?)

Anyhoo; like Churchill, Shakespeare the man has been largely replaced by Shakespeare the Myth, one promoted to ludicrous levels wherein his flaws such as his sanctioned plagiarism, tax dodging, food hoarding, and price gouging, are ignored by Shakesperean scholars who are presumably aware of the man's less than savoury food dealings but who choose to seal these facts in the clingfilm of concealment before hiding them in the pantry of propaganda. (See Archer et al, 2015). Once you start examining Shakespeare's life, you'll find he was (like everyone) a product of his time and privilege, meaning his work and

123

views reflect this cultural straitjacket. Shakespeare's schooling was the perfect preparation for his later career in the playhouse as the curriculum demanded religious study, grammar, and close study of approved (i.e. classical) texts. The pupils of these schools then proceeded to composition, in which they would copy this approved history, or be given a style or theme to emulate, following which they would be taught to give the old theme their own unique spin – for taking a classical scene and reworking it was considered the height of creativity and genius in Elizabethan culture. Yes, really. Which explains why so many of Shakespeare's plays are copies of pre-existing stories. (You can look that up with Bate, 1998).

You'd *think* this would give the "Shakespeare as Genius" narrative a damn good kick in the fundamentals, given there was no attempt at originality as we would understand it, but no; "Shakespeare is a genius", lather, rinse, repeat, and no other views will be tolerated. (On a side note, I think for my next book I'll do a story about an orphan boy sent to boarding school who discovers he's a secret agent with a license to magic. And he's part of a superhero team pledged to defend the Earth from intergalactic mobile dustbins armed with sink plungers. The money should just roll in).

Shakespeare, then, was squeezed into a pre-determined mould to come out in a pre-determined form, which is the central point of this novel; we are all the products of our culture, and hence an elitist training ground will sustain and replicate elitism, while state-controlled education for the masses is little more than a capitalist sausage-making machine in which the lower orders are trained to obey. And oddly enough, Winston Churchill was born into an upper-class Victorian family and went through an upper-class Victorian upbringing and emerged – can you believe? – as a typical upper-class Victorian archetype.

How weird is that?

(iii)

Continuing with Shakespeare's Establishment conventionality, we should briefly consider how many supposed "geniuses" required a collaborator (or several) throughout their careers. We've already noted (footnote #75) how Churchill used hordes of unacknowledged spectral researchers and ghost writers to do his work for him, but there are other examples. The Old Masters (i.e. those painters of the 16th – 18th centuries who are now labelled as Old Masters by the Establishment) employed the guild system, meaning an apprentice would be used to fill in backgrounds on the Old Masters' latest painting before they were finished off, signed off, and sold off by the Old Masters themselves as a piece of original Old Master art – and yet the fledgling artist would have no rights whatsoever to the pictures. A very nice piece of capitalist investment ...

The official striking of these collaborators from the public record through the policy of admitting to their existence before hardly ever mentioning them again is also seen with Shakespeare. We could, for example, ask about his collaborators such as George Wilkins, Thomas Middleton, and John Fletcher, and while it's true their names are out there, we have yet to see an entire industry based on the figure of Fletcher, or a conspiracy theory stating Middleton's works were written by the Earl of Oxford, or find a film entitled *Wilkins in Love* at our local cinema. Yet all these people – Churchill's assistants, the Old Masters' young apprentices, Shakespeare's co-writers – have all been glossed over on the windowsill of time by the painter-decorators of history. You can still see their outline on the wood, but only if you already know where to look.

As such, we again see the common threads of Mythical genius begin to unravel; early education, cultural context, the world these heroes are born into – all these aspects form the child who becomes the (often morally repugnant) adult who later becomes the socially constructed myth.

(iv)

Returning to the concept of the 'Hero as National Myth Used by the Establishment to Maintain Cultural Conformity and Control' brings us to the moment Shakespeare's reputation really started taking off for him. Which was after he was dead. *Long* after he was dead. You might think from the current level of Bardwank he was recognised in his own time as a genius, but although he was popular, and rated highly by fellow playwright Ben Jonson, theatrical writing in general was seen as a lower form of endeavour, a bit like soap opera writing is today. So, Shakespeare was just the *EastEnders* of his era, albeit without his characters screaming 'You slaaaaggg!' at each other.

In fact, his reputation in his own time, because of plays being viewed with suspicion, was based more on his poems than his stage writing, but even here, while some contemporaneous lists of leading poets mention him, he seems to have been less well regarded than Philip Sidney or Edmund Spenser. Admittedly, one of his works, *Venus and Adonis*, was enormously popular at the time, but it was actually a dirty poem and the public lapped it up for the titillation. Which means the great Willy Shakespeare, as well as being the *Eastenders* of his day, was also the *Fifty Shades of Grey* of his day. Think on that. (And think also on the fact that many years later, the Gothic genre justified its own existence by referring back to Shakespeare's preponderance for horror, the supernatural, the sensational etc. Which means as well as being the *Eastenders* and *Fifty Shades of Grey* of his day, Shakespeare was also the *Twilight* of his day. The horror!)

It wasn't until Ben Jonson printed his own works in 1616, the year Shakespeare died, that attitudes toward playwriting started to change. It was Jonson who pioneered the canonisation of plays (and therefore playwrights) by producing his own works in folio format. Shakespeare's plays did appear in his lifetime, but only as cheap and unauthorised quartos which were usually produced (badly) from memory – the norm for many playwrights at that time. And Shakespeare was very normal for his time.

Shakespeare did eventually get a poor-quality folio in 1623, but it didn't go into a second edition until 9 years later – suggesting the first edition didn't sell especially well, or it was intended only for the wealthy elite, or else the publishers were given cash up front by someone (possibly Shakespeare's widow) to produce it. And by 1668, his reputation had declined to the extent that Beaumont and Fletcher's plays were being performed more frequently than his own.

What finally established Shakespeare's reputation was plain good fortune. For one thing, not many plays had survived from before (and during) his era, meaning Shakespeare's output took up quite a chunk of the available market. Literacy also began increasing in the 18th century, and hence textual criticism was emerging – and textual criticism (obviously) needs texts to feed on. Cue the first copywrite law, established in 1709, which were exploited by numerous publisher who could now produce their own editions of Shakespeare's work, meaning his plays were everywhere and he was the Enlightenment equivalent of an Internet meme.

The enormous ego of actor David Garrick (1717 – 1779) was also essential in founding today's Shakespearean myth; Garrick ruthlessly used Shakespeare to boost his own profile by appearing in the plays, commissioning several portraits of himself as various Shakespearian characters for the people to ogle and admire, and by organising the first Shakespearean celebration (sans any Shakespeare, apparently) in Stratford Upon Avon, all of which promoted Shakespeare's reputation and visibility.

And the dictionary also helped, odd as that sounds. Dictionaries like to use a quote to show the word you're looking up, to give it some sort of context. Most dictionary compilers therefore reach for an approved source, and the most approved source of all would be a line from Shakespeare, and thus we get the myth that Shakespeare practically invented every word in the English language. (In truth, he would have used words already in use; how else would the theatregoers of the time understand anything? See D McInnis, 2016, for more.)

(v)

Another aspect that boosted the bard was, depressingly, good old-fashioned English xenophobia. Voltaire and other continental critics had beef with Shakespeare because his plays weren't really any good by neoclassical rules, which (broadly speaking) place emphasis on symmetrical form, the exploration of flawed characters, and perhaps most importantly, a focus on rationalism and logic. This criticism inspired Shakespeare's bitches – sorry, his *defenders* – to move the goalposts by declaring such things weren't that important after all, because it's the emotional aspect that matters. (See Desmet & Williams, 2009). Or, to put it another way, if your side is losing because you're not good enough, change the rules, do away with intelligence in favour of emotional reactivity, (very Daily Crier), and then claim to be the victor. If you have an Empire to back you up, not many are likely to disagree.

Having established some historical context, we can now explore the truly disturbing ideology behind the bardolatry; Shakespeare's complete lack of any truly revolutionary ideals in his work, which made him the perfect figure for the ruling elite. The Governmental Licensing Act of 1737 was a piece of legislative censorship designed to prevent theatrical outbreaks of critical satire against the government – and it meant the only works allowed on the stage after the ban were those deemed acceptable by the Establishment. Enter Shakespeare, stage right (wing), and his entire theatrical output, which was *not* affected by this governmental suppression. Which leads to the question; what was there in Shakespeare's plays the government approved of so much that when they literally cancelled other writers and productions, they left Shakespeare untouched?

The answer is simple; the Bard's conservative attitudes, in which social disorder is always controlled and the Establishment reaffirmed, suited the elite perfectly. Even *Hamlet*, which ends in a royal genocide, sees stability and normality restored with the immediate acquisition of a new imperial household for Denmark. And so Shakespeare became a political/cultural weapon to hammer the population into unthinking obedience – very handy after the power of the church had been damaged by the developing sciences, meaning a new form of cultural control was required.

And this happened when the British Empire was *the* dominant force across the globe, (providing a neat echo of Christianity's arrival into Britain on the back of the Roman Empire several centuries earlier, destroying the indigenous pagan beliefs in a tidal wave of colonial suppression). Shakespeare was exported out to the world along with English Christianity and English cultural imperialism, all three aspects of which fit snugly together with the shared central messages of do as you're told, accept your lot in life, and don't ask awkward questions. And so Shakespeare became *the* cultural touchstone for the UK, meaning anyone looking for legitimacy had to use Shakespeare for their cause; hence the chartists (workers with no rights) and the suffragettes (women, ditto) would quote Shakespeare to give themselves some credibility in the eyes of the powerful elite. (Morris, 2015).

Some claim this is Shakespeare's true genius – that we can find points of reference with him and recognise ourselves in his work. But you can also do that with parts of the Bible, Christopher Marlow, Ben Jonson, Terry Pratchett, crime fiction, romance, farce, Marvel films or even the *Beano* – yet these don't get the same level of academic posturing that Shakespeare enjoys. And, of course, *anyone* can use Shakespeare for their own ends. The Third Reich *loved* the plays, with *Hamlet, Macbeth* and *Richard III* all proving to be very, very popular, so clearly the Nazi High Command found much to admire in the Shakespearean canon. And what if we step outside this dominant Eurocentric view; would Shakespeare still be seen as universal? Or would we, like Erik Rolfsen, start asking some basic questions on how a white 16th century man can possibly represent all people of all ages? Especially given the white 16th century man spent his business life screwing over the poor and his playwriting life preaching conformity to the masses ...

What this ultimately seems to prove is how thoroughly the Establishment controls everything; want to change society? You can only do so by *becoming like the ruling elite*, in this case by co-opting Shakespeare for support, which means you are playing the elite's game, by the elite's rules, on the elite's playing field. Shakespeare was a gift for an Establishment looking to maintain social dominance, while his reputation has become an industry blindly reproducing itself in theatres, popular culture, and educational institutions, as each generation slavishly worships and repeats the assumptions of yesteryear. No wonder our political masters insist on Shakespeare being taught in the school curriculum, for Shakespearean attitudes are a cornerstone of cultural oppression.

And on top of that, many of his plays are as boring as fuck.

(vi)

Having started this monstrous footnote with a fictional comic book character, let us end there also, not just because of the symmetry but because Churchill himself became a comic book character in 1957-8, courtesy of *Eagle Comics*. In this depiction of reality, Churchill is posed in front of a Union Jack overlaid with the (white and wholesome) British people while making his "Finest hour" speech. It's no wonder the Right has such a moronic, jingoist view of the world, given their hero has been rendered (both literally and figuratively) as a two-dimensional character. And this goes some way to explaining the Myth that Britain won World War II alone, (therefore overlooking the Russians, Americans, Indians, Australians and countless others), as most English people are fed this tripe from birth onward.

Indeed, one is tempted to speculate that right-wingers honestly believe the war ended when Churchill was dropped by Q branch in an experimental Aston Martin Rocketcar into Berlin to prevent the Nazis from detonating their secret Hun Atomic Bomb. After which he personally duelled with Adolf Hitler in hand-to-hand combat. With Excalibur. Which is also a lightsabre. God save the King/Queen! (Delete as applicable).

Churchill the Lone Saviour of Everything and Everyone from the Nazi Hordes is as much a fictional construct as Batman or James Bond, (himself a right-wing wet dream denying the reality of Britian's declining power and importance). Fiction and reality have entwined, with the declining imperial power of Little England recreating itself (at least in pop culture) as a force to be reckoned with. Churchill has been employed by the UK political and media Establishment as a cultural weapon of oppression, one which keeps the bulk of the tabloid readership compliant and on-side. Hence the Establishment's horror at the idea of real history being revealed.

The point being made here, just so the reader doesn't have to tease the meaning out, is that Churchill the Myth is a multi-faceted kaleidoscopic construction used by the Establishment to draw lines between "us" and "them", for people living in squalor and depravation will not question their place if they have someone different to hate, i.e. woke lefty immigrant atheist PC Muslim Marxist trans gay people. (And the mental contortions which must accompany this, as those with nothing fold themselves into ever smaller shapes so they can consider themselves superior to the person next to them who also has nothing, is quite mindboggling, and says something depressing about the average Little Englander's lack of intelligence – as well as their eager willingness to eat the shit of deference shovelled at them by the Establishment).

And this is why the Establishment seems to be predicated on perpetuating the myth over the man, the jingoism over the reality, the propaganda over the truth. In doing so, the Establishment regurgitates itself through its own version of history, consolidating its cultural hegemony and thus bolstering its own legitimacy and power, knowing the fuckwits of society will lap up Churchillian Myth as a baby suckles milk from the teat.

And so the cycle continues.

Chapter Ten

A red-letter day for Yvonne (who is oblivious to the hideous cliché of "a red-letter day", for she is inexperienced in editing) as she has her first direct interaction with a real live author, a breed she has long deified as wondrous creators inhabiting a higher realm of art and abstract thought.

As such, her illusions are about to be exposed to the awful reality; writers are just like everybody else. Only worse, because we're supposed to be better, peering through the veil to share our wisdom on how the world works – instead of which, the majority simply reinforce *the way the world works.[84]*

Yvonne was sitting quietly at her desk in the late afternoon, alone as the rest of the staff were in a meeting across the hallway, when the outer door slammed open and a man strode into the office, his face resting in its natural expression of social superiority. It was the expression that confused Yvonne, for it meant she didn't immediately recognise the man she had seen on innumerable television

---

[84] See, for example, Bram Stoker's *Dracula*, in which a foreign pagan immigrant invades England to corrupt our impressionable weak-willed women, until his foul-fanged scheme is undone by a confluence of upper and middle-class rational Christian westerners who kill the foreigner before entrapping the surviving woman in matrimony and motherhood by making her believe it is her natural role in life.
If Stoker were alive today, he'd be writing for the Daily Crier.

shows ruthlessly plugging the "Terrance Rogerson, affable chap of the old school" brand.

'I'm here to see Michael Vansittart,' announced Rogerson, his tone making it clear he expected to be shown straight to the publisher's office. His gaze, which up until that point had been flicking around the room in the hope of seeing a more important (and less ethnic) person he could deal with, finally came to rest on Yvonne's face.

'Have you an appointment?' asked Yvonne, nervously, for the man's posh accent and air of command was sending socio-encoded signals to the personal deference program culturally imprinted onto her character.

'I emailed Michael I was coming in,' replied Rogerson, emphasising he was on first name terms with the head man while glossing over the timeframe of the email, which only extended back some forty minutes. He wouldn't normally have talked to a coloured unless there was a television camera around, but in the absence of anyone else, he had no choice.

'So, you have an appointment?' asked Yvonne, timidly.

'I emailed him!' repeated Rogerson, his patrician voice moving up the social scale as he put the Black girl in her place, for this was the way his world worked. Though he suspected she probably liked his tone; the firm white hand of the experienced older man ...[85] 'Kindly tell your employer

---

[85] The reader may have noticed that Vansittart, Hutchinson-Cockburn, and now Rogerson all view Yvonne as a girl, while Felicity views her as a woman. This may seem an unremarkable fact, but when unpacked, some rather unpleasant assumptions start to spill out – and all revolve

around the dehumanisation of Yvonne as a person. Starting with the men, one reason for their automatic infantilization of Yvonne is power and sexism; rendering a full-grown woman into a girl/girlie/filly/totty etc belittles not just the woman, but her entire existence, and thus makes it clear that 'she' is not as great as 'he', thus reinforcing standard patriarchal power norms.

A quick glance at Chapter Eighteen will reveal how Hutchinson-Cockburn regards himself as the Alpha Male of the office, while in a similar manner Vansittart considers himself the older, sophisticated man, yet both are ultimately the same as they categorise Yvonne, and thus diminish her, by viewing her as little more than a girl – a sexualised girl who, in their view, is receptive toward (even craving of) their male attention. (And Chapter Nineteen will also reveal Hutchnson-Cockburn's similar attitudes to working-class women, thus demonstrating that, in certain ways, there is very little difference in the Establishment's view on women of any background and ethnicity, for in this schema all non-Establishment women are sexual, disposable, and less than fully human).

Welcome to the traditional male gaze.

As well as the infantilising sex/power angle, however, we must also be aware of the racial/historical view. The attitudes still held today by those in the real world (of which Vansittart, Rogerson, and Hutchinson-Cockburn serve as illustrations) toward Black women can be traced back to Empire, colonialism, and slavery, in which Black women were viewed as the Jezebel; inherently sexual, decadent, insatiable – and available to their white masters out on the plantations. In contrast, eighteenth and nineteenth century patriarchal 'standards' viewed (or classified) white women as demure, passive, virtuous, and innocent – and available to their masters out on the marriage market.

That Yvonne, or any woman, should have any autonomy is never considered by Rogerson, Vansittart or Hutchinson-Cockburn, for they cannot fit this idea into their world view; Rogerson and Vansittart are aware of the 'male gaze', but only as a piece of faux lefty rubbish from the cinema, while Hutchinson-Cockburn has never even heard of it. To them, girls are fair game, to be lusted after equally but differently, with white girls (of good breeding) needing the sexualised cage of masculine/patriarchal protection, marriage, and motherhood (male heirs preferred), while Black and working class girls/women are regarded as little more than animal, something to be enjoyed as spectacle or fuck-toy before being thrown back into their poverty traps, out of sight and mind.

Having looked at the male gaze, we should now look at what could be termed the 'female glare', as seen in Felicity's objectification of Yvonne, albeit as a woman rather than as a girl. Superficially this may seem an unremarkable thing; Yvonne is about eighteen or so, a full legal adult, so why worry about Felicity viewing her as a woman? The answer lies within the racial issue of Adultification, in which society will often assume white teenagers are children (and thus victims) in any given scenario, whereas Black teenagers are viewed as perpetrators and adults, as seen in 2020 when a Black fifteen year old, referred to in reports as Child Q, was strip-searched at her school by Metropolitan police after she was accused of drug possession.

No drugs were found.

When faced with Yvonne, Felicity can only view her in one way; as a potential racialised adult threat. Not as a girl, or a vulnerable teenager, or someone who just happens to be there, but as a threat. But this leads to an issue; young girls are not easily classed as being threatening, and hence to get round this issue they must be encoded as women, for a woman is an adult (who can therefore cope in a way that children cannot) and an adult can be viewed as a danger, thus shifting any moral blame or guilt away from those who have, for example, just stripped a Black teenage girl naked based on nothing more than an accusation.

Hence throughout the novel Vansittart et al perceive Yvonne as a sexualised girl, while Felicity perceives Yvonne as a guilty and dangerous adult, for this is how they have all been trained by their respective cultural norms.

And you could now ask yourself who disseminates those cultural norms, and why ...

that Terrance Rogerson of the Daily Crier, and author of *And There She Rides a Revenant*, is here to see him on a matter of utmost importance.'

'He's in a meeting,' croaked Yvonne, feeling her vocal cords tightening with anxiety; she was in the presence of an author; and a posh author at that.

'Then go and get him from the meeting,' swayed Rogerson, for the lunch at the Chummo Club had been well lubricated.

'Um, well, I'm not sure,' said Yvonne, desperately worried that interrupting the meeting would see her dismissed, though she also felt (again with no conscious thought) that she had to defend Vansittart's domain as he was both her boss and her social superior.

'You think this is an acceptable way to treat the editor of the Daily Crier?' demanded Rogerson in outrage, sending a whiff of brandy into the air.

'Um,' said Yvonne, doubtfully; she had heard of the Daily Crier, and she knew it had a rotten reputation in most of the Black community for its barely disguised bigotry against all minorities. 'If you wouldn't mind waiting, I'm sure he'll be out soon.'

'You need to sort your priorities out,' snapped Rogerson, making it clear he was referring to both the business in general and Yvonne in particular. 'I've worked hard to get where I am, and I had to fight for everything!'[86]

---

[86] In fact, Rogerson had worked reasonably diligently at university, but only by regurgitating his tutors' ideas into his essays and final exams to

'Ah, Terrance, I thought I heard your voice,' said Vansittart, drawn from the meeting, for like truly did attract like. 'How are you?'

'Very upset,' replied Rogerson, his tone and manner modulating to something approaching equality, for he was now talking to a social[87] and racial equal, something noticed by Yvonne though she didn't realise the significance until that evening, after she had calmed down and her brain had kicked back into gear. 'I have sent numerous emails to your office which have not been answered.'

'I do apologise; we've had a lot of staff turnover and illness,' replied Vansittart.[88] 'What can I do for you?'

---

gain their approval. Rogerson, however, is totally oblivious to this fact, thinking his ability to get a pass on almost every paper was a sign of his intelligence and ability, rather than a simple stimulus-response of writing up approved answers to find approval with approving authority.

[87] Rogerson and Vansittart had, after all, been at Eton together, albeit in different years. Not that this made any difference to the old school tie.

[88] This standard excuse fell without any conscious thought from Vansittart's lying lips. In truth, he had seen all of Rogerson's emails complaining about his lack of sales, but he had employed his usual policy of ignoring them in the hope the author would eventually give up contacting him.
This, incidentally, is based on real life. When my old publisher, Accent Press, was sold to a larger concern, (Headline Publishing Group), the few original Accent authors Headline were interested in were contacted immediately by the new hierarchy. The rest of us were treated appallingly. Emails and phone calls asking what was going on,

'My sales of *And There She Rides a Revenant*,' replied Rogerson, glowing in contentment; he was the injured party, meaning he had the moral high ground, which strengthened his bargaining position. 'They are totally unacceptable!'

'Oh? I thought them quite encouraging,' said Vansittart, flipping through his phone app to find the latest sales figures.

'Encouraging?' snorted Rogerson. 'My last royalty statement showed only one hundred books sold in the last quarter!'[89]

---

did we have a future with the company etc, were dismissed with the glib excuse mentioned above or else were ignored completely.

And this does seem to be typical for traditional publishing. You may as well just do it yourself on Amazon or Lulu. You get treated with the same level of contempt by Amazon, (Lulu is an unknown quantity for this author), but at least you know in advance that the corporation doesn't give a damn about you. And while you get no advertising or marketing unless you do it for yourself, this is no different to traditional publishing which now expects their authors to do most of this donkey work themselves – unless the author is already famous, of course, because they've been on telly or kicked a football about for a few million quid each week, in which case a marketing campaign will be launched.

But for everyone else, the novel you poured yourself into will just sit there, unnoticed, unloved, and unread.

Welcome to the (book) club.

[89] One hundred books is a pretty good target in publishing, and yet Rogerson, a man born with everything, still wants more. See also Churchill, W, and his ambitions.

'Not a bad sales record by any means.'

'*Not bad?* I'd expect a work of such profound insight to be pulling in five times as much. At least! And what about the literary prizes? Where are they?'

'Of course, we actively promote our authors,' said Vansittart, who in truth hadn't submitted *And There She Rides a Revenant* for any prize, for while he knew the novel had a good chance of success, (given most book committees were made up of his and Rogerson's peers), it cost a lot of money to enter literary contests.[90]

'The book clearly needs greater distribution!' snorted Rogerson.

'It is out in the bookshops,' pointed out Vansittart, fully aware the book's presence on the high street shelves was down to Rogerson's public profile as "that bloke on the telly".[91]

'So, you admit your marketing team could do better?' exclaimed Rogerson in triumph, feeling he had trapped

---

[90] In 2016, the costs of entering a literary contest could range from around £2500 to £4000. Which explains why Vansittart would rather spend the money or some tangible aspect of the business. This suited Vansittart enormously as he was saving money which could then be spent on other important areas of concern. Such as his quarterly family holidays to Tuscany, Capri, Skiathos etc.

[91] As of 2020, your chances of being put on the shelf in a typical bookstore is less than 1%. Note Rogerson is on the shelves and yet this still isn't enough for him and his sense of entitlement ...

Vansittart with cunning verbal dexterity, though he flashed his trademark charming smile to show they were old friends together. Which indeed they were, as long as Vansittart and his company remained useful to him.

'The marketing team can only do so much,' said Vansittart, fully aware the "marketing team" consisted of whoever was free to post a title or two on social media. 'But authors must now do their fair share, as laid out in the contract.'

'Harumph, yes, well,' muttered Rogerson, moving away from the dangerous territory of legal certainty. 'There should still be more sales.'

'I'm afraid *And There She Rides a Revenant* is in a very crowded space at the moment,' soothed Vansittart, though he didn't specify how many other books existed which featured a demonic woman with an anagrammatical name of Rogerson's first wife seducing and betraying a man of genius before symbolically living off his corpse for years. 'You need to build up a platform, as more books means a greater audience and more sales.'

'But the quality of *And There She Rides a Revenant*,' insisted Rogerson.

'Indeed, but you need a platform,' reiterated Vansittart. 'Have you considered moving into other areas? YA fiction might be making another comeback next year.'

'Children's fiction?' snorted Rogerson. 'I do not intend to waste my gifts – such as they are,' he added with a quick burst of entirely bogus humility, 'on writing for those who could not appreciate it. Wait until I am senile, and then I will be at the right level for that!'

'Or books which have relevance to women and women's issues?'

Rogerson snorted again; he would never put a female writer on his own level, for all they dealt with was banality and domesticity. He was a writer with something to say and a voice which needed to be heard, not a woman with too much time on her hands thanks to her hard-working husband.

'And you could use your magazine more,' suggested Vansittart. 'Make use of your contacts, attend all the literary luncheons, get the industry newsletters. And are you sending copies out to your personal contacts in the press, as we are?'

'Of course,' snarled Rogerson, petulantly.

'Then keep it up, keep it up,' soothed Vansittart. 'Now, you must excuse me as I have an important meeting to attend.'

'Very well; but I shall expect to see improvements with *And There She Rides a Revenant* forthwith,' said Rogerson. 'And sort the movie rights also! I can just see Veronica Laurent in the main role.' Rogerson's eyes clouded as he thought of his actress of choice in her nude roles. 'If we wait much longer, she'll be past it,' he added, for Laurent was already in her late twenties. 'Oh, and what's happening with the Churchill biography?' he added in a forced casual manner.

'Early days,' said Vansittart cautiously, recognising the hungry look in Rogerson's face.

'Submissions coming in, I should think?'

'A few,'

'Anything good?' queried Rogerson, impressed with his own forensic investigative technique.

'Some possibilities,' shrugged Vansittart, edging toward his office.

'But nothing suitable?' pressed Rogerson.

'We've had some very good ideas from writers of a non-traditional background,' said Yvonne, bravely dropping a hint in front of her boss.

'Non-traditional?' echoed Rogerson in horror. He had no idea what the dusky maiden meant, but he was sure it was going to be utterly unpalatable.

'Yes; writers from marginalised groups who usually don't get a chance,' began Yvonne, before being interrupted.

'Good god!' exclaimed Rogerson as he wheeled backward, partly from drink and partly from the idea of someone so fundamentally *dubious* getting anywhere near the hallowed ground of Sir Winston himself. 'It sounds like the cranks are crawling out of the woodwork!' He bellowed in laughter at his own wit, inviting Vansittart to share the humour aimed at the non-Eton, non-Oxbridge world in general, and the young Black girl in particular, while also making a mental note to use the phrase 'hallowed ground of Sir Winston' as soon as possible.

'Indeed, but we keep an open mind here at Clavier and Coldwell,' said Vansittart, smoothly, for he knew the value of keeping up the public face of tolerance.[92]

---

[92] Vansittart (and his peers) do indeed know the value of tolerance. Tolerance is not acceptance. Tolerance is not respect. Tolerance is

'Oh, indeed, indeed,' nodded Rogerson, for he too knew the code of espousing values in public he would never endorse in private. 'Well, I'd better be getting along. Think about what I said, Michael. I'm sure we'll be meeting soon.' Rogerson shook hands with Vansittart and left the building, ignoring Yvonne completely as she was probably a fringe voter, given her colour and mad lefty politics. *To think!* he pondered; *the looney left lurking in Michael's office!*

But that's multiculturalism for you!

---

letting people know they are only there on suffering. No wonder the Establishment is so keen on tolerance; tolerance means they don't have to change anything about who they are, the way they live, or the way they treat others.

Tolerance is a hierarchy.

Chapter Ten (continued)

In which Rogerson, musing on the political possibilities the Churchill biography will open up for him, his sacrosanct right to write the Churchill biography, multiculturalism as a failed experiment imposed by lefty dogma, and the issue of people not knowing their place, begins rolling a few phrases around in his traditionalist orthodox mind ...

... and perceived his astounding cognizance was on the verge of another truly prodigious article on the threat to Great British History from the woke lefty immigrant atheist PC Muslim Marxist trans gay agenda, the threat to Great British Values from the woke lefty immigrant atheist PC Muslim Marxist trans gay agenda, and the threat to Great British Business from the woke lefty immigrant atheist PC Muslim Marxist trans gay agenda mob.[93] Always go British; that was Rogerson's very public motto.

---

[93] This chapter sees the prole author back up on the main page, where he can mock Rogerson and all those like him. Though once again the footnotes continue, like this one, pointing out that Rogerson's rage at the woke lefty immigrant atheist PC Muslim Marxist trans gay agenda is in truth nothing more than him stoking the flames for his own ends – and that of the Establishment, for whom the culture wars were a godsend for their ability to divide the public and distract from real news stories of Establishment corruption and incompetence, for a fractured country is an easily ruled country.

And why wouldn't he? After all, if stoking the flames does result in society burning, Rogerson knows damn well he will be protected, as

Rogerson pulled his Yamamoto Voice Recorder from his pocket and began speaking into it, aware of the stares he was getting from the public but enjoying the attention, for his self-image saw himself striding down the pavement toward his Destiny, while around him the common people would know they were in the presence of someone truly special, and they would love him for it.[94]

'Er, right, Grenville, new article for the magazine, to go in the new edition, pride of place, page eight,' orated Rogerson, laying down the law to his young unpaid intern. 'Headline: *How the lefties are infiltrating our most cherished arts exclamation. Er, make that art institutions. Er, or maybe our sacred areas. Exclamation!* Er, just tidy that up, will you, Grenville? Right, first paragraph.

'*We all know Churchill is a hero full stop we know it comma the world knows it full stop even Germany knows it comma though the sausage-sucking denizens may not publicly admit it* er, you'd better run that past the lawyers, just to be safe,' added Rogerson. He wasn't sure if an entire

---

will his peers, by the police and army, as well as big business, the banks, parliament etc, because that is what the Establishment is for; protecting the status quo and people like him.
And fuck everyone else.

[94] Rogerson did, however, increase his speed as he walked, for fear of being approached by the common man, synonymous in his mind with criminal lower-class types. It was Rogerson's unwritten, unspoken, but perfectly articulated belief to never be in proximity with the lower orders unless there was a photo opportunity in it.

country could sue, but he wouldn't put it past them to try. Probably using the European Court of Human Rights. And what a travesty that was!

'Second paragraph. *In honour of this comma a new and exciting announcement was er announced* tidy that up as well, Grenville, *by one of our oldest and best publishers comma Vansittart's Publishing who called for a new biography of our greatest man* oh, er, comma in there, of course.

'Fourth paragraph. *Ordinarily comma this would be a reason to rejoice full stop'.* That was better; he was beginning to run smoothly now. *'After all comma what man achieved more than Winston Churchill question mark*[95] *born to humble stock comma despite his aristocratic lineage*[96] *comma Churchill would shape the nation and the world but even here* er by which I mean here in publishing, Grenville, not here in Churchill's life, *even here comma the lefty*

---

[95] In this, Rogerson is oblivious to a point made earlier in this narrative – Churchill was *allowed* to be Churchill by his privileged birth. Had he been born in a slum to working-class parents without wealth and contacts, he would never have got anywhere in life, even if his character had been exactly the same, i.e. egocentric, brave, depressive, sentimental, callous, manipulative, bigoted, corrupt etc.

[96] If challenged, Rogerson would have retorted that Churchill was humble in *essence*, meaning he was simultaneously aristocratic *and* salt-of-the-earth, for Churchill was so large, so amazing, so unlike any and all who had come before, that even contradiction was possible in His great character!
Rogerson considered himself a man of contradictions also …

moaners will not stay away comma and they insist on intruding on the hallowed ground of Churchillian … er … of Churchillian grandeur full stop.

'Next paragraph. *Incredible as it may seem comma the lefty presence is making itself felt at all levels comma spreading its intolerance of greatness into all our sacred areas for the left can't stand the idea that one man can be better than another comma and in the future they will demand we will all be alike with no difference between us exclamation point.*' Ha! This was the stuff, and it was amazing how easily the words flowed from his lips. The fact he'd used an almost identical phrase three times already that week did not register as he continued his oration.

'New paragraph *for dear friends what did I find when checking out the background story of this new call for a life of the Greatest Ever Brit I found lefty sedition*[97]er, exclamation mark there, Grenville, of course. And some commas.'

'Story continues: *For in the sanctified land of publishing so long a symbol of our heritage and tradition I found the moaning voices of the socialist demanding Churchill books be written to show Churchill facts* er, no, scrub that last bit, Grenville, I mean, er, *Churchill books be rewritten to show*

---

[97] The idea that Yvonne could hold any sort of valid opinion was an alien concept to Rogerson for she was Black, female, from a lower-class background girl and she held a different opinion, meaning she was (in his worldview) morally wrong, factually wrong, and economically wrong.

socialist facts comma facts which appear in no official history exclamation.' By God, he was on a roll now.

'New paragraph *instead the left now demands only certain types of facts be allowed in Churchillian biographies exclamation only facts showing how horrid Churchill was* oh, er, better put quote marks around that last fact, I think, to show we're aware these are not facts at all, continue, *but these are not facts at all they are fictions exclamation Churchill was the greatest Brit of all time comma but listening to the left you'd never know this exclamation according to them he was a racist and a warlord well I mean* oh, er, exclamation there, by the way, after warlord.

'Continue *I mean he was of a different era semi colon of course he was different exclamation and maybe his views are a little old-fashioned now comma but when push came to shove it was comma Churchill comma and Churchill comma alone comma who stood up comma for everyone* Black *comma white blue and green,* er, put commas in there, will you? Um, *Brit and Indian Scot and Eskimo and round eyes or slitty eyes* ah, actually, delete that last bit, just in case the chinks get offended continue h*e stood up for us all and his supposed faults became virtues as he fought for you for me for everyone exclamation point did Churchill do all this through the greatest catastrophe we have ever seen the second world war started by the jackboot Jerry Germans just so the left can rewrite history in this way I think not* oh and punctuate that, Grenville, there's a good lad.'

Rogerson nodded, agreeing with himself on everything he'd said. However, he knew he had to pay some lip service

– and here he thought of the Black girl and her mouth, and he snickered at his wit while admiring his refusal to bow down to lefty PC strictures on perfectly legitimate humour – to the notion Churchill had some flaws, and he flipped the recording button once more as he marshalled his thoughts, ready to deal with the matter fully and conclusively.

'Of course no great man is free of flaws and Churchill himself had er *some.'*

Rogerson nodded, wisely. All great men had flaws; it was what paradoxically made them great. He found this thought so profound, he jotted it down on a piece of paper pulled from his jacket pocket, ready for later recycling, while reflecting on how some claimed Rogerson himself had flaws with tiresome accusations of racism, infidelity, and corruption made by those who were simply envious of him. And in any case, Rogerson knows that far from being flaws, these personal attributes simply emphasize the massive, uncanny parallels between himself and Churchill. Smirking uncontrollably at the undoubted similarities, Rogerson hit Record and continued his self-absorbed oratory.

'Of course Churchill was a man of his time not to be compared with men of our time for he was born when the great British Empire still ruled the waves and it's a pity we ever lost it and besides oh, er, exclamation mark again, there, Grenville. Or delete the comment about the empire. Or, no, keep it in, for we must dare speak the truth and shame the devil! Oh, and add a bit from any biography to defend the Indian famine, will you? There are several in the office.'

149

Rogerson's thoughts shifted to the shelves heaving with reassuring Churchillian biographies, most within arm's reach but all too far away to be bothered with. At least by him. Not when he had staff on hand to do the work. 'Oh, and put a conclusion on the article, there's a good lad.'

Rogerson smirked afresh as his destiny unfolded before him, just as it had unfolded for Churchill, the other Great Man of Destiny! Feeling he had more than justified his salary for the day, if not the week, Rogerson glanced at his watch and decided to seek out some convivial company at the Chummo Club. Drinkies before tea, then some drinkies after tea, then home for dinner and drinkies.

Nodding in satisfaction, the Man of Destiny hailed a taxi on expenses, trying to remember if he was booked in for dinner with his ex-wife, his almost ex-wife, his mistress, or his fiancée.[98]

---

[98] A key question of this book is whether the legion of Establishment politicians, journalists, historians, biographers etc are *knowingly* replicating the status quo with each generation, or whether this duplication is being done by a bunch of vacuous inheritees and arse-lickers who lack the wit, insight, empathy, self-awareness, and intelligence to see how they themselves are nothing more than ever-turning cogs in the Establishment machine.

We have already looked briefly at political sleaze in footnote #78, and if politicians really are so disturbingly separated from morality they think this sort of behaviour is normal, (as well as acceptable), then maybe our most scathing criticism should be reserved for those journalists who are wholly aware of the inequalities of society but who clearly choose to do nothing about it, therefore keeping the status quo (and their own privilege) in place.

One ex BBC journalist spoke of how she was told from above (i.e. by posh public school Oxbridge BBC executives) which stories she could cover, what she could say etc, which would suggest journalist as a breed are weak, spineless collaborators with the enemies of a genuine meritocratic society.

However, on a closer inspection of the species, it's hard to avoid the conclusion that many journalists are just thick as shit; consider how they spend all day, every day, upholding the status quo, with not one of them seemingly thinking to question the assumptions underpinning their world of privilege, thus giving the impression they are collectively about as bright as a dead glow worm buried under several layers of compost. And this view has some evidence behind it, such as when a high-profile BBC television presenter and "journalist" insisted they had never been told what they could or couldn't report on, which is a self-own of epic proportions given this simply reveals how they, and others like them, don't even *need* to be told to support the elite, attack any alternative viewpoints, and generally distort the news to fit the Establishment agenda. They just do it anyway.

But then, this is hardly surprising, given the posh homogenous nature of the industry in which (as of 2021) 9 out of every 10 journalists are white, while 80% of journalists come from the highest social classes. Though one tabloid found a workaround to this particular issue by attaching the names and pictures of Black quisling commentators to articles written by... posh white male journalists. Which proves three things; firstly, my cynicism is nowhere near deep enough to match real life. Secondly, journalists have no shame and no ethics. And finally, in the regard to the quislings just mentioned, the oppressed truly do become the oppressors. (See also footnote #159 for more on this final point).

The result of this unholy inbreeding can be seen in the utter corruption running through the press and political classes alike, such as when the recommendations of the Leveson report for media regulation were abandoned by the Conservative government, while Leveson 2, the promised independent enquiry into the relationships between the press and the police, wasn't even held. And bear in mind the original

Leveson report laid bare the corrupt relations between politicians and the press, with the latter influencing the former with bribery and threats so they could influence the "democratic" decision-making process.

And these trustafarians are the people who control access to the media, meaning they control who gets to present their views to the public. And the vast majority of those views are going to be those which already harmonise with their own attitudes because they all went to Eton and Oxbridge together. They probably don't even need to explain what sort of views they want; they already share them completely. In 2022, pupils at Eton college erupted into misogyny and racism when seeing some visiting girls from a local state school; this pretty much tells you everything you need to know about the elite; those who will be obtaining positions of power in the coming years are even now fully supportive of misogyny, racism, class hatred and xenophobia, and they will have no desire, and absolutely no reason, to examine and eradicate their own prejudices and systems of power.

And this reinforcement of cultural norms replicates itself with each generation, with the means of communication (education, literacy, access to the wealthy people who own the means of publication etc) forever being concentrated in the hands of the few who can impose their views on everyone else. After all, how often do the working classes appear in any detail in Establishment history, or Establishment story telling? And when the working-classes do appear, are they represented fairly?

And Churchill? He certainly seems a prime example of a man wanting his privilege (embedded in the past, the empire, and in the class structure) to continue forevermore, but again, how self-aware was he in this? Was it (to him) simply the way the world worked because he was a selfish, blinkered, small-minded bastard, or was there something altogether darker going on? Did he know full well the misery he was perpetuating, thus making him a selfish, callous, evil-minded bastard? For the purposes of this book, and to make things easier for the reader, it can be revealed that Terrance Rogerson regurgitates Establishment dogma in the belief he is a true original, but he is a borderline

sociopath only interested in two things; his own advancement and keeping his small, selfish, elitist world of inherited privilege and gross inequality protected from any outside scrutiny, law, or morality.
But bear in mind Rogerson is a fictional character. In fiction. Unlike in the real world.
Which is no doubt entirely different.

Chapter Eleven

A chapter making use of a flashback within a flashback, which may not be appreciated by literary purists. Featuring a sojourn to India, where the call for a new biography on Churchill triggers the memories of one man closely bound to the living history of his country. Be warned; these memories of the dead and dying of the Indian famine of 1943 may be distressing to those with empathy, so caution is advised.

The reader may also wish to question if the author has succeeded in creating a believable illusion of a foreign land and people, or is this chapter populated with nothing more than examples of the Exotic Other? And should this section even exist, given it is taking real-life horror and then rendering it into cheap fiction?

Although Clavier and Coldwell's submission call was put out on their website, Vansittart had no real conception of it being seen, or responded to, by anyone outside the United Kingdom. (Truth to tell, he probably couldn't conceive of anyone outside the Home Counties having the ability to respond to the Churchillian challenge). Notwithstanding this insularity, the call was indeed seen worldwide, including by Mr Umang Joshi, of Hauz Khas, Delhi, India, lately retired from the Civil Service.

Umang was, at that moment, shuffling slowly down his family garden. It had once been Nani Prisha's pride, this oasis in the city, at a time when English conventions on what constituted a garden were very much to the fore. Weeds were never tolerated, trees and shrubs were tended, and small boys who dared play on the grass in shoes or sandals would feel a quick, sharp thump around the ears.

Then, after the illness, it was his mother who tended the long plot, stealing away from the housework for the equally hard work in the garden, timing her absences carefully from the house to coincide with the limited shade offered by the taller trees and bushes against the scorching heat, working on the flowers in the morning, a little light edging thereafter, and tending the fruit trees in the late afternoon. In Umang's young eyes, this was nothing less than a choreographed dance between his mother and the sun, two partners moving gracefully around each other in perpetual movement.

Umang smiled faintly at the memories, far and distant in his life yet still remarkably vivid in his mind. He poured a little water over the wilting jasmine shrubs, just as his mother had done, and her mother before, as had his wife for so many years before she too had been taken from them. And although he now had daughters who performed their servitude to the garden, he liked to potter about himself, walking the sandstone path and breathing in the sweet scents of the remaining flowers and parched lawn.

For although it was not spoken about openly, at least with Umang himself, the garden was dying as the increasingly arid summers blazed down, burning away any hint of moisture and destroying the earth beneath. The sandstone walk had been steadily enlarged over the years to disguise this fact, and now the garden was almost two thirds covered with hot brick, the living earth receding with each passing generation. And yet, despite these changes, each part of the garden still contained many lingering memories for Umang, and here he felt a true sense of peace.

The ping of his mobile phone coincided with the screaming of the latest train thundering along the embankment some ten feet or so from the bottom of the garden, bound for New Delhi Station. Metallic weeds sprouted from the railway line, crawling inexorably over the blurring boundary between the public railway and the private land adjacent to it.

Umang rummaged in his hip bag, covered in the latest cartoon characters enthralling his grandchildren, pulled out his phone and activated it via his thumb print, frowning at the slow reaction as the device was now at least two years old; it would soon be time for another. The cause of the ping was a text from his old friend, Ramesh Lucknawi, once a figure of authority in the Indian Information Service, resplendent in his smart suits of exquisite cut and texture, a man of dignity and substance.

Yo! You seen this, bro?? asked the message, followed by several grinning emojis. Umang smiled; old Ramesh was exercising an impish sense of humour in his dotage, of which his favourite joke was echoing the speech patterns of his youngest grandchildren.

Umang tapped the attached link and was taken to the Clavier and Coldwell call for Churchillian submissions. His eyes misted over as second-hand memories of the war years enveloped him, for his Nani – his grandmother on his mother's side – had witnessed this era at first hand, and had told him about it, and it was these conversations which now tumbled down the years, pouring into his mind.

Nani Prisha had never forgotten the Indians marching off to war as part of the British Empire, ordered to fight for a land they had never seen and a people they had never been allowed to meet on equal terms. And neither had she forgotten those left behind to die as famine swept the land and Churchill refused to release food to the starving. She and her son-in-law, Reyansh, Umang's own father, had argued long and hard on many aspects concerning the British, the Empire, and Churchill.

Umang could still recall Nani's bitterness, spoken in the garden when Umang himself was but a child. 'They took everything,' the old woman had said, gesturing vigorously with a trowel in the direction of a passing train – for Nani, the trains were synonymous with the British. 'They said it was progress; they said it was good for the people, for the economy, to get goods moving quickly from one place to another, but whose goods were they? Who made the money from them? The British, that's who!'

'The trains helped everyone,' replied Reyansh, the exchange clear and lucid in Umang's memory.[99] 'The trains

---

[99] This demonstrates the dangers of relying on memory alone – it was a series of later conversations Umang was remembering, some of which had drifted from their original setting and attached themselves to his recollection of a hot Saturday afternoon when he was six, though in

helped to create modern India.'

'They were designed for British investors!' shot back Prisha, slicing through a root with a vigour which suggested she regretted it wasn't her son-in-law's neck underneath her trowel. 'They were intended to transport coal and iron and other raw products to the ports to be taken on to Britian. And the British shareholders were paid back double from Indian taxes; they made a fortune by exploiting us!'

'But it was long ago,' said Reyansh, looking at the train as it disappeared into the distance. Reyansh was the consummate civil servant, for he believed whatever the ruling elite believed. Should those beliefs change tomorrow for social or political reasons, he would smoothly change with them, barely registering the transition. 'And look at what they left behind; unity, education, and an excellent political system!'

'They destroyed the original system and replaced it with their own divisive control!' snorted Prisha. 'You only believe in it because you're a government man; the system benefits you.' This obedience to the political system was the chief reason why Prisha despised her son-in-law.

'The government today is different!'

'There is no difference!' exclaimed Prisha. 'When we were ruled by our own people, in the time of the Mughal reign, the land workers only had to pay fifteen percent in taxes to

---

reality it took place on a Monday evening when Umang was ten. And in any case, the conversations were not exactly as he remembered.

the rulers, which gave us plenty of protection when famine came. But under the British, we were paying fifty percent taxes – and we had no security when famine hit us all. We had nothing in reserve, while the British racked up ever greater profit.'

'It was no different under Mughal rule,' sneered Reyansh, whose dislike of his mother-in-law was prompted largely by the elderly woman's strong hold over young Umang. 'I remember my grandfather saying they were little more than parasites who took what they wanted while living in luxury.'

'Things were better,' snapped Prisha, brushing aside the faults of the old rulers. 'The death toll under the British was catastrophic and they didn't give a damn about us. Instead of showing any compassion for the dying, they just raised taxes on the living, to cover the shortfall. And they made us grow food to be exported, rather than grain we could eat ourselves, so when the famines came, we suffered while they grew rich and fat!'

'But things had changed by the time Churchill was in charge, surely?' asked the young Umang, for his father venerated Churchill as a gentleman and a hero, and this attitude was already insinuating itself into Umang's young soul.

'They got worse,' seethed Prisha. 'He diverted food and medical aid for the war in Europe. He condemned thousands to death by neglect. I still remember them, the dead and dying, lying in the streets, nothing but skeletons covered in thin flesh, sacrificed to British profit and

159

Churchill's hatred!'

Prisha angrily blinked back the tears as her early memories carried her unwillingly back to her village in 1943, the sun beating down, the ground baked hard as stone, great cracks opening in the water-deprived earth as though the land itself was begging for sustenance while dust, dirt and sand lay over the dead and dying alike.

The dead lay where they had fallen, in doorways, in streets, in fields, by rivers, wherever the last spark of hope had disappeared as they finally succumbed to the inevitable. Those still alive didn't have the strength to do anything for the dead – no funerals, no ceremonies, no rites – for they too were near their final collapse, their hope in their leaders, the future, of even just seeing tomorrow, eroded by the famine covering the land. Only the dogs and vultures tended to the corpses, pecking and ripping at what was left of the flesh, locked in their own desperate fight for survival.

Prisha blinked again and the scene changed; now she was in the city, where she and her mother had travelled in a last desperate attempt to find sanctuary, but the city only held further suffering for the rice was gone, taken, politicised, and all that remained was the keening of the dying who knew their time had come, inflicted on them by nature and the evil that privileged men do.

'That was the result of the famine!' exclaimed Reyansh, deftly echoing the view which was politically convenient to his government. 'It was nothing to do with Churchill!'

'That was just a cover,' retorted Prisha. 'The worst of it

was over by the middle of the war, so what happened to all our food, eh? Where did it go? To the British, that's where!'

'The Japanese were taking it also,' replied Reyansh, referring to the fall of Burma.

'Not all of it,' replied Prisha, digging with savage intensity and spilling soil onto Reyansh's highly polished shoes. 'There was enough for everyone – or there should have been! Churchill redeployed our food because he only cared about the West, not India!'

'How come I've never heard of any of this?' asked the young Umang, tears gathering in the corners of his eyes.

'Because those in power keep the people in ignorance,' replied his grandmother. 'But more than that; people keep *themselves* ignorant.'

Umang was drawn from his reverie by the rushing of another train passing by the garden, carrying with it a hot wind and the foul stench of blistering metal and burning fuel. He shook his head at the memories, dabbing at the unexpected tears gathering in his eyes. His poor grandmother. His grandmother who had hated the British for what they had done to India. And his grandmother had written down her thoughts and memories in a series of diaries, as had her mother and grandmother before her, for the whole family believed in the importance of history.

And surely that was important? Real accounts from those who had witnessed history at first hand, facilitated by the official documents Umang knew he could call upon after his long career in the Civil Service? A genuine ground-level view of an entire country?

Pulling out the latest iPad from his hip bag, Umang opened a text file and began tapping away, composing fluently as he recalled his grandmother's tales of happiness and horror, of triumphs and defeats, each memory evoking a long forgotten feeling or a lost sensation, such as the faint smell of Jasmine which he always associated with both his Nani and his mother, or the smell of ink and paper clinging to his father's suit.

Chapter Twelve

In which we see a publisher at work, (necessitating several new counter-culture footnotes), gain an insight into Helen's broken dreams, and witness Yvonne's first direct attempt to launch the ship of her ambitions. Which will shortly founder on the choppy water of elitism before striking the iceberg of corporate reality and sinking into the cruel sea of lost hopes.[100]

'Michael,' called out Yvonne the following morning as Vansittart appeared promptly in the office at twenty-three minutes past eleven. 'You've had a call from the man who was here the other day; Terrance Rogerson? He says can you call him back about the matter in hand? By which I assume he means the Churchill biography.'

'Christ on a crutch!' exclaimed Helen. 'Terrance Rogerson wants to do the biography?'

'Is there any reason he shouldn't?' demanded Hutchinson-Cockburn, who knew Rogerson socially; his father and Rogerson had been at Eton together. Though not actually *together;* a few years apart. But it still counted.

'Have you read *And There She Rides a Revenant?*' asked Helen. 'Biggest pile of elitist misogynist shite I've seen in a long time. And I had to do most of the work on it as he was too lazy to do the edits himself.' She glared at Vansittart, for

---

[100] Not all metaphors are worth pursuing. That one certainly wasn't.

she had complained bitterly at the time over the quality of the work and the lack of quality in the author, but she had been overruled by the Old Boy Network. 'Rogerson is the sort of man wouldn't piss on you if you were on fire, unless you offered him something in return.'

'I'm sure he'd do a splendid job,' objected Hutchinson-Cockburn, for the unwarranted confidence he held in his own abilities also projected onto others within his social circle.

'It would be a travesty that serves one purpose,' countered Helen. 'And that purpose is Terrance Rogerson.'

'Yes, well, no decision has been made yet,' said Vansittart, somewhat huffily, for he did not appreciate hearing his friends being criticised.[101]

'Shouldn't a good biography be about the whole man?' asked Yvonne, seeing an opportunity to turn her (hitherto ignored) hints about doing the work herself into an open declaration. 'Don't we deserve the truth about Churchill, as a society?'

'Well, yes, obviously, clearly,' spluttered Vansittart in dismay, for the last thing he wanted was the truth; it would be *ruinous* to book sales. This, however, was a shameful thought buried deep within his bookseller's psyche, safely walled off from his social persona which was only aware of one reality – that of Churchill's greatness. All other views

---

[101] That Helen was right in her observation was not something that bothered Vansittart, for he could (privately) rationalise her comments away as envy or female hysteria.

about Britain's war time leader could then be safely dismissed as either wrong or, if corroborated with inconvenient facts, an irrelevance.

'Won't happen,' said Helen. 'Too many Establishment hacks around,'

'But surely the world of biography is better?' pleaded Yvonne. 'I mean, don't you need intelligence and depth and intellectual rigour?'

'Not really,' replied Helen. 'I mean, you do get the occasional bio like that, but not often.'

'But why not?'

'Writers are usually already part of the Establishment. Which means they think like the Establishment, act like the Establishment, and they do the Establishment's bidding. Probably without even being aware of it.'[102]

'But that's totally unfair!'

'It's the way of the world. You think I wanted to be an editor stuck wet nursing a bunch of posh self-entitled authors? Real life gets in the way. Like needing to pay for food and housing. Whereas those from privileged backgrounds can do what they want as they have the

---

[102] Think of it this way; you're the Establishment, and you want a biography written about you. Are you going to hire an outsider who will raise uncomfortable questions about your unethical behaviour, or do you go with a chap from your social circle who holds the same views and values as you do, and who can be trusted not to ask any untoward or unseemly questions?
Truly, the Establishment knows how to serve up a sausage while claiming you're getting the whole hog ...

money and contacts before they even start. So, the chances of finding an Establishment biography which isn't just a generic panegyric is remote, to say the least.'

'Um,' mumbled Yvonne, deciding Helen's comments were unduly negative, for Yvonne desperately needed to believe her ambition of becoming of a millionaire author could happen. And she did have a pipeline into the industry, given she was working for a publishing company ...[103]

'Michael,' smiled Yvonne, giving her boss her most appealing look. 'Why don't *we* do the biography?' She gestured around the office, though the shrewd swing of her hand ensured the main focus was on herself. 'We could write it ourselves,' she added, by which she meant she could write it herself, with help as and when needed, but definitely with her name and picture on the cover, and the royalties in her bank account.

'Do it ourselves?' gasped Vansittart in a shocked tone, for he was a *publisher*, not a *writer,* though Vansittart knew he *could* be a writer, should he so choose, for he undoubtedly had a way with words and maybe one day, as a gentle retirement, he would take that option up. But not today, where his income came from paying (rather poorly) other people to write on his behalf. 'We're *publishers.*'

---

[103] This is only true in the physical sense; in the social sense, Yvonne is the invisible woman to those in charge.

'But just think of the publicity; the publishing staff doing the biography of our Greatest Leader, rather than a traditional writer.'

'Well, yes, but no, yes, I mean,' stuttered Vansittart, still taken aback by the assault on the sacred demarcation within Clavier and Coldwell's hierarchy. Such was his shock, his evolutionary 'fight or flight' response kicked in and he began edging toward the office door. And to think; he'd only popped in to grab a contract for reference purposes.[104]

'We have the skill and knowledge in here,' insisted Yvonne, by which she meant she herself represented the business skills, with the historical knowledge being silently projected onto Helen.

'Oh, yes, undoubtedly, I mean, I choose my team most carefully, the best in London I always say,' blathered Vansittart, creeping ever closer to the door.

'So, we *could* do it?' insisted Yvonne.[105]

---

[104] Vansittart had an appointment with an agent who had supposedly discovered the next A.T.L.T.K. Hansen, whose *Darkwing Dragon of My Soul* had proved an unexpected hit in the summer, (much to the consternation of the press, until they were able to label – and thus sneeringly dismiss – the novel as "retro-Scandinavian-post-punk-alt-historical-fantasy"), prompting a wholesale scramble by wholesale publishers to discover their own retro-Scandinavian-post-punk-alt-historical-fantasy authors.

[105] Yvonne could see Vansittart was against the idea, but she subconsciously reinterpreted the scene until she developed a false representation of reality in which Vansittart was merely hesitant, meaning she just needed to work on him gently, discreetly, and diplomatically, so she could finally begin her literary odyssey.

'Er, well, maybe, but in the meantime we have other duties to attend to,' replied Vansittart, desperately searching for stability and familiarity as the unexpected appearance of lower-class thought and ambition threatened to destabilise his office and existence. 'There are invoices to answer, paperwork to prepare, boxes to be moved, and I want us to make a start on preparing for the Chelsea Book Fair next year – it's only eleven months away, so chop-chop everyone, and let's get on with our paid work.'[106]

Yvonne then decided to get one of her shorter skirts out of the wardrobe to wear the following day. But only because she felt she hadn't worn anything to make her look like an attractive woman for a while.

This, sadly, is the result of living in a patriarchy, in which women judge *themselves* on their appearance as much their ability. See Ellemers, 2018.

[106] Making the poor work hard all day is another way of preventing the workers from developing their own agency, which could otherwise lead to all sorts of dangerous ideas like creating an egalitarian society. In dumping an excessive amount of extra work on his staff, Vansittart was unconsciously calling on generations of Establishment behaviour to help him in his time of need.

Chapter Fourteen

In which we see the disadvantaged worker trying to put her plan into action ...

'Does he really want us to start writing a biography?' asked Sarah as Vansittart scuttled away to his office.

'Yes,' said Yvonne, firmly, for she needed a little help in chasing her literary dream. 'Er; how do you begin, exactly?'

'I think you need to answer that yourself,' said Helen, who knew it would be best to let Yvonne find her own way to her inevitable disappointments. 'An essential part of any creative endeavour is understanding your medium.'

'So I – we – need to do some research?' asked Yvonne.

'It would probably help,' nodded Helen, though not in an unkind manner, for she recognised and understood Yvonne's intent; she had once been like her.

'OK, let's see what I can find online,' said Yvonne, her fingers flying over her keyboard, oblivious to the disdainful yet furtively interested expression from Hutchinson-Cockburn. 'Ah, let's see what this site says; "Notes on writing a biography", by Leonard Harris.[107] Huh; the first point it makes is "You won't make money"!'

---

[107] Yet another fictitious representation of a real piece of work.

'Damn true,' said Helen. 'Publishing makes money for the publishers, mostly. And not always then. Very rarely does a writer share in it.'

'Um," said Yvonne, her throat warbling in shock. The media had successfully sold her the lie of wealthy writers living off their best-selling tomes, and this insight into the reality of authorial earnings was a severe blow to her daydreams of unimaginable wealth and fairytale castles. 'But you can earn enough to live on, can't you?'

'Nope. Another reason why publishing favours those who are already wealthy,' shrugged Helen. 'Or have access to wealth.'

'Um …' repeated Yvonne, her confidence badly dented, though her subconscious was pointing out with the resilience of youth how there were still some authors sipping at the champagne of success. '"Remember a biography is about the subject, not the writer"'.

'Try telling any author that. Bunch of egomaniac weasels, always inserting themselves into the narrative.'[108]

'Next is; "No biography can be about the truth, no matter how hard you try"'.

'Ha!' snorted Helen. 'A biography *should* be about the truth, but it's usually nothing more than an interpretation.

---

[108] I am stung by Helen's contempt. My role as the self-inserted author is *essential* for dramatic tension, deeper philosophical truth, and the occasional double entendre.
When I can fit one in.

Sometimes quite a loose interpretation, to put it mildly. But that's biography for you. And historians.'

'Bloody hell; listen to this! "A biography is a story, not a factual account."'

'Again, sounds about standard,' said Helen. 'And I don't think many popular historians would see anything wrong with it. And neither do publishers. They all want to sell their books, so the truth usually takes a running jump.'

'By this criteria, I suppose Trumper is supreme at biography, given the way he conjures a story and a narrative of Churchill which makes you want to read more,' observed Yvonne, though rather quietly, for fear she would be sued for even hinting at the suggestion Trumper had written a one-sided grovelling account.

'Any other advice?' asked Helen.

'"Make sure you know the era, so you can show the historical context."'

'I agree,' interrupted Hutchinson-Cockburn, feeling excluded by the two women who were having a conversation without him and his expertise. 'You can't ignore the era.'

'"Always go to the primary sources for dependability,"' said Yvonne.

Helen barked with laughter. 'Bollocks! Even back in his own time, Churchill's contemporaries realised he was deliberately speaking and writing for the public record, so he'd look good for history. And he took stuff out of the official archives which reflected badly on him. And hoarded notes and memoranda so he could present himself as he wanted to be seen. And he refused to write down anything that would reflect badly on him. Primary resources are sometimes no more valid than any other.'

'"Non primary sources are only useful if their content can be verified."'

'I wonder how many writers bother to verify?'[109] asked Helen. 'After all, how many Churchillian biographies are based mostly on Churchill's own interpretation and presentation of himself?'[110]

'"Ensure you know your subject fully,"' continued Yvonne, feeling a little forlorn from Helen's observations.

'Go on, I'll give 'em that one,' said Helen. 'But speak up,' she added as she headed for the door, a cigarette already on the voyage from packet to mouth.

---

[109] One historical writer (Gordon Corrigan) consulted the war diary of the 2nd Battalion Grenadier Guards to compare against Churchill's own cheery recollections of winning over the entire regiment and being their de facto leader, and found a certain number of discrepancies between the two accounts.

[110] This is a key issue, for this novel is *not* concerned with primary or original research, but instead with how history is prepared, sliced, diced, packaged, delivered, reheated, served to and then consumed by the public in a perpetual orgy of self-replicating Establishment veneration. Churchill is a prime example, glazing himself heavily before anyone else had the chance to examine his rump. In short, this chapter exemplifies the entire point of this novel; biographers write what they are *conditioned* to write, and to treat them (or their work) with Biblical Reverence is foolhardy in the extreme. (See Chapter Thirteen for further details, as well as Clive Ponting's *Churchill*, 1994).

'"Tell the reader what you think."'

'Ha! Some of them do nothing else,' coughed Helen, already lighting a follow-on cigarette from the smouldering dregs of her first.

'"Ensure the subject's successes are front and centre of the biography; you must justify why your biography sits on the shelf."'

'Churchill certainly did something successful,' hooted Hutchinson-Cockburn 'He stopped the Nazis!'

'I'd forgotten you were there, Rupert,' replied Helen, returning to the office and temporarily crushing the young man. 'The silence was so unusual. And misleading. And Churchill's role in "stopping the Nazis" is contentious at best.'[111]

'Anyway; how's that for a start?' asked Yvonne, closing her Internet tabs.[112]

---

[111] And Churchill's intransigence reportedly very nearly lost the conflict, as noted (again) by Gordon Corrigan. Plus, Churchill wasn't fighting the enemy alone; a few other people were involved. Politicians. Civil servants. Generals. Industrialists. Civilians. The armed forces. The Empire. Leaders and citizens of other countries such as America, Russia etc etc etc ...

[112] Having looked at what a biography is and how it should be written, (according to one source, anyway), some readers may now be wondering why *Constructing Churchill* has been written as fiction (and more specifically, metafiction) rather than as a simple biography or academic study. The reasons, thankfully, are straightforward. Metafiction, as a genre, tries to draw attention to its own inherent artificiality to provoke thought on what reality really is – or isn't. From the very beginning, *Constructing Churchill* was concerned with how

history/biography is formed, created, and presented, but writing only began after about two months of research, jotting down ideas, and struggling to work out who the characters were going to be, where they would be, and what they would be, an issue which vexed the author considerably during the early planning stages.

Eventually, however, the obvious and practical idea of setting the action at a small independent publisher finally occurred, allowing different perspectives to be brought in and explored as various would-be-authors approach the publisher with their submissions. This idea was then refined further, resulting in Yvonne Jones becoming the main character and (possible) audience identification point, as even focusing on just a few characters would result in a tranche de vie novel which would probably have required a million words or so to adequately cover just one aspect of the whole.

Approaching this via a meta narrative rather than as a "straight" novel, (or even as a non-creative historical/sociological study) allowed me a greater flexibility in tackling the subject matter, for metafiction can break rules, ask questions, and raise issues that biographers and historians may not be able to tackle, or even be able to acknowledge, because you have to behave yourself when writing a proper piece of academic work, presenting both yourself and the thesis as quiet, sober, reflective, and above all, respectable. Whereas with fiction, and especially metafiction, I can be as subversive, rude, and as childish as I want to be.

Especially in the footnotes.

Chapter Fifteen

In which we have a quick discussion on the concept of traditional biography and how it relates to the "Great Man of History" trope...

'OK, let's compare with what traditionally published material has to say on the subject,' said Helen, reaching to a small shelf opposite her desk and selecting a slim volume which she passed to Yvonne.

'*How to Write Biography* by Dudley Crawford,' said Yvonne, assuming her "reading out loud from a book" voice which, oddly, was far more artificial than her "reading out loud from a webpage" voice. And in contrast to Hutchinson-Cockburn's self-confident oratory, Yvonne's demeanour when reading from a book fell into the *Oh God, someone's looking at me* school of self-mortification.

'Right. On page five, he says; "Biographies must, at times, contain fictional threads. These are required to create drama, to show your subject in the best possible light, or to provide essential information to the reader ..."'

'Or you could just present the evidence you have,' muttered Helen. 'You know; keeping it honest for the reader.'

'"The more you look at your subject, the more you will understand him or her."'

'Bull crap,' said Helen. 'Churchill influenced – or warped – perceptions of him by writing down *his* history, *his* way, with *his* slant, and almost every writer thereafter just followed his lead like dutiful little sheep. Meaning practically all our understanding of Churchill has come from Churchill himself. That's not understanding; it's regurgitating bollocks.'

'Skipping ahead,' said Yvonne hastily, '"You may think to ask yourself why the subject of your biography needs a new book written about them?"'

'Because some sod, somewhere, is making cash from it,' muttered Helen, feverishly searching her pockets and handbag for her cigarette stash. She was beginning to fret as she could only find three packets when she thought she had five. 'Churchill is now an entire industry,'[113] she added, breathing out in relief as her fingers closed around the

---

[113] The Churchillian Myth/Industry is, in truth, little different to any other English cultural Myth/Industry, (Shakespeare, the Brontës etc), in which the Myth fuels the Industry and the Industry fuels the Myth, thus making the real Churchill as elusive as the real Shakespeare, or the real Brontës in their respective industries. They're all part of the status quo, keeping little England chugging along on the same smug track, spreading the message that to be accepted you must agree with, and think like, the rest of society.

No wonder homogenous bland white fiction which lauds the status quo is so popular on the literary syllabus; *Jane Eyre* is little more than a smug masturbatory capitalist racist patriarchal right-wing fantasy, as the plucky heiress rebels briefly (and safely) against not having any family love before conforming to saintly gender stereotypes of teacher, nurturer, wife and mother – and that's just in relation to her wealthy landowner aristo husband – before the book ends with fulsome praise for Jane's devout brother-in-law as he literally gives his life to Jesus by converting the Black heathens in Foreignlandia.

If Charlotte Bronte were alive today, she'd be writing for the Daily Crier.

missing packets. The thought of trying to last the day on only three packs had been sending panicked signals into the ancient part of the human brain usually concerned with outrunning apex predators on the prehistoric African landscape.

'I'd say behold new writers doing new things,' sulked Hutchinson-Cockburn, still smarting from Helen's putdown while also being upset at the Black girl being the centre of attention. Especially when one considered her awful speaking voice which had zero projection, zero dramatic emphasis, and zero class.

'This bit will please Rupert,' observed Yvonne. '"Be aware morality changes over time, and good people from once held opinions which today would be deemed unacceptable."'

'There, you see?' demanded Hutchinson-Cockburn as though all his values had been supported while Helen's lefty madness had been rebutted, secure once more in his world of thoughtless privilege.

'So you agree Churchill's opinions were unacceptable?' asked Helen with a wide grin.

'The point I'm making, as you know full well,' snapped Hutchinson-Cockburn, 'is you can't judge him by today's standards. The book just said so!'

'Then let's judge him by his contemporaries, shall we?' said Helen. 'One of them said there wasn't much difference between Churchill and Hitler, in terms of Churchill's hatred of Indians.'[114]

'It was a different era,' snapped Hutchinson-Cockburn through the tightest of tight lips.

'You've gone quiet,' said Helen of Yvonne, who was frowning over the book.

'Because she has heard the truth!' declaimed Hutchinson-Cockburn, hoping to bury the awkward facts on Churchill's contemporaries under sheer volume.

'Because of what I've just read,' replied Yvonne, her voice threatening to break. '"Slavery, as an example, was not considered a great wrong or moral issue for many years by the majority of people. Everyday citizens could be seen to be good and true in their thoughts, words, and deeds, and yet they participated in the slave trade. There is no reason at all for a modern writer to ascribe modern sensibilities to past situations."'

'Again, truth from the book!' declaimed Hutchinson-Cockburn, who seemed to be turning the short guide on writing biography into a religious text, complete with cherry-picking of useful verses and wilful ignorance of any other historical or moral source.

'The book just admitted there were some who were against slavery,' snapped Yvonne, 'so surely Crawford's just contradicted himself within a few lines? Slavery, and the

---

[114] Helen is referring to Leopold Amery's comments on Churchill and his attitudes.

178

racism that went with it, were not held to be universal truths. People were pointing out the evil of both, well before Churchill was even born.'

'But *most* people held the view!' replied Hutchinson-Cockburn with considerable exasperation.

'Are you including the twelve million slaves themselves in that reference to "most people"?' demanded Yvonne. 'Or do you only count the white slave owners and their supporters as being "people"?'

'All right, most *other* people held the view!' snarled Hutchinson-Cockburn, mentally glossing over the fact that his comment hardly reflected well on white British culture. Or his own views.

'Apart from the half million or so who signed a petition against slavery, and all those who boycotted sugar in a demonstration of consumer power,' fumed Yvonne.[115]

'It's the way things were,' sulked Hutchinson-Cockburn. 'And it was the English who stopped slavery, but we never hear anything about that, do we?'

'Along with all the other countries that outlawed it,' pointed out Helen.

'And only after considerable pressure was applied over the years by anti-slavery activists,' spat Yvonne. 'And who got

---

[115] Yvonne is here referring to how the Quakers led a consumer campaign against slavery and its associated products. By 1791, almost 500,000 Britons supported the campaign.

paid compensation after abolition? The bloody slave owners, that's who!'[116]

'It was how most people saw the world back then,' muttered Hutchinson-Cockburn.

'Then shouldn't your precious Churchill, as the supposed Greatest Man Ever, have seen past the traditional colonial views of his time and realised what the real truth was?' demanded Yvonne, sarcasm dripping from her words. 'Doesn't the fact he held the same Establishment views as the Establishment itself make him Bog Standard Man? After all, he seemed to have been as trapped in the colonial mindset as much as you are!'

---

[116] Equivalent to around 300 million pounds, in today's money.

Chapter Sixteen

A continuation on the Great Man theory – and how our fictional constructs within Clavier and Coldwell react to the hidden side of Churchill …

'Is there any work going on here?' demanded Vansittart, re-entering the office with a contract in his hand and disapproval on his face. His finely tuned corporate antenna had picked up the lack of work going on in the front office, as well as the worrying outbreak of intelligent probing against Establishment norms. It's also possible he'd picked up a telepathic distress call from Hutchinson-Cockburn, who had absolutely no answer to Yvonne's questions.[117]

'We've just blown the justification for defending Churchill's ongoing racism as "being of the times", grinned Helen. 'People should have known better back then, but most still sided with hatred and bigotry. Just like today.'

'I'm sure he wasn't *perfect*,' said Vansittart, feeling himself to be a great beacon of liberal modernity for his sensitivity and ability to see the other person's point of view, no

---

[117] Vansittart and Hutchinson-Cockburn both live in posh, safe, comfortable worlds, where inconvenient facts are as about as welcome as a dose of venereal disease in a brothel. Is it any wonder they refuse to scratch the buboes of pub(l)ic conformity, for fear of witnessing the oozing pus of social injustice?

matter how wrong it was. 'But who is perfect? No one, that's who!'

'Well, I've never starved millions of Bengalis to death, so I think Churchill may be a little less perfect than me,' replied Helen.

'I'm sure he had nothing to do with starving people,' announced Sarah,[118] her Daily Crier sensibilities ruffled by the attack on their Greatest Ever Leader.

'And there was an actual famine in India at the time,' muttered Vansittart, giving Helen a dirty look as her attention was safely focussed on Sarah.

'A natural disaster he exacerbated by diverting resources away from those who needed it,' replied Helen, searching her bag for any loose cigarettes. She had a feeling she'd be needing a few extra before the end of the discussion.

'We needed food during the war shortage, what with all the rationing.' said Vansittart, staring at the far wall in noble martyrdom.

'So did the Indians, but hey, they only grew it in their own land, so what rights did they have to their own produce?'

'Churchill never gave up!' yapped Hutchinson-Cockburn. 'Unlike the French!' he added, glossing over 200,000 dead French fighters.

'I'm not sure how "He never gave up" excuses the famine, but maybe I'm funny that way,' replied Helen.

---

[118] Bet you forgot about Sarah, didn't you? And Felicity. Alas, this is the fate of most secondary characters in a work of fiction.
And real life.

'He was a hero; everyone knows it,' mumbled Vansittart, for though he was Helen's employer, he was intimidated by her higher intelligence and alarming gender. Which partly explained why he underpaid her.

'Really? My grandfather thought of him as a warmonger and self-serving egotist. Grandad fought in the First World War and refused to idolatrize Churchill throughout the Second. He had him down as a charlatan from the beginning. My parents spoke about it often, but because they were working class, their testimony was never recorded. Unlike the posh Establishment boys who get to write about how great Churchill was in book after book on the subject.'

'He stood alone against the Nazis!' barked Hutchinson-Cockburn.

'He thought just like a Nazi,' said Helen, rummaging in her bag again for her lighter. 'He hated people who were different, especially when they were darker, and he wanted a permanent British Empire, rather like Hitler and the Thousand Year Reich.'

'It was war!' snapped Hutchinson-Cockburn, answering a point no one had raised as this was easier than dealing with Helen's comment.

'And what about after the war, and the establishment of concentration camps in Kenya in the early 1950s?' replied Helen. 'Around one hundred and fifty thousand men, women and children were herded into the camps where rape, torture and mutilation were part of the policy of suppression. And all done on Churchill's watch as he was back in power by then. And he personally favoured taking the best of the Kenyon lands for white colonial settlers, not the native Kenyans.'[119]

'I'm sure it was only done for the best of reasons,' huffed Hutchinson-Cockburn.

'Really? How is mass torture of an indigenous people done for the best of reasons?'

'The empire had a civilising influence!' snapped Hutchinson-Cockburn.[120]

'How is raping and torturing thousands civilizing, exactly?'

---

[119] Churchill was at least consistent in his hatred. In 1921, he held forth to Edwin Montagu, Secretary of State for India, on how Kenya – an East African country whose first human settlers arrived around 3000BC, and which saw no European colonisation until around 1500BC – was (somehow) a white man's country.
Montagu's response to this was to label Churchill a fanatical settler type. And just to reiterate the point; *this was in 1921*. Which again knocks a hole in the "judge Churchill by the standards of the day" arguments made to defend him. But then, this perennial discourse is a favourite of those in the media, as seen when the right-wing magazine [name redacted] defended Establishment clone Lady Philomena Tabletop-Cuttlefish-Mopbucket [real name redacted] for repeatedly demanding to know (at a Buckingham Palace reception) where a Black UK-born woman was *really* from. The defence was that Lady Philomena Tabletop-Cuttlefish-Mopbucket was merely old and unfamiliar with modern thought ... and this was in 2022. 101 years *after* Montagu's reaction.
The more things change, the more they stay the same.

[120] Sadly, many English would agree, according to a survey of 2016.

'Security!' blurted Hutchinson-Cockburn after several seconds of frantic thought. 'For the good of society!'

'Whose society? The natives, or the invading overseers?'

'Both, obviously,' muttered Hutchinson-Cockburn, secure in the scientific knowledge that those from primitive or bad backgrounds could never achieve anything without assistance from people higher up the social and evolutionary ladder. After all, genetics counted for something – and explained pretty much everything in terms of who was on top and who was at the bottom of the social hierarchy.[121]

'Care to elaborate on that point, with historical references?' asked Yvonne, feeling she was learning more history from one hour of Helen's company than she had ever managed in an entire year at school.[122]

---

[121] A government advisor had to resign when several past social media comments with his name on them were made public. The comments themselves mostly revolved around Black people being of lower intelligence, the advocating of compulsory contraception to prevent a permanent underclass, and a general approval of eugenics.
Presumably, no one in the government saw anything wrong with these views.
Don't we have some lovely people in charge of us?

[122] This is not surprising; Tower Heights was a mediocre academy run by a board of middle-management freeloaders sucking as much government money into their bank accounts as possible while regurgitating officially approved conformity into the minds of the young.

'It was the times and you should move on from it!'' snapped Hutchinson-Cockburn, standing up to signify the conversation was over, the Last Word was his, and his Word was Law, before disappearing with a newspaper to the staff toilet.[123]

---

[123] Hutchinson-Cockburn's reactions and beliefs in this chapter may stem from a well-known psychological issue known as cognitive bias, in which the sufferer creates a false view of reality owing to faulty perceptions of the world. Unfortunately, the human brain – percolating in confirmation bias and self-deception – can be easily fooled, deliberately or otherwise, when receiving (mis)information, with the result that if one belief is absorbed, such as Churchill the Hero Beyond All Reproach, then this must be reiterated for evermore, and all facts to the contrary must be rejected.
The above chapter also raises another interesting question; why do we *need* heroes? And why do we so readily overlook their flaws? The term "hero" originated with the ancient Greeks, though to them a hero was someone who performed a feat far beyond the ability of most other people, thus becoming an example of what everyone else could aspire to – even if the feat wasn't morally laudable.
Jump forward a few centuries and we are still defining ourselves by our heroes, explaining why we – both individually and as a society – project so much onto them. Which is fine if the hero is indeed genuinely heroic, (in the modern sense, not the ancient Greek way), but this hero-worship can have negative effects on our personal and collective identity if it turns out our hero is less than perfect, for this forces us to question our own choices and who we consider ourselves to be.
Which may explain why our cultural/national/mythological heroes remain heroes even when stories of their insalubrious actions start bleeding out into the public sphere, as we can't bear to admit we could be wrong in our beliefs.

Chapter Seventeen

A rare glimpse into Yvonne's homelife – rare because trying to create an authentic picture of anyone's domestic situation is difficult enough, and the issue is even more problematic when dealing with lived experiences which are completely different to your (my) own, i.e. being a Black family in modern Britain. Hence this descriptor to remind the reader how Yvonne and her family are constructs of the imagination, and exist only as authorial interjections rather than as representations of real-life people.

Also, the chapter demonstrates the difficulty of getting on in life if you don't have financial and familial support – which is the main point of the narrative. And yes, I realise this goes against the high literary philosophy that multiple meanings can be teased out from a single text, but some books really are about just one thing.

And this novel is a prime example of that.

'What on earth is all this?' asked Yvonne's father, Derek, as Yvonne got home and immediately laid out the books Helen had loaned her on the dining room table.

'Just some research,' replied Yvonne, sorting out the notebook and pen she had purchased. She already had several notebooks and pens of different types and colours in her possession, as she knew from the Internet these were the essential props of any budding writer, but she believed the new plain pen and notebook set signified how she was now getting down to the real work of authorship, rather than simply dreaming about getting down to the real work of authorship.

'Research? For what?' asked Yvonne's grandmother, Mary, entering with a tablecloth. Despite her increasing frailty, Mary was still an active member of her local church, and she was also a frequent visitor in the Jones household, resulting in innumerable outbreaks of bickering between herself and her son-in-law.

'It's sort of a project,' began Yvonne.

'You can tell me after helping to set the table,' interrupted Mary, flapping the tablecloth with practised ease so the end billowed out over the books, obscuring them from view.[124]

Yvonne, recognising a lost domestic battle when she saw one, helped set the table before sitting down with her chosen volume, aware of her father's sceptical gaze.

'That's better,' nodded Mary, smoothing the tablecloth before giving her granddaughter a quick kiss on the forehead.

---

[124] This gives a pointed example on how, for those outside the elite, everyday chores hamper any chance of sustained creativity, because reality gets in the way. And now extend this artistic metaphor to everyday life, and you realise how capitalism has moulded an environment in which daily necessity – such as working so you can (if you're lucky) just afford to live – controls every part of our lives. When people are forced by necessity to work so hard for so little, then escape becomes impossible. No wonder so many do the lottery; the 1 in 45,000,000 random chance of winning offers far better odds of getting ahead through your own talent and effort in England's moribund oligarchical class-based capitalist system.

'What are you reading?' asked Yvonne's mother, Lily, as she hurried in with the plates.

'Books about history, and also Winston Churchill,' replied Yvonne before being interrupted by her father.

'Ah Churchill! Without him, we'd all be speaking German,' announced Derek, clearly thinking he was making a profoundly original observation.

'Churchill would have hated us because of our skin colour,' muttered Yvonne, her mind on Helen's comments.

'Rubbish!' snorted Derek, though he offered no argument against Yvonne's statement.

'One man's terrorist is another man's freedom fighter,' said Lily, trying to broker a dining table peace with the panacea of cliché.

'There's too much cynicism about these days,' muttered Derek.

'There's not enough godliness about, more like!' exclaimed Mary. 'People should ask; "What would Jesus do?" That would set them on the right path.'

'Or maybe we just need to have a better idea on who our heroes are, and remember they're all human and have human failings,' said Lily, again playing the peacemaker.

'If only,' replied Yvonne. 'You try criticising Churchill and see where it gets you.' She blushed as her father glared at her, realising he felt he was the target of her comment, though she'd really been thinking of Vansittart and Hutchinson-Cockburn.

'Churchill was a hero,' grumbled her father, laying down the law by tapping one stubby finger on the table, for he

189

had imbibed society's assumptions rather well over the years. 'That's what the focus should be on.'

'And ignore everything else?' asked Yvonne. 'Even if the rest of the person is awful?'

'We all need someone to look up to,' said Lily, noting her husband was lacking any coherent response.

'And that raises another interesting question,' said Yvonne, flipping through the pages of her notebook with her free hand. 'Who gets to decide who our heroes are?'

'How do you mean? asked her mother.

'Who decided that Churchill should be presented as a hero? Who decided what the narrative would and wouldn't include?'

'Easy; other people just like him,' said Mary, unexpectedly, for she rarely left the confines of theological statements and domestic routines. 'The rest of the establishment. They're the ones who control everything, so they're the ones who have the power to control Churchill's narrative.'

'Exactly, Nan!'

'Cobblers,' muttered Derek before flushing under his saintly mother-in-law's reproving glare. 'And you haven't said *why* you're reading those books.'

'It's for work,' mumbled Yvonne, correctly guessing the reaction to this statement.

'Paid work?' demanded her father, eagerly. 'Have you finally been taken on?' His tone suggested Yvonne had somehow been deficient in not immediately being employed within the company at upper managerial level.

'No, this is extra.'

'Extra paid?'

'No.'

'Why are you doing *more* unpaid work?' demanded Lily. 'You need to think about where you're heading in your life!'

'You need to think about the future, my girl,' agreed Derek.

'This *is* for my future,' replied Yvonne.

'I don't see how doing something for free is helping,' sniffed Lily.

'This could get me noticed by Michael, and maybe get me a paid post with the company.' Yvonne kept quiet on her hopes of working on the biography; she doubted either parent would view such an activity as being worth anyone's time, unless it came with a salary.

'Get you noticed?' echoed her mother. 'Working hard gets you noticed!'

'I am working hard,' muttered Yvonne, thinking of the eternal cleaning, scrubbing, and vacuuming waiting for her at the office. And that was before dealing with the never-ending tedium of her administrative duties which seemed to envelop the rest of the day.

'You don't just get things handed to you,' stated Derek. 'You have to *work* for them!' [125]

---

[125] The author is tempted to ask why those who work long and hard in administration, motor engineering, mining, assembly lines, cleaning etc are not all living in mansions while being made the Chancellor of the Exchequer or similar; if hard work really does equate to success, surely this should be a given?

'Rupert Hutchinson-Cockburn gets everything handed to him,' muttered Yvonne, blinking away tears at her parents' tone.

'We're not talking about him,' said Lily, firmly closing the lid on any attempt to open the box of social inequality, as per her social training, which saw any such Pandoran action as being nothing more than excuses and social envy.

'Exactly!' snorted Derek. 'This is the real world![126] You're eighteen now; it's time you acted like it! What are all these books going to do for you?'

'They're improving my knowledge and critical thought processes,' muttered Yvonne.

'Pah!' snorted Derek.

'We can't keep you forever,' said Lily. 'Have you made your five-year work plan yet?'

---

[126] This demonstrates how effectively both Derek and Lily had been indoctrinated with the belief that wealth is the yardstick of success – and societal acceptance. This represents an astonishing accomplishment by society, which has warped an otherwise amiable couple into holding the ideology imposed by the elite, (judging poverty as being synonymous with immorality, believing hard work will be rewarded etc), while giving them absolutely nothing in return except for a false sense of superiority over other people.
In doing so, Derek and Lily have been condemned to the pursuit of an existence interpreted purely through the prism of capitalist dogma. It's like Stockholm Syndrome but for an entire society, with the captors being the wealthy elite, their weapons being cultural indoctrination, and the hostages being the general citizenry.

'No,' mumbled Yvonne, who was beginning to suspect any such document would be a greater work of fantasy than *The Lord of the Rings*.

'And how do you expect to get anywhere without planning your life and applying yourself?' demanded Derek.

'And don't think you'll be able to laze around on benefits, like some do!' added Lily before her daughter could even speak.[127]

'Damn right,' nodded Derek. 'We worked hard without claiming any benefits or handouts!'

'No handouts?' exclaimed Mary. 'Who gave you the loan to start your first nursery? All my life savings! And Richard's, God rest him,' she added, belatedly recognising the money left behind by her husband after forty years working on the London buses, supplemented by innumerable cash-in-hand musical gigs in many a pub backroom.

---

[127] By this, Lily is referring to the so-called "feckless poor", aka the benefit cheats/benefit scroungers/lower orders/the working classes etc; all easy stereotypes inculcated within her by the Establishment. It's worth saying again how the true working-class isn't represented in this novel as they can't get close to an opportunity even in a *fictional* world, never mind the real one.

And this also explains the complete absence of any LGBTQIA+ characters within the novel. And the near-complete absence of any intelligent people. Or empathetic people. Or any lefties. None of them have any place in the Daily Crier society depicted in this novel.

Or in the Daily Crier society you can see by looking out of the window.

193

'That was business, and you got it all back!' snapped Derek, waving the inconvenient facts away, as well as the lack of interest on the loan.

'After you were turned down by several banks, as I recall,' smirked Mary. 'And you were still living with me, rent free, in the early days.'

'And we kept on working until we succeeded!' retorted Derek. 'Lily and I did it all alone.'

'Oh, *you* succeeded all alone, did you?' replied Mary. 'And who was looking after Yvonne when she was born? Who took care of her when Lily went back to work at the nursery? And all for nothing, as I was living on my pension!'

'That was family,' muttered Derek, a double standard that reduced Yvonne to an incoherent stammer of utter frustration.

'And was "family" the reason I was making your breakfast before you left, and dinner when you got back, and doing all your laundry, and doing any other jobs for you while you were out at work? And you sit there and say you did it *alone*?'

'Being self-employed is hard work and requires sacrifices!' snapped Derek. 'That's what Yvonne needs to learn. She needs to learn the value of money!'

'Sweet Lord,' replied Mary. 'I hate it when men talk about "the value of money". They always sound so smug about it.'

'Yvonne has to learn self-reliance, like I did!'

'Did your self-reliance come before or after I gave you several thousand pounds?'

'Yvonne has to learn life owes you nothing!' shouted Derek as he leapt up and stalked from the room, pausing to deliver a final line from the safety of the door. 'We all work the same hours and have the same chances, and the sooner she learns that, the better!'[128]

---

[128] Once again, I urge the reader to revisit footnotes #22 and #125 for a rebuttal on this. (Or perhaps I should *enjoin* them, for the sake of literary merit?)

The reader may also wish to consider the points raised here by Mary; Derek and Lily only succeeded in their business as they had family wealth and support (no matter how modest) to fall back on. Without Mary's money and help in looking after them, (feeding, homing and loaning), their endeavour would most likely have failed, or at least it would never have been as fruitful, as they would not have had the same time, energy and finance to build their business. And perhaps even more importantly, they had the security of knowing they could fail without any real consequence of losing everything, for Mary was there to catch and hold them.

And yet they genuinely believe they did it all themselves, and they sneer at all those who don't – i.e. who can't – even try owing to the lack of spondulicks, support, and a safety net. To risk your savings, house, health etc when you have no support network is to truly risk everything, something the wealthy don't have to worry about as they will always have the family mansion to return to each night, and dear old Uncle Algernon Tyce Badger-Border-Bodger (of the Kent Badger-Border-Bodgers, not the dreadfully vulgar Worcestershire Badger-Border-Bodgers) will no doubt find you a nice little crib in his company if things do go south with your start-up scheme.

See also Chapter Thirteen.

Chapter Eighteen

A contemplation of the assumptions of the publishing world, in which we see how Vansittart's claims for diversity and inclusion are little more than performative, for Clavier and Coldwell publish only a very few "non-traditional" writers – and then only on the presumption these writers will adhere to certain subject matters.

Note also how a smidgeon of extra snark is filtering onto the main page again ...

Hutchinson-Cockburn watched in suspicion as the Black girl gathered several sheets into a large file marked *Churchill Biography Submissions.* He'd been ogling her for the past few days owing to her recently upgraded fashion sense, for she was now favouring skirts or dresses accentuating her figure, and he instinctively knew she was dressing to please him; he was an attractive Alpha Male, so it was inevitable. But duty before pleasure, and given he strongly suspected the papers had something to do with submissions for the Churchill biography, he followed both folder and figure as they headed up to Vansittart's office.

'Are those the Churchill biography submissions?' asked Vansittart, his gaze flicking from the folder labelled *Churchill Biography Submissions* to Yvonne's short skirt. The contents of the folder warmed him in the wallet as he thought about the potential profits, while the skirt warmed him elsewhere for he instinctively knew Yvonne was dressing to please him; he was an attractive, sophisticated man, so it was inevitable. Not that he'd ever act on it, of course. Not with his wife calling and texting regularly throughout the day.

'I've separated out the more interesting ones,' replied Yvonne, removing some of the printed sheets. She was momentarily distracted by Hutchinson-Cockburn walking in behind her and leaning against the far wall, hence she missed Vansittart's reaction to the word "interesting". "Interesting" was not what he, as a publisher or as a man, was looking for. Rather, he wanted familiarity, for the familiar was comfortable, stable, and reassuring. And he knew his readers felt the same way.

'This comes from a Doctor Ferdinand Ndam, of Cameroon, who has the idea of exploring Churchill's colonial ideology. Doctor Ndam says he can offer a unique insight as he has access to many records from both the German occupation of the area after the "scramble for Africa," as well as the carving up of the country under the French and British after World War One.'

Yvonne spoke with the illusion of confidence, hoping she wasn't pressed for details; she wasn't too knowledgeable about the "scramble for Africa" because foreign history, like British history, geography, art, and indeed most of the humanities, had been deemed by her school to be of less capital importance than economics and business studies.[129]

'Too wide a remit,' replied Vansittart, his cultural instincts rising against any in-depth examination of colonialism. 'It wouldn't be popular with the paying public. And remember this is a biography about one man and his role in destiny, so a specific tone is required.'

'All right,' responded Yvonne, shuffling the printed sheets. 'How about this? Churchill and India? A Mr Umang Joshi has family diaries going back all the way to the early eighteen hundreds ...'

'Again, it's not really going to be commercial enough,' interrupted Vansittart, alarmed at Churchill's "old fashioned" attitudes toward India being given airtime. As a publisher and as a man of culture, he knew discretion was the better part of valour – which was the closest he could ever come to admitting, even to himself, that not everything about Churchill was commendable. 'We need something unique to this country.'

'How about this?' continued Yvonne, glad to have dropped the Indian approach because, when all was said and done, it was Indian. 'A postgraduate student wants to convert his PhD on how Churchill has been constructed by the Establishment as one of the Greatest Myths of the Modern Age, and so he – the student, that is – asks questions about the morality of Churchill's character and actions given he –

---

[129] Yvonne is by no means stupid, but she is culturally stupefied. Hence her increasing awareness under Helen's cynicism. See also the next footnote.

Churchill, I mean – was ready, willing, and able to destroy countless lives across the world to preserve his own privileged and exclusive existence.'

'That sounds like an excuse for socialistic Churchill bashing,' interrupted Hutchinson-Cockburn, reminding everyone of his presence by wilfully misinterpreting the PhD under discussion.

'Exactly, Rupert,' agreed Vansittart, wearing the expression of a man reluctantly sniffing a dead fish. 'What are we, the looney left? I think not!'

'Then how about this idea from Doctor Jayne Griffiths?' asked Yvonne. 'She's already done a lot of research at Wolverhampton University, and she wants to approach Churchill from a working-class perspective ...'

'Absolutely not,' snorted Vansittart. Wolverhampton? Where even was that? It sounded suspiciously north. And as for the notion of the working-classes being able to write...

'But she's already written three very successful histories on the working classes through the twentieth century,' pointed out Yvonne, waving Doctor Griffiths' covering documents which ticked off all the criteria specified in the original submission call. 'She comes with an inbuilt market. And academic credibility!'[130]

---

[130] The reader may notice Yvonne has taken something of a quantum leap in terms of her knowledge, (though not, unfortunately, her racism). This is the artificiality of the novel, as personal development – which would normally take place over some considerable time – has to be concentrated into the artificial form of 60 - 80,000 words.

Vansittart weakened for a shameful moment at the mention of an existing market to tap into for commercial return, but his innate good sense reasserted itself almost immediately.[131] 'No, I know our readership; the solid, silent majority who make up this country. They know what to expect from Clavier and Coldwell Publishing, and we must never break our contract with them!'

Vansittart glanced at the printout and saw another issue missed by the young and inexperienced Yvonne; Jayne Griffiths' age was down as thirty-six. Which meant she either had children, which would distract her from the work, or else she would soon be having children – assuming she was one of those pushy career women who put off marriage until it was almost too late – which again would distract her from the work. And that was an unacceptable business risk for Clavier and Coldwell.

There was nothing personal about it, as Vansittart told himself; it was just good sense and economics. After all, it wasn't as if he *enjoyed* being the Arbiter and Gatekeeper of That Which Was Proper, but it was a *duty* nonetheless, and he would be *nothing* if he did not *serve* as his father, grandfather and great-grandfather had served before him – with *care, diligence,* and *professionalism*. He glanced at the

---

[131] Research into reading habits found very few men – around 19% of the total readership – will read top selling women authors. In contrast, top selling male authors attract a closer demographic of 55% male to 45% female.

clock, wondering if he could slip away for an early lunch.

'Then what are you looking for?' asked Yvonne, spreading the papers out on the desk. 'You did say this was going to be a new and innovative approach.'

'Yes, yes, but the work must also have sound scholarship behind it,' replied Vansittart.

'You mean a biography on the Establishment by the Establishment?' replied Yvonne, sounding rather like Helen.

'Market forces make these decisions.'

'Market forces alone are choosing posh white men for publication?' asked Yvonne with considerable restraint.

'We publish Black voices,' protested Vansittart, picking up a handy catalogue as proof and quickly flipping through to the *Commitment to Diversity* page. 'Nina Rogerson's *The Estate;* a harrowing tale of growing up Black and disadvantaged in modern Britain. Elizabeth Giraudy's *The Slave Trade*. Martin Clarke's *The Slave Trade in Africa*. Richard Huntingdon-Reyes *How the British Stopped the Slave Trade*.'

'Huntingdon-Reyes is white.'

'Yes, but it's all here; the representation,' said Vansittart, wondering if he should chide Yvonne for her racism against Huntingdon-Reyes. He decided not to in case she got upset, as her kind were wont to do. 'And all these volumes sit proudly on my own bookcase.' He gestured at the relevant shelving against the far wall, where the volumes in question did indeed sit, at the bottom, untouched. Apart from the Huntingdon-Reyes, of course.

'And do you notice anything about these examples?' asked

Yvonne, her smile trembling as it threatened to turn into a snarl.

'Yes; they're all about Black people,' replied Vansittart, confused by Yvonne's tone. 'They all show our diversity,' he continued, proudly.

'Diversity? Every non-white writer here is pigeon-holed into "acceptable" areas; the slavery narrative, the racism narrative, the growing up poor and disadvantaged narrative. Where are the Black writers on Churchill, or the Duke of Wellington? Why are all non-white authors forced down the road of writing only about racism or slavery? Why do they have to follow certain tropes to be accepted?'[132]

'I suppose they have their own interests, in their own history, you know, in Black history, not white,' spluttered Vansittart.

'And Britain is the least racist country there is!' exclaimed Hutchinson-Cockburn, parroting a phrase he'd often seen on social media. And in the tabloids. And heard spoken by many right-wing pundits.

'And you think that's somehow laudable?' demanded Yvonne. 'Being slightly less bad than somewhere else makes you better?'

---

[132] A known issue within the publishing industry, but not one which is being addressed in any meaningful manner. Certainly nothing will ever change within Clavier and Coldwell, given Vansittart's routine promises to bring out new and exciting works before defaulting to his usual practice of disseminating more of the same.

'Things are changing,' muttered Vansittart, feeling he was being personally attacked and found unjustly guilty just for being a genuinely nice guy.[133]

'So, you agree we need more Black people doing this sort of biography? This sort of work? To show how British history is everyone's history, and is not just the preserve of the wealthy elite?'

'Well, yes, of course,' mumbled Vansittart in financial, historical, and cultural horror at the idea of "Churchill by a Black Writer". After all, if the world was ready for such a thing, it would already have happened. The fact it hadn't happened was proof it couldn't happen.

'So wouldn't it make sense to employ someone to do it?' continued Yvonne, excited at pushing her ideas forward while simultaneously feeling societal shame in demonstrating ambition while being female.[134]

---

[133] A nice Establishment guy who does absolutely nothing to challenge or change the inherent bigotry within Establishment society. Not that Vansittart would ever recognise this fact.

[134] Ambition and leadership in a woman are still viewed far more negatively than in a man, as demonstrated by a professor's experiment when he handed half his students a scenario revolving around "Howard", and the other half the same scenario but involving "Heidi". The students pretty much all took against Heidi.
It's interesting to wonder, as my PhD supervisor did at this point, how this scenario would have played out in the UK; would the insular English be against Heidi just for her Germanic name? After all, anti-German feeling still runs deep in this country, what with the "We'd-all-be-speaking-German-if-it-wasn't-for-Winston" attitudes out there, the

'If the right person should apply,' stuttered Vansittart, before remembering Yvonne had already mentioned doing the project herself. He hadn't given the matter a first thought since, never mind a second, but now his horrified mind realised Yvonne was being serious. 'Er, are you ready to submit a fully costed proposal on the submission call?' he asked, retreating into official language while squirming in the face of naked female ambition.

'I have been researching ideas, yes, though I need some guidance on how best to present the facts,' replied Yvonne, determined to butter Vansittart up in order to pin him down.

'Er, well, yes, in all things we must, I must consider, how in all things, we must all be considered,' waffled Vansittart in dismay, trying to show he was fully supportive of any and all Black endeavour while not actually agreeing to support any Black endeavour if he could possibly help it. 'Or Helen can help,' he blurted in relief, realising there was no reason he had to deal with the issue when he had a paid underling who could do it instead. Along with all her other work.

'So, I can start looking into it, can I?' demanded Yvonne, pressing Vansittart for a firm decision. She was slightly ashamed she was using such an important sociological issue to manipulate events to her own advantage and so, rather like Vansittart assuring himself his company was a beacon

---

very phrase revealing the racist superiority complex oozing from every English pore.

of modernity and tolerance, she hastily framed her behaviour as noble altruism on behalf of the entire Black community. Which at least enabled her to maintain her own self-image.[135]

'Oh, yes, indeed, jolly good, we'll have to meet, I mean schedule a meet, but not for a few weeks, give me time – give you time to get something down,' mumbled Vansittart, edging toward the door and lunch. 'See you tomorrow,' he called out, deciding he would get more done by working from home, without any further interruptions.

Behind him, Yvonne recognised (once again) that Vansittart wasn't interested in her taking on the project, but she (once again) vigorously reinterpreted the scene until she arrived at a fantasy version in which he was merely *hesitant* about the idea of her doing the project, meaning she just needed to work on him gently, discreetly, and diplomatically.[136]

And on a completely unrelated note, Yvonne decided tomorrow she would get one of her low-cut tops out of the wardrobe.

Because it really was very warm in the office.

---

[135] Though Yvonne does at least have the genuine excuse that she is outside the elite, and so she has no choice but to exploit any advantage going.

[136] And thus self-deception keeps Yvonne's hopes alive for a little longer. Though whether this is a good thing or not is one for the psychologists.

Chapter Nineteen

A symbolic chapter, and I should probably apologise in being so crass as to point out the symbolism within – but alerting the reader to the inherent artificiality of our cultural norms is basically what this novel is all about.

As such, we have the significance of Yvonne expanding her perceptions by learning about the very essence of history, while in contrast Hutchinson-Cockburn merely bolsters his position by quoting from traditional historical authority, thereby using the past to support the present.

The following morning saw Yvonne staggering to work under a considerable weight of books. Having decided that knowledge of Churchill the man was not enough for a decent biography, she had done her best to equip herself (via an Internet search) with a selection of tomes on the nature and construction of history itself. Unfortunately, Yvonne didn't have any spare cash for these essential items, so she paid an early morning visit to the Kensington Manor library, wherein she hit upon another snag; the library didn't have the latest editions of any of the items on her list.

Yvonne inquired about ordering the updated versions, which the helpful librarian was very happy to do, but this carried a charge of £5.99 for each individual book, something Yvonne just could not afford as she was earning no money at all at Clavier and Coldwell. Indeed, the only cash she had in her purse came from her father's grudging pocket money which barely covered her travel costs, and Yvonne had felt a hot flush of shame at her relative poverty.[137]

In contrast to Yvonne's plight, let us now turn to Hutchinson-Cockburn. He was uncharacteristically worried he was being outshone by a girl, (and by a Black girl, at that), so he decided to bone up on a little history; hence some two hours after Yvonne had entered the library in search of her books, Hutchinson-Cockburn was browsing a major high street book retailer before continuing to work.

Inside, Hutchinson-Cockburn found it difficult to know what to choose, but he knew he could trust his innate good taste and breeding in making his selection. Grabbing the volumes nearest to hand, he made his way to the till to pay for his goods, openly ogling the filly behind the counter for she had very large breasts, and Hutchinson-Cockburn felt it was an excellent mark of his character that he should pay attention to a shopgirl, for it demonstrated he had no snobbery or side about him whatsoever.

---

[137] If you think it utterly deplorable that anyone should feel ashamed about their financial situation after being born outside the wealthy elite, then you are neither a politician nor a journalist.
Yvonne's financial situation, incidentally, also explains her habit of making a sandwich at home and carrying it in for lunch each day, rather than popping out for a quick bite or, as in the case of Vansittart, a full meal of at least two courses, more usually three. With a bottle of wine. Sometimes two. And a full cheeseboard. And a choice of liqueurs. And coffee. And probably a brandy thereafter.

'Just these three, my darling,' he leered, wondering whether to ask the girl out as she was bound to be a right little slapper in the bedroom.[138]

'Ninety-six pounds, ninety-seven pence,' replied the woman, giving him a cold stare.

Bloody lesbian, though Hutchinson-Cockburn as he riffled through his wallet. *Bet she could put on a show for me, though, and then I'd her give a bit of dick, show her what's she's missing … Get her and the Blackamoor in from the office, we all know what they're like in bed, and wahey!*

He abandoned his pornographic line of thought to focus on money. He'd accidentally taken out the bank card for his trust fund rather than his current account, and he was momentarily dithering between which card to use, though in truth there was little difference between them; the trust fund clocked up an ever-increasing balance from his innumerable inherited dividends, while the current account was kept healthy by the fortnightly allowance direct from his father.

Hutchinson-Cockburn finally decided to use the current account, though he would have to be frugal until his next payday; although the new shoes he'd bought yesterday had been a very modest one thousand, one hundred pounds, he'd also treated himself to a new jacket, watch, cap, and

---

[138] Hutchinson-Cockburn's thought processes could be summed up as; she works in a shop, therefore she is working class, therefore she is sexually promiscuous. It wasn't exactly a syllogism, but it was certainly close enough for his purposes.

several nights out with his friends, meaning his current account was now dipping down alarmingly low – almost as low as five figures.

He would have to cut his cloth accordingly, and maintain an austere lifestyle until the next cash injection arrived; he'd only be able to enjoy three or four nights out at *Tranters*, the exclusive nightclub of choice for the Bright Young Things, and he would have to cut back on dining out, limiting himself to no more than two or three days in the week at his favourite restaurant. And maybe postpone buying the rather splendid watch he'd seen in a jeweller's window until next month.

Truly, he suffered.

On arriving at the office, Hutchinson-Cockburn perched his books ostentatiously on top of his desk for all to see and admire, in contrast to Yvonne who had carefully hidden her elderly library books out of sight as she was still feeling the shame of her poverty.

The office was quiet for a few hours as everyone got on with their work; Sarah was busy on a contract which would give the company twenty percent of all authorial royalties, both home and abroad. Helen was proofing a romance novel, one of the few financially successful series helping keep the company floating upon the sea of incipient bankruptcy, though the leaks of a changing marketplace coupled to the choppy waters of bad business decisions were deflating the dinghy of solvency with every passing nautical mile. Felicity was ordering a fresh supply of pencils, while Hutchinson-Cockburn was glancing over a historical submission on the War of the Roses, though his real focus was on one of the history books he'd bought earlier, now secreted on his lap.

'Interesting,' boomed Hutchinson-Cockburn over the office space as he carelessly copied and pasted a standard rejection email to the War of the Roses submission, for the writer had attended state school and some unknown provincial university.

'What is?' asked Sarah and Felicity, both of whom were rather fond of Hutchinson-Cockburn's insouciant manner, delightful pedigree, and charming wealth.

'This book on the War of the Roses,' beamed Hutchinson-Cockburn as the female gaze focussed upon him, though he noted he was missing fifty percent of the female gaze as neither Helen nor Yvonne looked his way. He glanced approvingly at the new history book on his lap, and the chapter entitled "Invalid History" by Anthony Fitzwilliam.[139] 'It's got me thinking about how you can't change history, no matter what *some* may say.'

Yvonne looked up from the book on her lap by which she was continuing her education not only on history, but on how to *think* about history. 'You mean?'

You cannot change the past,' replied Hutchinson-Cockburn. 'Facts are facts!'

---

[139] All the history books used in this chapter are, once again, entirely fictitious. Apart from being based on real history books, of course. But apart from that, they are entirely fictitious.

'Come on, be specific,' challenged Yvone.

'"It's ridiculous to say any historian imposes a slant or story upon his facts,"' intoned Hutchinson-Cockburn, his face turned to the office, his plummy speaking tone rising to the heavens, his eyes straying to the book on his lap as his mouth passed off someone else's words as his own.

'Then what are facts?' asked Helen, sarcasm edging her tone.

'Well,' replied Hutchinson-Cockburn, glancing down again. '"Any historical event is a fact ... a historian gathers certain events and pieces them together, with no fear or favour."'

'Codswallop,' replied Helen. 'The historian can't help but interpret history according to their own biases.'[140]

---

[140] In support of Helen's statement, you could seek out and compare two books both bearing the same title, *Churchill and the Jews,* in which the separate authors (Martin Gilbert and Michael Cohen respectively) explore Churchill's attitudes and feelings towards Jewish people and yet come to differing conclusions on the matter.
Gilbert takes the view that Churchill was a supporter of the Jewish people, whereas Michael Cohen believes Churchill's actions were motivated only by the payback he would receive, either to himself directly (such as by gaining votes from the large Jewish population in his constituency or receiving loans from Jewish benefactors) or else because it would be good for the Empire.
Delving into one specific occasion; both books explore Churchill's fight against the Conservative Government's 1904 Aliens Bill, a piece of legislation ostensibly concerned with foreign immigration but which was primarily aimed at Russian Jews looking to settle in the UK. It is striking to see how Gilbert portrays Churchill's part in defeating the bill as heroic and decent, while Cohen is rather more cynical, noting that Churchill himself never believed the Government would pass the bill

'"Cold hard facts alone lay down the truth of history,"' quoted Hutchinson-Cockburn.

'Ah; so you think a posh white historian, who knows nothing outside his posh white world, will suddenly become aware of the issues facing the non-posh white population by reading up only on diaries, reports and histories written by posh white people?'

'Facts are facts!' insisted Hutchinson-Cockburn.

'But are they?' countered Yvonne, riffling through her own hidden pages to find an extract to support her developing view of history, while also breathing a silent "thank you" to the library for stocking Clare Thompson's *The Story of History*. '"Facts alone do not exist. All facts are sorted, arranged, and placed before the reader in a particular manner, with some facts being emphasised while others are marginalised. And it is the historian who makes the judgment on how the facts are to be laid out."'

'Balderdash,' sighed Hutchinson-Cockburn, rolling his eyes upward before hastily spinning them back down to his lap. '"All history is a process, and all processes lay out our history. There is no other way of viewing this."'

'Yes, there is,' said Yvonne, glancing at her knees for another quote. '"School history books have long echoed the

---

for fear of alienating their own affluent Jewish allies – hardly the attitude of a man free from stereotypical prejudice.
Why and how can two accounts of the same historical event be displayed so differently? Is it all down to unconscious bias? Or is it a deliberate distortion to further a conscious agenda?

official line laid out by the political elite, focusing as they do on the establishment's greatest achievers while marginalising those without power, wealth, or access to historians. Even though the marginalised were present at so many great historical events."'

'Facts are facts,' snapped Hutchinson-Cockburn. 'You can't change them!'

'Really?' said Yvonne, glancing back down. '"Recent years has seen the visibility of marginalised groups rise in the public consciousness as their stories and identities have finally been acknowledged; new facts have emerged, and old facts have been exposed as inaccurate, or even entirely wrong."'

'Pah!' snorted Hutchinson-Cockburn, desperately flipping for an agreeable quote. '"If anyone can now write a history, then everyone else can now be marginalised. What good does it do to have the great men and women of each era swept away in favour of some unknown characters who just happened to be there? And who decides who we focus on? Will black historians demand the erasure of non-black participants?"' He nodded in a pointed manner at Yvonne, noting afresh her suspicious skin tone, but refrained from saying anything out loud.[141]

'Traditional history has already marginalised the underdog,' retorted Yvonne, her eyes returning to *The Story*

---

[141] It's interesting to note how Hutchinson-Cockburn automatically swerves away from articulating his racism – but then, people do live in denial about their own prejudices.

of History. 'You'd think there were no Black or working-class people in Britain, the way some people go on. And bear in mind "no fact exists independent of its context, or the context of the historian who examines that fact."'

'"Why not give time to the Marxist historian, so he may marginalise those he politically disagrees with?"' boomed Hutchinson-Cockburn, wrapped up in the sentiments which reassured him that his way of living, his way of *existing*, was correct. '"Trendy Marxist history makes the apolitical political. It denies human agency from the top down, rendering us all as slaves to economic forces. And this is the real oppression against people of all societies." There is the truth on the lefty historian! [142]

---

[142] My PhD supervisor's response to this chapter was to note it was almost turning into a rap battle between Yvonne and Hutchinson-Cockburn – which inspired me to do a posh boy rap on behalf of the boy from the grim urban ghetto of Kensington and Chelsea:
"I'm the Rupert H to the C
I'm so posh I can use the Royal We
I'm a gangster straight outta Eton
So well-bred I can't be beaten
Mother so loose she wears only fox fur
Scandals in the family? They do sometimes occur
Standing up for my brothers out in the ghetto
To escape Kensington and Chelsea, we gotta let go
My class don't benefit me, I keep it real
So down with the poor, I make do with veal
But come at our man, Winston our hero
I'll take you down, You're Rome to my Nero
(chorus)
Churchill was Great
Churchill was Lean

'And Churchill was the greatest Brit ever!' added Hutchinson-Cockburn. 'And that's an indisputable fact!'

'And where do these "indisputable facts" come from?' demanded Helen.

'From history, obviously.'

'And where does history come from? Does it just appear in history books by some divine hand? Or does it have to be written down by people?'

'Tcha!' snorted Hutchinson-Cockburn. 'Historians are trained specialists. They know what they're doing.'

'That's debatable.'

'And I suppose you think history is a conspiracy?' sneered Hutchinson-Cockburn.

'It certainly smells of a conspiracy of unthinking elitist tradition,' replied Helen, 'with every writer simply taking their cues from the writers who came before, with no original thought going on anywhere in the process. And it's those attitudes and beliefs which go into everything. Books. Plays. Newspapers. Films. Nothing exists in a vacuum.'

'Except dust!' replied Hutchinson-Cockburn, the smug expression on his face demonstrating he had scored a palpable hit.

Churchill beat the Germans
By playing it clean
All you communists hiding in the buisson
This is the Church-Hill I will die on."
Etc.

'So those with power are able to describe and define everything, meaning they also control everything, because they get to tell us *how* to look at the world, which in effect tells us what the world is?' asked Yvonne.

'Exactly,' nodded Helen. 'Which is why an unregulated government of posh rich elitists, supported by the billionaire-owned press is so dangerous to democracy; we don't get the news in a newspaper; we get the *filtered interpretation* of news.

'Rubbish!' snorted Hutchinson-Cockburn. 'Facts are facts, and you can't change them!'

'Facts are not facts, as we have been trying to explain to you for the past hour,' sighed Helen. 'Those with the power to be published, by which I mean the wealthy elite and their sycophants, are the people who get to describe how the world is; they control the very definition of what our reality is, and how it is consumed. This is why Churchill the man has been effectively turned into Churchill the Myth.'[143]

'We'd be speaking German if not for him!' exclaimed Hutchinson-Cockburn.

'Behold the stock phrase from the stock man,' sniggered Helen. 'It's what Churchill's supporters always say – and I bet the anti-German racism comes to them very easily. But do they ever look at what he did in office during the war? The decisions he made? The decisions other people –

---

[143] Again, bear in mind this novel is concerned exclusively with how the populist perception of Churchill has been formed – and how it is maintained. See also Chapter Thirteen.

people in the government or the military – made? No, they just trot out the same repeated phrases and deny any chance of establishing a more balanced, nuanced approach to history.'

'Facts are facts!' exclaimed Hutchinson-Cockburn.

'Facts are never just facts. When someone researches an area, everything passes through their own filters and perceptions. And their work then passes through the *reader's* perceptions because they interpret it according to *their* preconceived biases. Beliefs usually formed by the status quo. Meaning their beliefs are usually little more than biases.'

'I'm not biased!'

'You parrot the pro-Churchillian line without considering if another point of view could be equally valid,' interrupted Yvonne.

'Yup,' agreed Helen. 'Blind replication.'

'Historians don't blindly replicate!' whined Hutchinson-Cockburn.

'Then why did Thomas Becket become known as Thomas à Becket for centuries?' asked Helen. 'Some bugger bunged a letter "A" with an acute accent into his name and it stuck. By replication. For generations.'

'Lefty rubbish!' seethed Hutchinson-Cockburn.

'Rupert is part of the system, and a beneficiary of it, meaning he can't see the value of critical thought,' said Helen.

'Lefty rubbish!' repeated Hutchinson-Cockburn.

'Good critical practice tells us to be aware of our own biases – which is a lesson *some* people could do with learning. Here, try reading this; Johann Herzlos's *Constructing History,* a collection of ninety-seven essays on how dodgy history is forever repeated as Holy Writ by the elite.' Helen selected a solid book from one of her shelves and skimmed it over to Hutchinson-Cockburn, striking him in the assumptions. 'You might discover a new way of thinking, and become a better person as a result.'[144]

---

[144] Hutchinson-Cockburn becoming a better person is highly unlikely to happen in real life as he is essentially a social parasite preserved in cultural amber, perfectly insulated from criticism by his social privilege. And this is one of the reasons why nothing will ever change in society. So, if you've enjoyed watching Hutchinson-Cockburn getting his arse handed to him, please bear in mind this can only happen in a work of fiction.

However, for those (unlike Hutchinson-Cockburn) who are interested in expanding their horizons, this might be a good place to look at qualitive research which, broadly speaking, is designed to allow us to see how others see the world. The qualitative research methods used in this PhD were ethnography, autoethnography, media framing and semiotics. (The other methodology was "snark", though this isn't technically an academic discipline, alas). These will now be briefly examined in turn, (except for the snark), after which we can get back to the story.

Ethnography is the study of the beliefs, assumptions, and behaviours found in any given group, be it a country-sized group, a group comprising a community, a religion, a social level, a workplace, or even just a few friends down the pub. Autoethnography, meanwhile, came about as researchers started to realise those with power, (political, educational, media etc) were able to describe, define, and therefore control (to an extent) that which they were describing. As such, rather than simply writing something down as a fact, the good qualitative researcher will employ ethnography to ask whether the supposed fact is indeed a fact, where it comes from, and why people believe it, while autoethnography encourages the researcher to be aware of their own assumptions and attitudes, to avoid repeating the assumptions and attitudes of those who came before.

Media framing, meanwhile, focusses on how the media handles any given story, and examines how a news event can be filtered, edited, and distorted to present a particular perspective or ideology. One clear example of media framing can be found in the documented lies told by the right-wing press in their presentation of the 'loony left', i.e. any non-wealthy/posh/white/male/hetero entity. One Sunday newspaper, for example, told of Haringey Council's supposed policy of banning black bin bags as the bags were deemed to be racist – but the story was at best garbled, at worse a lie, though the paper never admitted this. And why would it? It had done its job of throwing shit against the wall, meaning its credulous dim-witted readers would remember the stains and not the lack of content.

And it's not just the media who manipulates us into a particular worldview; our very language influences and even controls our thoughts and ideas. This can be seen in the study of semiotics, aka the study of signs and meaning, an academic field which, like media framing, strongly supports the notion that the Establishment's use of language to control society is truly deliberate.

Language may appear to be neutral and obvious, but it is anything but. The *denotation* of a word is the meaning of the word/sign/symbol itself, whereas the *connotation* is what the word/sign/symbol ideologically represents, and thus words *create meaning,* and that meaning is political because it has both a role to play and a mission to perform. Churchill is a perfect example; what do you think of when you hear the name or see a picture of the man? Most probably (if you're a tabloid reader) you'll immediately think of bravery, tenacity, standing firm etc. But why do you think that? Because the words *tell you to do so*. And who controls the meaning behind the words? The journalists, the historians, the writers ... and thus the Establishment.

219

The words used to construct this reality appear time and again in Churchillian discourse, regurgitated almost without fail, with 'We'd all be speaking German if it weren't for Winston' being the most common refrain. And with each replication of these words, the sign-system is renewed afresh thanks to binary thinking, an important aspect of sociological construction and semiotic research, for in a binary society things can only be right or wrong, black or white, up or down etc.

This tendency to structure the way we view the world is seen clearly with the media's framing of Churchill into a series of binary oppositions, (Churchill v Nazis, or Churchill v fascism), which can then be elaborated into the (slightly) more complex forms of Churchill/Freedom v Nazis/Oppression, or more simply, Churchill/Good v Anti-Churchill/Bad.

This semiotic 'them' versus 'us' narrative division is manufactured by the Establishment, in which a deliberately constructed facade of reality – created by the careful selection, presentation, and omission of facts – is pushed forward as the *only* legitimate way of viewing the world, thus replicating the status quo in the minds of all those who live in it. (See also footnote #98 for further consideration on whether journalists are doing this deliberately, or if they are unthinkingly employing the language and tropes used by those who came before them, blissfully unaware how they themselves are merely cogs in a bigger machine. And see also Roland Barthes for more on the sinister use of myth, and Daniel Chandler for a comprehensive run down of semiotics).

The methodologies outlined above warn us to be aware of our own socio-economic prisons, and to be cautious of the cultural prejudices held by society's dominant hierarchal voices who are able (thanks to their socio-economic privilege) to impose their views on society – though it should be noted qualitative research is prone to the criticism that it doesn't deal with raw, physical data which can be counted, measured, or weighed, meaning it doesn't exist to the material mind which only wants neutral facts and figures.

If you still believe in the concept of neutral facts and figures ...

Chapter Twenty

In which our characters go to lunch and Yvonne has another revelation concerning the differences in behaviour, attitudes, and expectations between the classes.

Seething over the woke lefty immigrant atheist PC Muslim Marxist trans gay agenda attacking the Greatest Man ever, Hutchinson-Cockburn turned to sociological conformity for support; namely, he glanced at his watch before invoking the incantation guaranteed to summon his kith and kin and restore order to his world. 'I see it's lunchtime.'

'Time for a bite, Rupert?' asked Vansittart, materialising by the door without any apparent movement from his office.

'Lovely,' replied Hutchinson-Cockburn with the deep pangs of one who hungers after a busy morning's work – despite having barely been in the office for longer than an hour. And besides, he felt he was owed something after being harangued by the office harridans, and he fully intended to alert Vansittart to the festering socialism under his very nose.

'Good idea,' said Helen as Vansittart and Hutchinson-Cockburn scurried out. 'Let's grab a bite to eat and get a change of scene.'

'I'm far too busy,' replied Felicity, rattling her fingers over her keyboard as an example to the other staff who, in Felicity's view, should stay over their breaks to continue their work rather than spending time on luxuries such as eating.[145]

'I've brought my lunch in,' said Sarah, heading for the staff fridge. 'I've got more contracts to sort.'

'You won't get any real thanks for it,' replied Helen before glancing over at Yvonne. 'It's just you and me, then. My treat.'

Yvonne hesitated; she too had bought her own lunch, but the thought of the wilting bread and cheese easily lost out to being treated somewhere. 'Lovely, thank you,' she smiled as she grabbed her coat, scarf, and bag.

The two women paused outside the office as Helen lit a cigarette and inhaled with almost orgasmic delight. 'That's better.'

'Isn't smoking going to kill you off?' asked Yvonne, giving a nervous laugh to show she meant no offence.

'As long as I die after the cat, that's all I ask,' replied Helen. 'Where are we heading, by the way?'

'Sandwich bar?' suggested Yvonne, nodding over the road.

'Too busy,' replied Helen, destroying half her cigarette with one puff. 'Pub?'

'That creep with the union jack t-shirt keeps trying to chat me up in there.'

'Ah, I know; we'll try *Klytaimnéstra*.'

'Try what now?'

---

[145] An attitude inculcated into the workforce as 66% - 82% of them will work through their lunch break, according to research.

'Clytemnestra, in our lingo. You know, the old Greek myth? Killed her husband in the bath? After he raped her, married her, got her pregnant several times, and then sacrificed their daughter to the gods in return for good sailing winds.'

'I wouldn't normally try somewhere like that,' mumbled Yvonne, abandoning the confusion of Greek myth for the confusion of the authentic artisanal demitasse, authentic artisanal goat's cheese milk, and authentic artisanal Padrino sandwiches advertised on the board outside the shop, no doubt all written up in authentic artisanal chalk. 'What on earth is a Padrino?'

'Let's find out,' said Helen, stubbing out her second cigarette and marching forward.

A woman who probably had 'middle-class' stamped through her like a stick of rock hurried forward with a menu and the sort of false smile Yvonne dreaded; it was the type which said "I'm not racist – I'm talking to this coloured person normally" while staying out of range in case they got mugged. 'Would you like anything to drink?' she asked, her question only just on the right side of being a demand.

'Two coffees, please,' replied Helen, 'and what is a Padrino?'

'It's a spicy fusion of soppressata, calabrese, mortadella and provolone, all entrenched between wood-fired bread,' replied the woman, her lips twitching in contempt that the question had to be asked.

'Cheese and ham toastie, thanks,' snorted Helen. 'How about you, Yvonne?'

'The same, thanks,' mumbled Yvonne.

'And what sort of coffee?' sneered the owner, who hadn't borrowed from her family to create an authentic taste of international cuisine just so she could serve ham and cheese to the lower orders. 'We do a very fine jamocha.'

'White, with three sugars,' responded Helen, firmly, as she and Yvonne settled down at their table.

'It's a bit ...' muttered Yvonne, looking around.

'Poncy as fuck?' asked Helen, cheerfully. 'Certainly is. I'm guessing the place reflects the posh bint who runs it, and that means its carefully screening out the poor.'

'How so?'

'The lower orders are excluded from success not just by the usual factors of wealth inequality, but by social factors as well. They don't know how to behave when in wealthy situations as they have no experience of it, and this creates further barriers between the classes as they don't fit in.'

'Not knowing which knife to use at the dinner table?'

'Exactly, though it goes much further; there are layers of cultural signifiers which people don't understand if they're not from the right class. It all boils down to like recognising like, so if you don't know the codes, you're automatically excluded and hence you don't get the opportunities being passed round.'[146]

---

[146] Helen is here referring to the observations of David Brooks (2017), if you want to learn more on the topic.

'Oh no,' muttered Yvonne in dismay as the door opened to admit Vansittart and Hutchinson-Cockburn. 'How did we get here ahead of them?'

'They probably stopped at the bank first,' guessed Helen. 'Let's see how they navigate this place.' They watched the two men saunter across the café and settle at a table before glancing casually over the menu, each clearly at home with the content of the contents. 'See? It's not just money,' said Helen. 'It really is the whole social system.'

'How so,' asked Yvonne, looking in hope for their order; the sooner they ate, the sooner they could get away from where they clearly did not belong.

'The whole socialisation process basically prepares posh kids for a lifetime of success rather than failure, because the wealthy come from a background in which networking is as common as breathing. Even as children they're meeting people who will be useful to them in later life, who'll hold the door open so they can walk through.'

'Henry!' bellowed Vansittart in his "Hail fellow, well met!" voice, gesturing at a red-faced man in an expensive suit who had just entered. 'How are you? How's the family?'

'Not bad, Michael, not bad, thanks. Hello, Rupert, how are you?' asked Henry Sommerville-Davies, beaming complacently at his two socio-economic colleagues.

'And does it start appearing early? The advantages?' asked Yvonne, observing the posh social interaction.

'God, yes. Imagine you come from a background in which writing is common; because of that, it becomes a familiar, easy thing to do. Now, compare that to a background where

225

writing is something that's only done as and when needed, and you can see how you end up with a massive difference in the way children from different socio-economic backgrounds approach an application form.

'A kid from a wealthy background,' continued Helen, 'will sit down with far more confidence than a working-class kid – so even though they may have the same sort of ability in real life situations, because the wealthy kids have developed a far better way of expressing themselves thanks to their environment, they're the ones who will fill in the application form in a way that stands out.'

'But won't any competent admissions officer or employer realise what's going on?'

'Highly unlikely, because they'll only see what's on the page, not what lies *behind* the page. They be too busy being impressed with how the wealthy kid has included pages of stuff about their extracurricular activities in the Tennis Club and the debating society – all the things working class kids can't usually access.'

'But what about talent?' asked Yvonne mournfully. 'I worked hard on all my school subjects. Was I wasting my time?'

Helen shrugged. 'I've seen Michael turn down applications from people who didn't go to Oxbridge as he genuinely believes they "chose" to go to a lower ranking university, which in his view demonstrates something about their character. That was before he twigged about using unpaid volunteers.'

'But that's totally ridiculous and unfair!'

'Yup.'

'But why do those outside the elite follow and replicate the system? Why do those at the bottom of the social hierarchy just take all the shit society pushes at them? *Why*?'

'Being charitable; cultural conformity and brainwashing,' replied Helen. 'Some say it all starts at school,[147] when kids are taught how to behave and what to expect from life.'

'And if you're not being charitable?'

'People are as thick as shit,' said Helen. 'Mind you, I also think some humans are born bigoted; as long as they can blame outsiders for all their problems, they gain validation and a feeling of being superior to someone else.'[148]

---

[147] And here Helen is referring to Louis Althusser; you may wish to glance over his observations on the Ideological State Apparatus back in footnote #17. When it came to education, Althusser noted that schools teach children what to expect from life; high achievers (i.e. those from privileged backgrounds) will learn how to give orders, while low achievers (i.e. everyone else) will learn to accept those orders. (Of the 53 ministers in charge of UK education from 1900 to 2020, only two went to comprehensive schools. Hence everyone learns their place in life, thus replicating the status quo down the generations and keeping the system of socio-economic serfdom intact.
No wonder Edward Frederick Lindley Wood, (1st Earl of Halifax, grandson of the 11th Earl of Devon, son of the 2nd Viscount Halifax), declared that schools should exist to train up servants and butlers ...

[148] Psychological studies have revealed a definite relationship between low cognitive ability and conservative right-wing ideology. A sense of deference and a desire for order may be the key aspect as to why people are so invested in Establishment narratives rather than taking an unflinching look at all the evidence on any given subject. Though we

'But that's horrible!'

'That's humanity. There's always someone ready to chain themselves down in service to the status quo. And they're willing to chain everyone else down as well by deriding anyone trying to better themselves through school or university, or getting a better job and moving to a nicer area.'

'It's horrible,' repeated Yvonne, too shocked to say anything else by Helen's cynicism, though she was increasingly becoming aware of the difference between

---

could also speculate on how a fear of being different drives many Little Englanders to docile subservience, for conformity is a powerful tool of control and most people are too afraid/shallow /stupid/untaught (delete as applicable) to question established norms.

But then, who these days is going to be foolish enough to say anything critical of Churchill? The biographer John Charmley noted in the paperback edition of *Churchill: The End of Glory* that he suffered considerable cultural fall-out simply for asking a few questions about Churchill's actions in the war. As such, one can only assume the average historian probably feels it is better to keep quiet rather than risk the seething outrage which greets independent thought.

Hence Establishment Myths persist, for people lack the will, the knowledge, or the backbone to counter the dominant beliefs encountered in newspapers, books, films etc, and thus the beliefs of the privileged elite (i.e. those creating the articles, books, films etc) become (via cultural imposition) the beliefs of the rest of society, and so the model is set forevermore.

Which also explains how an entire nation can be gaslit into thinking society can only be structured in one way, with no alternative being possible or even imaginable – see *Capitalist Realism* by Mark Fisher, 2009, for further particulars.

How's that for a depressing conclusion?

Hutchinson-Cockburn's *wealthy* education, which he had been given, and Helen's *worthy* education, which she had to acquire for herself. And this, Yvonne suspected, was a deliberate educational policy by those who held power.

'It's capitalism,' observed Helen, who knew she and Yvonne would never get anywhere near the real opportunities. They weren't the right class. They knew Vansittart, but they weren't *of* Vansittart. The best they could hope for was enough money to pay their bills and have a bit left over for their own interests. As long as those interests didn't impinge upon the social order. Hence Helen's joint obsession with cigarettes and cats.

'Look at the time!' exclaimed Yvonne as their food arrived, noting their half hour break was nearly up.

'Toss those sarnies in a bag, please, and we'll have them to go,' said Helen to the scowling owner, who was appalled to hear of her gastronomic creations referred to as "sarnies". Helen and Yvonne rushed out, leaving Vansittart and Hutchinson-Cockburn – both of whom looked to be in no hurry to return to their respective duties – chatting with Henry before being joined by Camilla, then Joyce and Tristian, and finally by Allegra and Tarquin, all greeting each other as old friends, current networking contacts, and future opportunities as they ate, drank, and made merry on the expenses tab.

Chapter Twenty-One

In which Yvonne tries to get to grips with some real history...

'What are you looking puzzled about?' asked Helen of Yvonne the following morning.

'I was wondering about Tonypandy,' said Yvonne, trying to read through four Churchill biographies spread over her desk while simultaneously keeping her attention on two Internet tabs on the same subject, all in her doomed quest to impress Authority into giving her an opportunity.

'Ah, right,' grunted Helen.

'What's Tonypandy?' asked Sarah.

'A town in Wales where Churchill sent in the troops when the miners were striking,' answered Helen. 'The arguments have festered ever since as to what their orders were, the appropriateness of the action, and whether the troops shot anyone or not.'

'Troops shot at their own people?' goggled Sarah, unwilling to believe any such thing could ever happen in England; that sort of thing only ever happened in foreign reports. In foreign places. With foreigners.

'Maybe not at Tonypandy, but using the army to suppress or even kill strikers was a typical response, back then,' said Helen. 'I bet the buggers would do it today as well, if they thought they could get away with it. Which they probably could, given the supine nature of the English, coupled with the country's police force which exists to protect the status quo, not to serve the public or pursue justice.'

'How can you say that?' demanded Sarah, supported by vigorous nods from Vansittart, Hutchinson-Cockburn, and Felicity.

'How heavy handed are the police at any democratic protest against the government or any other form of power?' asked Helen. 'And then compare that with how the police refuses to do its job of investigating government corruption, unless forced to do so?'[149]

'Well, I still don't believe the troops shot anyone,' replied Sarah, though "won't believe" would have been closer the truth, for she was thoroughly indoctrinated by the tabloid media and she was already blaming the strikers for their poverty.

'It was a text-book response,' shrugged Helen. 'You can look up the Llanelli riots as well, where troops shot and killed two people, one of whom wasn't even a rioter.

---

[149] A parliamentary inquiry criticised the police for their violent approach in stopping "Kill the Bill" protesters (i.e. those marching against the draconian Government legislation which would allow the police to suppress just about any form of legitimate protest) in 2021. The police also brutally suppressed a vigil in the name of Sarah Everard, a woman who was falsely arrested, kidnapped, raped and murdered by... a serving police officer.

Meanwhile, the then Commissioner of the Metropolitan Police refused to investigate Downing Street parties during the Covid lockdown until legal proceedings were initiated (by a private group) against the Met for its failure to do its job of actually investigating criminality.

Tell me again how we're all equal under the law ...

Churchill was the Home Secretary then, and he suspended the act stating troops had to be called in by the local authorities, meaning the army could instead be despatched on the government's say so. Without waiting to see what was actually happening in the situation.'

'What does the Trumper biography say on it?' asked Sarah, clinging to the hope it was all a mistake. Surely, the thick, solid, reassuring biography would explain all?

'It seems to gloss over it,' said Yvonne, rifling through the pages of *Churchill the Brave*. 'There's a reference here to some people – I assume he means Labour members – who never forgot about Tonypandy, but that's it. There's nothing else. At all. Which makes me wonder what the significance is of Trumper omitting it.'

'I'm sure Churchill did nothing untoward,' sighed Hutchinson-Cockburn in exasperation.

'No, he must have had his reasons,' said Sarah, briefly struggling with the cognitive dissonance of keeping her sociological indoctrination of Churchill as a Great Man intact against the knowledge he had been literally trigger happy when it came to the working classes. Sadly, it didn't take long for the indoctrination to triumph.

'Let's have a proper gander at Tonypandy, then, and see if we can find the truth,' said Helen. 'Though I doubt we will, as the truth rarely gets out in history. We just get the interpretation.'

'Here's one online article,[150]' said Yvonne after a quick internet search, printing out enough copies for everyone.

> Concerns have been raised over the future safety of statues of Winston Churchill and Mahatma Gandhi after a Welsh government report stated they were implicated in colonialism.

'It's manipulating the reader from the off, isn't it?' said Helen. 'I mean, stating there are "concerns" rather than, say, "discussions". And "future safety" is designed to immediately put you on the side of the statues, and thus the side of the Establishment.'

'Without Churchill, the allies would have lost the war!' sniffed Vansittart, ignoring the specific issues of colonialism in favour of a general point no one had raised.

'I think several million soviet and American soldiers would disagree,' said Helen, transmitting the most obvious look of contempt possible while remaining within the bounds of servile employment.

'The soviets were Nazi allies in the early days, before Hitler invaded and they switched sides!' jeered Hutchinson-Cockburn, following Vansittart's lead of ignoring the issue at hand in favour of focusing on something else entirely.

'Gosh, switching sides for the sake of power,' smirked

---

[150] Again, this is a fictitious article based on a real one. The book by Meredith in the following chapter is also a fictitious reconstruction of a real book by a real author.

Helen. 'Now, who does that remind me of? Oh, wait, was it Churchill in his early years, abandoning the Conservative party for a chance of power with the Liberals, before running back to the Conservative party after losing three contests?'

Vansittart and Hutchinson-Cockburn snorted simultaneously to show their contempt for these ~~historical facts~~ woke lefty ravings before finding refuge within the next part of the article:

> The report was released after questions were raised on several historical figures, including Churchill and Ghandi, by the Black History Initiative.

'The Black History Initiative?' sneered Hutchinson-Cockburn. 'Those woke lefty atheist PC Muslim Marxist trans gay thugs who want our children forced into being atheist gay woke lefty PC Marxist Muslim transexuals?'[151]

'They're fighting a system which routinely kills Black people for being Black,' snapped Yvonne. 'A system that discriminates against Black people at every level, from housing to the criminal justice system to jobs and education.'

---

[151] You may notice this accusation is long on hysteria but light on proof. But this is standard Establishment policy, raging against something largely (if not entirely) imaginary to deflect from reality.

'That's not true. The police are fair and even-handed!'[152]

'You only say that because of media manipulation,' said Helen. 'The police are often quoted freely and framed as justifiable, incorruptible authority. And whenever police corruption is reported, it's always presented as the cliché of one bad apple rather than as an issue with institutional corruption and systemic failure. The imbalance is obvious.'

Another double snort erupted from the two posh men before Hutchinson-Cockburn ventured a reply. 'And I suppose you want every monument to be torn down and history to be rewritten so it fits your narrative?'

'Why not?' said Yvonne. 'History has already been written to support your narrative – the white Establishment narrative. And it's been this way for centuries. So why not let others have their place in the history books?'

'Look at this next section!' proclaimed Vansittart, his face glowing with the smug righteousness of deflection:

> The Welsh report noted historical accusations against Gandhi for his negative attitudes toward Black South Africans.

'See?' continued Vansittart. 'Racism is a problem

---

[152] In the year ending 2019, Black people were 9.7 times more likely to be stopped by the police than white people. And when the Covid outbreak occurred and lockdowns came into effect the following year, those from ethnic minority backgrounds found themselves 54% more likely to be fined for Covid breaches than their white counterparts.

everywhere!'

'Exactly!' crowed Hutchinson-Cockburn. 'But you never hear about Indians being racist in the media, do you?'

'What, apart from right here in this media report we're all reading right now, you mean?' asked Yvonne.

'We're not allowed to talk about it,' whined Hutchinson-Cockburn. 'We can't mention the religion of peace, can we? Or their grooming gangs!'[153] With a smirk of triumph, he burrowed back into the article:

> The report also highlighted Churchill's role in the Indian famine.

---

[153] Hutchinson-Cockburn is here referring to the oft-repeated right-wing narrative that foreign Pakistani Muslims are responsible for most underage grooming and sex crimes. A Home Office report published in 2020 debunked this belief as false; most group offenders are, in fact, white. Unfortunately, the belief is still maintained over the reality – with significant help from the mainstream media.
This highlights the enormous overlap between right-wing extremism and the UK mainstream media; indeed, one is tempted to conclude it's not so much an overlap as a happy marriage of beliefs and bigotry. Only the behaviour is different, for while the extremist favours violence, the UK media prefers innuendo, lies, and propaganda.
And who are the journalists? As mentioned before, (see footnote #98) they are usually posh, white, and wealthy. And who are the owners of the newspapers? Posh, white, and super-wealthy. They mould the media narrative, and thus they mould society. No wonder most of the office staff, here cast as representatives of wider society, unthinkingly align themselves with racism, classism, sexism etc; for Vansittart and Hutchinson-Cockburn, it is their inheritance. For Felicity and Sarah, it is their indoctrination into cultural serfdom.

'Lefty nonsense!' snapped Vansittart, while Hutchinson-Cockburn hurried on to find a less contentious fact to be outraged about.

> As a result of the report, suggestions have been raised that the statues could be relocated to museums and have new plaques fitted, allowing the public to see a greater historical context.

'Vandalism!' gasped Vansittart. 'Cultural vandalism and suppression!'

'But the article just said the statues could be relocated,' countered Helen. 'Not exactly "suppressing" them, is it?'

'It's destroying their context and history,' flubbed Vansittart after several moments desperate thought.

'So, a statue with a plaque stating the person was great is proper history, but a statue with a plaque stating historical truths is destroying both context and history? Right, got it, that makes perfect sense.'

'Thankfully, we still have the right to reply,' sniffed Hutchinson-Cockburn, brandishing his printout. 'Here we have Bernard Meredith to fight our corner!'

> "Absolute rubbish" was the opinion of acclaimed historian Bernard Meredith. "This is lefty propaganda posing as history. Churchill did not make the Indian famine worse, and neither did he order any troops armed with bayonets to charge

at Tonypandy."

'Hang on a minute,' interrupted Yvonne, whose anger was growing exponentially as she learned how history was little more than an Establishment narrative. And the casual dismissal by her employer and her employer's favoured volunteer of anything they disagreed with wasn't helping her temper. 'The article doesn't mention bayonets at all, except for when this Meredith person dismisses them; where did he get them from?'

'Probably the original report the article is based on mention bayonets?' sighed Vansittart.

'If so, in what context?' demanded Yvonne. 'Why didn't the article specify? Especially as Meredith is explicitly rubbishing that particular claim.'

'Probably the reporter asked Meredith, received the reply, and then omitted asking the question, leaving Meredith's comment orphaned and without context,' boomed Hutchison-Cockburn. 'Typical lefty journalism!'[154]

'Or just typical shoddy journalism full stop,' said Helen. 'Then again, maybe Meredith brought up the bayonets himself, even though no one else mentioned them?'

---

[154] In Hutchinson-Cockburn's mind, any article criticising Churchill was automatically the work of the woke lefty immigrant atheist PC Muslim Marxist trans gay agenda. But then, *anything* Hutchinson-Cockburn disagreed with became the ravings of the woke lefty immigrant atheist PC Muslim Marxist trans gay agenda.
It's simply the way he's been made.

'Which means we've got no idea if the article is incompetent or deliberately disingenuous, or if Meredith was answering points no one had made,' observed Yvonne. 'So who, exactly, are we supposed to believe?'

Chapter Twenty-Two

A continuation of Chapter Twenty-One.

'We can at least ascertain the truth concerning Churchill's role at Tonypandy,' replied Hutchinson-Cockburn with smug pomposity.

'Really, Rupert?' simpered Sarah.

'How so, Rupert?' cooed Felicity, simultaneously.

'We have Bernard Meredith's very own *Churchill* right here,' announced Hutchinson-Cockburn, pointing at Yvonne's stack of biographies as though he were responsible for its presence. 'We simply have to reach out, open the book, and we will see exactly what the truth is.' He suited the words to the action, grabbing the book from the pile.

'Or more likely we'll see what Meredith *says* about Churchill and Tonypandy,' muttered Yvonne, whose remaining faith in biographers and historians was falling faster than a politician's trousers in a brothel. 'And that's not necessarily the same thing.'

Hutchinson-Cockburn smirked in derision, knowing Yvonne was going to have to eat her words. He was convinced Meredith, a gentleman[155] and a scholar[156] who

---

[155] i.e. posh and white.

[156] i.e. posh, white, and went to Oxbridge.

had so indignantly and scornfully dismissed the Welsh report, would prove to be the platform of truth upon which Churchill's innocence would be demonstrated.

That power lay beneath Hutchinson-Cockburn's hand. And he intended to use it.

He turned to the index.

And scanned down.

And found nothing.

Hutchinson-Cockburn looked again, rather more slowly, and then again, and then once more, until he finally found just three references, of which only the first dealt with what happened – but even then, nothing was really explained in depth. But he couldn't admit this (his reality would not permit it) so he instead read out loud as though Churchill was being triumphantly vindicated:

> '"Although Churchill dispatched several Metropolitan Police officers to act as a reserve force, they were under the control of General Sir Neville Macready, who in any case did not make use of them even after calamitous rioting hit Tonypandy. The damage done was considerable, with 63 businesses being attacked and/or looted. The police used rolled-up raincoats in controlling the crowd. A single rioter was killed. Churchill's tactical caution undoubtedly defused what could have been an even greater disaster."'

This, to Yvonne's developing critical faculties, seemed to raise more questions than answers. 'Hang on;' she said, causing a wince to flit over Hutchinson-Cockburn's face at her uncouth mannerism. 'Were troops used at all?'

'I don't know,' muttered Hutchinson-Cockburn.

'Who was the rioter who was killed?

'I don't know,'

'And who killed him?'

'I don't know.'

'And why is his death presented in the passive voice?'

'I don't know.'

'And how do we know he was a rioter anyway?'

'I don't know,'

'How exactly did the police *use* rolled-up raincoats?'

'I don't know.'

'How would that be effective?'

'I don't know.'

'And which police force? The Metropolitan, ordered in by Churchill, or the local forces?'

'I don't know,'

'Who directed them? Who told them what level of force to use?'

'I don't know.'

'Why is Meredith so vague here, but so specific on the exact number of damaged and looted businesses?'

'I don't know.'

'What proof is there that "Churchill's tactical caution undoubtedly defused what could have been an even greater disaster."'

242

'I don't know!'

'What proof is there that "Churchill's tactical caution" even existed?'

'I don't know!'

'And why is the final point made by Meredith pro-Churchill, which surely gives the impression Churchill is in the right as he's given the luxury of the last word?'

'I don't know! I mean, I think you're reading too much into things,' replied Hutchinson-Cockburn, looking for support around the office and receiving it in smiles and nods from three of the people present, which put him (and his views) in the majority and proved he (and his views) were right.

'Hey, look at this account by Belinda Knox,' said Yvonne, her voice rising in surprise at what she had found online:

> When discussing Churchill and Tonypandy, most historians (who are pro-Churchill) like to quote from fellow pro-Churchill accounts such as newspapers and other historians. This enables them to gloss over the fact that Churchill was ruthlessly pro-capitalist, and he was ready to use all the resources of the state to crush the workers and serve the wealthy.

'It's a hatchet job!' exclaimed Hutchinson-Cockburn. 'It's the tolerant left being anything but!' He barked with laughter at his own original wit – actually picked up from innumerable right-wing websites and message boards.

'And what if it's true?' asked Helen, gazing at her handbag

which contained her stash of cigarettes. 'Is it still a hatchet job if the facts are accurate?'

'Hey, it looks like Belinda Knox has a dodgy record as well,' said Yvonne, who – unlike Hutchinson-Cockburn – was determined to find out as much information as possible so she could reach a fair analysis. 'She got caught committing plagiarism. And editing articles on Wikipedia to attack journalists who criticised her.'

'There, you see?' bellowed Hutchinson-Cockburn. 'It's the lefty liars twisting things! Stick with Bernard Meredith; he's a real scholar!'

'Who utilises a typical right-wing narrative,' observed Helen. 'Deflect by focusing on something else and distract from the real issues or questions.'

'It shows the problem with history, doesn't it?' said Yvonne. 'We have to take it all on trust that historians and biographers and teachers[157] are being honest, rigorous and fair.'

---

[157] A perfect summary of the issues facing my project with regard to how Churchill is constructed through articles, biographies etc; all such material gives the illusion of truth and the concomitant illusion of authority, with both concepts feeding off the other in an eternal cycle of self referentiality, but these texts/truths are all carefully constructed façades for the facts therein, and their presentation to the public/reader is a careful selection, presentation, and omission of data. And how many school children, students or citizens think to question the authority of the classroom, the lecture hall, or the posh man on the telly presenting his documentary?

'You have to trust the system,' replied Hutchinson-Cockburn in shock, but then, he was genuinely unaware how much he was part of the system, and how he had been supported by it from birth.

Yvonne shook her head; it was impossible to know who to trust. She was clearly *meant* to believe the posh white privileged Oxbridge set, just as she was supposed to accept whatever the media spoon-fed her. But now, having learned so much under Helen's wide and intelligent cynicism, Yvonne felt unwilling to embrace any side, because in doing so she could potentially embrace falsehood.

Only one thing was clear; the UK Establishment, owned by a small cross-section of the wealthy cultural elite and staffed almost entirely by that elite and their quislings, was an institution of cultural oppression.

Chapter Twenty-Three

In which Yvonne she has another direct interaction with a real live author, except now she has lost her innocence having been exposed to cruel reality, and she now sadly knows that writers are just like everybody else.

Only worse.[158]

The following day, with the rest of the staff in a meeting across the hall, Yvonne was musing on the behaviour, attitudes, and assumptions of the elite when a facsimile of these behaviours, attitudes and assumptions flung open the door and stamped into the office, her face set in a belligerent scowl. It was this expression which confused Yvonne, for it meant she did not recognise one of Clavier and Coldwell's few token authors, Nina Rogerson.[159]

---

[158] See, for example, Virginia Woolf, who paid her servants £40 per year while she and her husband earned £4000. But then, Woolf was the product of posh privilege (she thought anything less than £500 a year was poverty) and she detested the working-classes, so the fact she paid her servants so poorly is not that surprising. And she was apparently (comparatively) left-wing in her views!
If Woolf were alive today, she'd be writing for the Daily Crier.

[159] Nina Rogerson's name and character have been chosen very carefully; her surname, shared by the ghastly Terrance, is a reference to her ancestors taken by force from Africa and hauled in squalor across the Atlantic, denied their home, their future, and finally their identity after being branded with the name of their slave master.

'I'm here to see Michael Vansittart!' snapped Rogerson, her tone making it clear she expected to be shown straight to the publisher's office. Her gaze, which had been flicking around the room in the hope of seeing a more important person she could deal with, finally came to rest on Yvonne.

'Have you an appointment?' asked Yvonne, leaning back slightly in her chair from the anger radiating off the outraged author.

'I emailed him to let him know I was coming in,' replied Rogerson in a haughty tone.

'So, you have an appointment?' insisted Yvonne.

'I emailed him!'

'And did he email back to confirm an appointment?'

'Don't you take that tone with me!' snarled Rogerson. 'Don't you know who I am?'

'No.'

'No wonder this publishing house is going down the drain, with this sort of ignorance on the front desk!' snorted the woman. 'Kindly tell your employer that Nina Rogerson, MBE, is here to see him on a matter of utmost importance.'[160]

The reader will thus easily grasp the business Terrance Rogerson's forefathers traded in. And he is not alone in this; there are several posh white wealthy descendants of slave owners ensconced in the English Establishment today, inheriting (by way of an example) plantations in the twenty-first century built on the back of slave labour some four hundred years ago.

[160] Born to a wealthy family which enabled her to attend private school and then Oxbridge (where she made many useful contacts), Rogerson

'He's in a meeting,' said Yvonne, feeling the last few remnants of her ideals wither and die. She had read – and identified with – Nina Rogerson's *The Estate*, an intense insight into racism as experienced by the author[161] as a child of the 1980s, but Yvonne was now seeing the woman behind the name. And that woman was merely a carbon copy of Establishment privilege.

'A meeting? This is outrageous! This tinpot company is a disgrace!'

'Can I take a message?'

---

had long demanded yet more from her life, career and opportunities – oblivious to the fact she has already been handed a life, career and opportunities denied to those lower down the social/financial scale. Rogerson, predictably enough, ultimately places the blame for her perceived lack of literary mega-stardom and super wealth on the woke lefty immigrant atheist PC Muslim Marxist trans gay agenda. Rogerson's attitude is making a point on how our own conduct is often little more than a replication of that we see above us, turning us into carbon copies of our oppressors. See Anne Bishop's *Becoming an Ally* for more.

[161] Or so Rogerson claimed; she had, in fact, appropriated several experiences from other people for her book before submitting it to an agent (and family friend) who was looking for stories of hardship and exclusion from the Black community. This, incidentally, was an extension of Rogerson's time at university, in which she had worked diligently by regurgitating her tutors' ideas into her essays and final exams to gain their approval. Rogerson, however, is totally oblivious to this fact, thinking her ability to get a pass on almost every paper was a sign of her intelligence and ability, rather than a simple stimulus-response of writing up approved answers to find approval with approving authority.

'You can tell Michael bloody Vansittart he's lost his best author; that's the message you can give him! His marketing is appalling, his sales techniques are risible, and I'm ending the contract.'

'I'll pass it on to him,' murmured Yvonne.

'And you can tell him I've had a better offer from Firefly Publishing for *The Estate*, so I expect the rights to be returned immediately, including all the overseas rights he's done nothing with, despite the novel being described as a work of great originality and depth!'

'I'll tell him you were here,' said Yvonne, noting Vansittart hadn't appeared in the office to deal with Nina Rogerson's complaints, in contrast to his rapid materialisation when Terrance Rogerson had been raising his posh white male voice a few days earlier.

'That is inadequate,' replied Rogerson, glaring in antipathy at the young Black woman who no doubt came from some God-forsaken part of Jamaica.[162] 'You think this is an acceptable way to treat an MBE and top author?'

'Um,' said Yvonne, feeling an uncanny sense of déjà vu about the whole exchange.

'You need to sort your priorities out,' snapped Rogerson as she strode to the door, turning only to make her exit line. 'I've worked hard to get where I am, and I'm not going to be pulled down by anyone!'

---

[162] A reference to the documented animosity between Jamaicans, Barbadians, and Trinidadians.

Chapter Twenty-Four

In which we start to explore how right-wing attitudes and extremist beliefs are not so far apart – and we see how Churchillian worship is a factor in both ideologies.

It was the last day for Yvonne at Clavier and Coldwell, though no one was aware of this as the staff started the Friday shift. The only abnormality was the early morning presence of Vansittart and Hutchinson-Cockburn, though this carried a simple explanation; an important client was booked in for an eleven o'clock meeting and Vansittart wanted all his staff present, to give the appearance of a unified, well-run operation.

'What's up?' asked Helen, noting Yvonne's distressed face and inadvertently causing the entire morning's chain of events.

'I found this article online, from someone called Harrison Taylor.'[163] As she spoke, Yvonne printed off enough copies for everyone. 'It's about Churchill's racism – but all the writer does is excuse it.'

> There has been a minor controversy, as mentioned by the *Established England* group, over the phrase "Keep England White", which

---

[163] Yet another faked example of the real thing, to avoid the legal issues of quoting without consent.

may or may not have been an election slogan suggested by Winston Churchill for the 1955 election. And to be fair to *Established England's* argument, there is far more nuance to this manufactured argument than we see at first glance.

The phrase is *only* to be found in Harold Macmillan's diary, who noted it down as a suggestion of Churchill's at a cabinet meeting. It is not, and never was, a public slogan.

'Well?' demanded Hutchinson-Cockburn, shrugging at his copy after skimming through it. 'What of it?'

'I see he takes pains to minimise the issue at the outset by calling it a "minor controversy", before emphasising the quote isn't found in any official documents, only in a private entry by Harold Macmillan,' observed Helen as she read through the document.

'I noticed,' said Yvonne. 'It seems like deflection from the quote itself. And saying the comment wasn't public is surely just cajoling the reader into thinking the remark was never made, or is unofficial, as though that somehow excuses it?'

'He's keeping to the facts!' snapped Hutchinson-Cockburn.

'The fact is that Churchill said it,' replied Helen.

'And everything else is just a series of attempts to excuse the comment,' fumed Yvone.

The phrase was nothing, an off the cuff remark that remained unused by the Conservatives and unspoken outside the meeting. And the context is more important than the quote itself.

'Why is he banging on about the context?' demanded Yvonne. 'I mean, a racist phrase is still a racist phrase.'
'Churchill was probably making a joke!' snorted Hutchinson-Cockburn. 'Look, it says so there!'

There is a good chance the remark, if it was ever made, was just a joke. And that Macmillan was being mischievous when he wrote it down.

'"Macmillan was being mischievous?"' echoed Helen. 'Or maybe Macmillan was disgusted by Churchill's remark, or astonished by it, or was even in agreement with it, yet Taylor only gives one interpretation, which is in defence of Churchill.'

Is it at all credible that a seasoned politician would suggest "Keep England White" as a potential campaign slogan?

'Exactly!' crowed Hutchinson-Cockburn. 'What politician would ever say such a thing?'
'A massively racist one, maybe?' replied Yvonne. 'One who was known to be racist by his own contemporaries? A racist

speaking in a time where open racism was even more acceptable than it is now?'

'Racism has never been openly acceptable,' snapped Hutchinson-Cockburn, turning to an entirely fictitious fact to salvage the argument.

'Except when landlords put "No Coloureds" signs in their windows,' observed Helen. 'And the race riot of 1919. The Notting Hill race riots of 1958. The Dudley race riots of 1962. Enoch Powell and his "Rivers of Blood" speech in 1968.'

'I'm just looking at the article in front of me,' huffed Hutchinson-Cockburn, quickly shifting his ideological defence. 'Churchill's comment was about immigration, not racism. It says so right here!'

> In any case, the context is clear; Churchill was obviously thinking over the complex issue of official immigration policy.

'Yes, a complex issue does require a racist soundbite, doesn't it?' said Helen.

'And "Keep England White" becomes so less racist when it's in the context of immigration policy,' sneered Yvonne.

'But look at this!' declared Vansittart, riding to the rescue of the sweating Hutchinson-Cockburn.

> These are the unvarnished facts. I leave it to the reader to decide on the truth.

'Exactly!' barked Hutchinson-Cockburn. 'He's given us the unvarnished facts, so we can decide for ourselves.'

'No, Rupert,' sighed Helen, wearily. 'He's spent the article excusing Churchill and generally manipulating the story, the prose and the presentation before claiming he's leaving it the reader to decide.'

'And look at his excuses in the comments beneath the article,' said Yvonne. '"If everyone had their alleged words taken out of context, we would all look bad." I mean, *one*; Churchill's words were not being taken out of context, and *two*; yes, we would look bad – if we said racist things!'

'Unless you're a member of the Establishment,' said Helen. 'Then you get away with it. And you're probably admired for it, as well.'[164]

'And Taylor ties himself in knots to minimise the racism and to defend Churchill' pointed out Yvonne. 'It's almost as though he doesn't know he's doing it.'

'That's the orthodox Establishment mind for you,' replied Helen.[165]

---

[164] This is quite true. One member of the Establishment claimed citizens in Britain feared being swamped by people with a different culture. Another claimed immigration was undermining Britain's pure Anglo-Saxon culture. A third described Black Africans as piccaninnies, and a fourth expressed the belief that the colonial system turned foreigners into gentlemen. These are all genuine incidents.

[165] Is Taylor unthinkingly replicating the "Churchill is Great" argument because he is so thoroughly orthodox? Is he so invested in Churchill as a *positive* that he genuinely cannot see any *negative* at all? Or is there

something sinister going on with Taylor's robust defence of Churchill's racism?

This is relevant as I have been told by my PhD supervisor that I must consider both sides of the argument(s) raised in this creative writing project, and this seems as good as place as any to state that my own feelings on 'bothsideism' (as it is sometimes referred to) is ambivalent, for the simple reason that sometimes the other side doesn't deserve to be heard as it has no scientific validity – see, for example, climate change deniers. But seeing both sides up on the same platform will fool the public into believing the views expressed by climate change deniers must have some legitimacy – especially as the deniers (funded by the wealth and power of the fossil fuel industry) will most likely get a very easy ride from the sycophantic Establishment interviewer.

This leads to the obvious question as to why the media deliberately fabricates a fundamentally dishonest world view which they then knowingly present as being entirely factual. The answer is simple and consistent: hate not only sells, but it deflects attention from the corrupt Establishment and all its little minions. And sadly, this policy is the mainstream, and is used by politicians, think tanks, and even academics, who all work with one thing in mind; preserve the posh white wealthy male Establishment.

This goes some way to explaining why we have a society in which the ruling elite can do as they wish with little or no genuine scrutiny, and certainly with no real repercussions for mistakes, incompetence, or even corruption. If we had a system in place ensuring politicians who made unforgivable mistakes were deselected, Churchill would have been out after Gallipoli – assuming he hadn't already been sacked for the siege of Sydney Street a few years beforehand. But Churchill was of the Establishment, and he therefore had privilege – the privilege to make mistakes with no real consequences, the privilege of corruption, the privilege to act only for himself and others like him without any sanction, and the privilege to lay waste to hundreds of thousands of lives.

And this privilege is still shared by his class, even today. Politicians can be unemployable serial incompetents, adulterers, liars, and bigots, and yet they rarely face any real repercussions for their actions; the police won't investigate even blatant illegality until threatened with legal action, (see footnote #149), while the capitalist media stands forever ready to defend the billionaire elite which holds power over the rest of us.

The lack of critical analysis from the mainstream media and the Establishment seems to be a deliberate process of sociological propaganda, a theory bolstered by their handling of Churchill; the public consciousness has been herded into a state of Saint-like veneration wherein Churchill becomes a Mythic Temple where all must enter with their heads bowed, voices hushed, and brains disengaged, for questions are a Sin unto the Almighty (Elite).

History truly is just a narrative. And those with access to the means of production get to write that narrative and feed it to the public. Which then dutifully swallows.

Chapter Twenty-Five

A continuation of the issues started in the previous chapter ...

'Some people just want to find things to complain about,' said Hutchinson-Cockburn, feeling a little sensitive as he had been recently finding so many uncanny parallels between himself and Churchill, and hence any attack on the Great Man's values were an attack on his own. Which meant calling Churchill a racist would infer that he, Hutchinson-Cockburn, was also a racist, which was clearly absolute rubbish because he had never once used the N word. At least not recently. In public. And then only *ironically*, as a joke with his Oxbridge friends, because he wasn't in the least like that.

'Complain about?' echoed Yvonne, her voice rising as weeks of being in close proximity to arrogant privilege finally burnt through her reserves of social conformity. 'Have you seen this group Taylor quotes from?' Yvonne waved a sheaf of printouts taken from the *Established England* website. 'It's a right-wing authoritarian party founded by posh wealthy bigots, based on the explicit idea of having other people conform to authority and tradition. Basically, the whole thing stinks of class hatred and white nationalism.'[166]

---

[166] The example of the class hatred and white nationalism alluded to by Yvonne in *Established England*'s manifesto is based on a real political group. Below is a fictionalised extract:

257

'Well, I don't see anything wrong,' muttered Hutchinson-Cockburn as he glanced over the first paragraph of *Established England's* paean to Churchill:

> Sir Winston Churchill was a prophet who saw the threat from Multiculturalism. His suggested political slogan "Keep England White" was a simple statement of faith and intent, not a racist proposition.

———————————————

> Leftism is a progressive disease. The symptoms can be easily seen; the pursuit of individualism, equal rights, trans rights, equality, gay rights, and no doubt paedophilia rights.
> This country was founded on Tradition, and Tradition made this country great. The tradition of the Church, strong leaders, the English Identity, and the freedom of all men.
> We stand opposed to immigration and wish to see our black brothers – for they are our brothers – returned to their homelands, where they belong, so we too may live where we belong, with our heads held high, as true Englishmen.

Hutchinson-Cockburn, incidentally, will find himself nodding along approvingly as he reads the above statement, and he will remain oblivious as to why the Black girl is making such a fuss about being proud of England's great traditions. (But then, Hutchinson-Cockburn is unaware how many traditions are in fact quite recent, and usually imposed from above on those below). And neither can he see a problem with the 'self-evident truth' expressed on tradition, multiculturism, and everyone knowing their place.

'Simple statement of fact,' nodded Hutchinson-Cockburn, approvingly.

> Churchill knew better than any how races fight each other for resources and survival, and how the stronger races will prevail – but only if they stand firm and do not allow any weak or treacherous ideology such as Cultural Marxism and atheism, or gay and trans dogma, to infect our strength of purpose.

'It all makes sense!' nodded Hutchinson-Cockburn.

'Sense?' demanded Yvonne, angrily reading aloud from the "About" section of the site. '"Ever since Labour opened the doors to immigrants and other criminals, we have seen our sense of identity and purpose be eroded under the weight of woke-minded Marxism, where the truth is labelled as being "racist".

'But listen to this,' countered Hutchinson-Cockburn. '"Our purpose is to restore the Lost England of our forefathers. To bring back the true legacy and inheritance of this once proud country." How can anyone be against that?'

'Because its rampart sexism, racism, class hatred and many other forms of bigotry masquerading as "legitimate concerns", maybe?' replied Helen.

'It's their belief and should be respected!' snapped Hutchinson-Cockburn, noting favourably the organisation's adherence to authority without once wondering whose authority was being lauded. But then, he didn't need to ask. He knew. It was the authority of him and those like him.

'"Our first act in power will be to repeal all aspects of the welfare state, which has done nothing but encourage scrounging by wastrels and idlers," read Yvonne in disbelief.

'Yes, that's true!' exclaimed Vansittart, nodding vigorously. 'We all have the same opportunities, but some people just don't want to work.'

'The same opportunities?' snarled Yvonne, angrily fighting back tears. 'Who outside the elite ever get any opportunities handed out by the Establishment?'

'And how many in the Establishment are scrounging off taxpayer-funded handouts like tax breaks, massive political expenses, and other subsidizations?' asked Helen.

'It's the typical lefty culture of envy,' sneered Felicity, a keen Daily Crier reader.

'It's why they want positive discrimination,' nodded Hutchinson-Cockburn, supremely unaware he was already at the front of the queue by virtue of the discrimination imbued in England's capitalist class system.

'Then answer the point about those from elite backgrounds being given opportunities denied to the poor,' retorted Helen.

'That's enough of that talk,' snapped Vansittart, thoroughly disturbed by the communism flooding through the office. 'We are here to do our jobs, not listen to socialism, and I'll have no more of this sort of talk in my family business!'

'It seems *Established England* shares your ideas,' snapped Yvonne, glaring at Vansittart. '"Our country can only be recovered by a return to older, traditional values of hereditary, Christianity, and a genuine commitment to the social order."'

'Bloody hell,' muttered Helen. 'Everyone should know their place and be happy with the boot of the oppressor stamping down on their face, forever.'

'And look at the people behind it,' growled Yvonne, her eyes still on the squirming Vansittart. 'Wealthy aristocrats, ex Conservative party members, churchmen, Oxbridge academics ... It's all the people who already have power and privilege but who want even more!'

Chapter Twenty-Six

A continuation...

'Hey, we're in the Daily Crier!' exclaimed Sarah in sudden excitement, for she had grown bored with the conversation she didn't (want to) understand and had decided to browse through the open post, wherein she found a courtesy copy of the magazine – with the appropriate article highlighted heavily on the contents page – sent to Vansittart as part of Rogerson's campaign to get the Churchill biography.

> *How the lefties are infiltrating our cherished arts!*
> *By Terrance Rogerson.*
> *Churchill is a hero. We know it, the world knows it. And in honour of this fact, an announcement was recently made by one of our oldest and best publishers, Clavier and Caldwell, who called for a new biography of our greatest man.*
> *Ordinarily, this would be a reason to rejoice. After all, what man achieved more than Winston Churchill? A humble man, despite his aristocratic lineage, Churchill would shape the nation and the world. But even here, the lefty moaners will not stay away, and they insist on intruding on the hallowed ground of Churchillian grandeur with their woke bleatings!*

Incredible as it may seem, the lefty presence is making itself felt at all levels, spreading its intolerance of greatness into all our sacred areas, for the left can't stand the idea that one man can be better than another, and in the future, they will demand we will all be alike, with no difference between us!

For, dear friends, what did I find when checking out the background story of this new call for a life of the Greatest Ever Brit? I found lefty sedition!

For in the sanctified land of publishing, so long a symbol of our heritage and tradition, I found the moaning voices of the lefty socialist, one Yvonne Jones, demanding Churchill books be rewritten to show supposed socialist "facts", facts which appear in no official history!

The left now demands only certain types of "fact" be allowed in Churchillian biographies! Only "facts" showing how horrid Churchill was. But these are not facts at all. They are fictions! Churchill was the greatest Brit of all time, but listening to the left, you'd never know this! According to them, he was a racist and a warlord!

I mean, he was of a different era; Of course he was different! And maybe his views are a little old-fashioned now, for Churchill was a man of his time, not to be compared with men of our time, for he was born when the great British Empire still ruled the waves! But when push came to shove it was

Churchill, and Churchill alone, who stood up for everyone: black, white and brown and yellow alike!

He stood up for all of us; he fought for you, for me, for everyone! Did Churchill do this through the greatest catastrophe we have ever seen, the Second World War started by the Germans, just so the left can rewrite history in this way? I think not!

Thankfully, level-headedness and common sense have returned to Clavier and Caldwell, thanks to a timely intervention by the Daily Crier: "Despite the more enthusiastic comments from our volunteer staff," said head honcho Michael Vansittart, "We at Clavier and Caldwell are committed to publishing a good, solid, traditional biography of the Greatest Brit ever."

What a relief! We look forward to seeing it, Michael!

'What in hell?' exclaimed Yvonne. 'Where did they get my name from?'

'They're the press,' babbled Vansittart. 'It's their job.'

'And what's all this crap about "enthusiastic comments from our volunteer staff" supposed to mean?'

'Well, they wanted a story,' shrugged Vansittart, glossing over how the story was obtained over a lengthy dinner and boozy evening with Rogerson (and his expenses account) at the Chummo Club.

'And you just told them my name and let them make up whatever shit they wanted to?' demanded Yvonne, her voice rising.

'Language, please!' barked Vansittart, for foul language was unnecessary and he would not allow it, would not listen to it, and would not respond to it.[167] I don't tolerate bad language in my business place, or any woke nonsense. We are here to do our jobs, and that job is to publish books. Now, there are several jobs which haven't been done today, like cleaning the bathroom and the kitchen, so let us all continue as normal.' So saying, Vansittart did as normal and hurried up to his office.

Behind him, Felicity jumped up with a small gasp of horror and made for the small tin containing the tea kitty, realising she hadn't done her usual daily check on the coins as she had been distracted by the early morning Churchillian discussion. She grabbed the tin from the shelf, her eyes straying suspiciously to the Bla — *young* woman sitting opposite.

---

[167] An expedient way of dismissing any points raised, and hence a standard response from the elite. Whenever anger breaks out at injustice, you will hear the Great and the Good sanctimoniously telling everyone how they will only respond to civilised discussions … despite the fact minorities have been asking for decades for genuine (social as well as legal) equality while suffering abuse from the police, employers, institutions etc. And then, when defensive and/or frustrated violence breaks out, the next standard response of the elite is to smugly note how the group in question should have just *asked* rather than resorting to violence …

'There's nothing missing from it!' bellowed Yvonne as the final walls of her reserve broke down.

Felicity swung round angrily. 'I'm just counting it!'

'You never count the petty cash when anyone else has been alone in the office with it!' snarled Yvonne.

'That's not true! How *dare* you say such a thing?'

'And you never clutch your bag to your leg when anyone goes past you, either,' snarled Yvonne. 'Don't think I haven't noticed that little signifier.'

'You're imagining things!'

'I'm seeing what's there!' shouted Yvonne. 'The assumptions of colour, of me being a criminal because I'm black!'

'I don't see colour when I look at someone,' retorted Felicity. 'That's your problem!'

'My problem is having my entire existence categorised and denied by racists!'

'How dare you?' shrieked Felicity. 'I know exactly what you go through as an oppressed minority; I'm a woman!'

'Gender oppression is not the same as racial oppression,' glowered Yvonne. 'You only experience one of them. You perpetuate the other.'

'How dare you?' sobbed Felicity, tears pouring down her face. 'I'm an ally and you're attacking me!'[168]

---

[168]A phenomenon known as "white women tears." A very handy way of deflecting accusations and centring the dialogue back onto the privileged and away from the oppressed.

'What on earth is going on?' asked Vansittart, reluctantly reappearing in the main office. His usual strategy for dealing with workplace drama was to hide until it was over, but the important eleven o'clock client would be arriving soon.

'She's calling me racist; it's a disgrace, I've never been racist!' shouted Felicity, getting her version in first.

'She is racist; every damn day!' snarled Yvonne.

'That's a lie!' wailed Felicity, bursting into a fresh surge of tears.

'And this is an official complaint!' shouted Yvonne in angry frustration. 'I'm complaining about the racism from her, and the fact she's just called me a liar.'

'You'd better both come up to my office,' sighed Vansittart, forced into action by the fact he was under silent observation from the rest of the staff. 'I'm sure we can sort this out by civilised discussion, as befitting rational adults,' he added.[169]

---

[169] By this, Vansittart was sending out a coded warning concerning the compliant and deferential behaviour he expected from his staff. After all; he didn't want to find himself in an awkward or embarrassing social scene. He was also consciously hoping he could persuade Yvonne to drop her complaint before it was committed to paper and thus became official, though if he couldn't, his subconscious was already musing on how easily memoranda could get mislabelled, misfiled, or else misapplied in the bathroom ...

And yes, he really would use the grief of the workers to wipe shit from his arse. What else would you expect from the Establishment?

Vansittart squirmed behind his desk for the next twenty minutes as his hysterical Office Manager and the Angry Black threw claim and counterclaim at each other until eventually silence fell, inviting Vansittart to demonstrate how justice, integrity, and equality ruled in his domain. 'What I need to know,' he said, ignoring justice, integrity and equality, 'is whether you can both work here professionally, as professionals, and not act as though you're in a school playground.'

'Playground?' echoed Yvonne. 'This is an official complaint about open racism!'

'Yes, well, I think you need to consider your course of action most carefully,' coughed Vansittart. 'Such things are not done lightly.'

'And what else should I do about her racism?'

'How dare you! I'm putting in a complaint about your lies and bullying and threatening behaviour!' cried Felicity, pulling a fresh tissue from her handbag.

'Then you'd better get an Industrial Tribunal ready to hear both of us and then deliver a judgement,' snapped Yvonne at Vansittart.

Vansittart twitched at the idea of any form of judgement in his domain. 'I think you'd both better go home and think very carefully about how you wish to continue,' he pronounced, making a mental note to deduct the hours left in the day from Felicity's wages. He also wondered if he could deduct anything from Yvonne before reluctantly deciding, as he didn't actually pay her anything, he couldn't. Which didn't seem right or fair to him.

'Fine,' snarled Yvonne. 'I'll get the complaint written up over the weekend and handed in on Monday.'

Vansittart stared at his desk diary to avoid making eye contact with either woman as they left the office. Swift, decisive action was needed to quell the protest and restore harmony to his fiefdom; Yvonne would have to be allowed to leave her unpaid post, for she was clearly a disruptive presence in the office, no doubt a result of her Bla – well, of her character in general. And if he wrote the letter now, timed and dated to that morning, thus making it official before the end of the day, he could then state that Yvonne would not be able to hand in her official letter of complaint on the following Monday ...

Vansittart nodded in self-approval. He'd quietly post the letter of termination at Yvonne's home that evening, informing her of the resolution and requiring her to clear her desk no later than first thing on Monday. And with the decision made, Vansittart phoned his wife to suggest a surprise weekend away, for he was concerned she was looking tired recently and he felt a good rest would do her the world of good, and there'd be no reason to hurry back, the office could do without him for a day, ha ha, they'd return late on Monday afternoon, and no doubt the baby sitter would be delighted to earn some extra money[170] for

---

[170] Rather less than the minimum wage. But then, the girl was only sixteen, and so she couldn't expect the same wage as an adult. Market forces said as much, and so it had to be true.

the weekend and also on the Monday[171] by looking after the children and no, it didn't matter she might be missing her Monday classes at the local college, she could always make the work up later, and that's quite all right, darling, I just thought you'd like a little surprise, I was only thinking of you...

So ended Yvonne's hopes and dreams, smothered by the status quo before they could even draw breath.

---

[171] Though Vansittart only paid her for the morning rather than the entire day, as they returned in the late afternoon and so the girl had not done a full shift. Market forces at work again!

Chapter Twenty-Seven

The End

Monday morning dawned bleakly for Yvonne, for she was travelling for the last time to Clavier and Coldwell. But rather than looking forward to a day in the office, a career in the office, and finally a literary career launched from the office, she was now going in simply to clear her desk.

She had got up on Saturday morning, her head dull and heavy after the previous day, and found Derek and Lily sitting in parental disapproval at the kitchen table, an open letter propped up ostentatiously against the condiments.

'This is for you,' said her mother, her voice carefully modulated to reveal the anger, disappointment, and distress she was feeling.

'Why's it open?' asked Yvonne, picking up the letter and seeing the envelope carried her handwritten name and a large slit at the top, evidence of her father's letter opener.

'I recognised Michael Vansittart's handwriting,' replied her mother, her tone shifting to betrayed accusation. 'I thought he was offering you a job. But instead, I found this!'

Yvonne pulled the letter out and read the short note of dismissal. Her services in the office were no longer required. A brief thank you for her hard work. And the request (command?) to remove all her personal belongings first thing on Monday morning.

'Well?' demanded her father.

'Well, what?' snapped Yvonne.

'What do you have to say about losing this opportunity your mother found for you?'

'Opportunity?' exploded Yvonne. 'What opportunity? The opportunity to be exploited and discriminated against? The opportunity to see how wealthy people get everything?'

'You have to make your own way in this world, like we did,' snorted Derek.

'You borrowed a shitload of money off nan!' yelled Yvonne. 'You'd have got nowhere if you hadn't guilted her into cleaning out her life savings!'

'She got the money back!' shouted Lily.

'That's all you can see, isn't it?' raged Yvonne. 'The money, the big house, the flash car; all the signifiers of success! Everything society tells you to get, even though society makes sure you can't – and we're supposed to be *thankful*?'

'You need to make your own way,' repeated her father.

'Why? So I can copy my social betters and dream of becoming like them one day? Because that's the truth, isn't it? I'm not even allowed my own dreams in this world; only the second-hand dreams imposed by the wealthy elite – work hard, don't raise your voice, and for the love of God don't think about anything! Just be a dutiful drone, doing everything you and society tells me!'

For a moment it seemed Yvonne's words had made an impression on her parents as they glanced uneasily at each other. 'Look, darling, we only want the best for you,' muttered Derek, modulating his tone to "male reasonableness".

'But your idea of the "best" is just status and money and being a wage slave your whole life. Isn't there anything more out there?'

'Well, what do you want to do?' asked Derek, his reasonableness quickly melting under his rising exasperation.

'We'll support you, darling, you know that,' added Lily, an unexpected spurt of maternal guilt prompting the unusual promise.

'I want to go to university and read History and English Literature.'

'What? You need to get a job, my girl!' snorted both parents simultaneously.

And now it was Monday. The weekend had been filled with recrimination and awkwardness, and Yvonne was glad to leave the house even if it was only for a few hours. She arrived at the office at her usual time, an hour before anyone else, though today this was because she didn't want to see anyone. What, after all, was there to say? Apart from "Hello, I've been sacked, goodbye."

And besides, Yvonne could already guess the reaction of Sarah, (mouth hanging open in a vapid O shape), Helen (coughing fit), Hutchinson-Cockburn (casually assuming Yvonne had a trust fund, family connections, or an old pal from university days to lean on), and Felicity, (smug racist superiority).

The thought of Felicity reminded Yvonne she hadn't written the letter of complaint; she'd been too upset to think of it over the weekend, what with the ongoing squabbling with her parents and her anxieties about the future and scouring Internet adverts for identikit dead-end jobs leading to identikit dead-end professions and an identikit dead-end life.

She unlocked the office door and saw the vast pile of Churchillian books still on her desk. It took some time to gather them together using the excess of carrier bags from under the kitchen sink but finally she was done, after which she awkwardly thrust her pens and notebook down the side of the lightest bag, furthering the likelihood of developing a tear before she got very far down the road.

She looked around for one last time before throwing the office keys onto Hutchinson-Cockburn's desk, hoping he would understand the message that he, and others like him, held the keys to life thanks to their birth and privilege and maybe – just maybe – he would recognise himself as a smug, arrogant wanker.

She then had to take the keys back anyway as she realised she needed them to lock the door as she left, after which all she could do was shove them through the letterbox and listen to the mocking jangle as they hit the floor.

Hauling the heavy bags along, Yvonne staggered to the library only to find a sign on the door announcing the services within were all permanently closed owing to budget cuts, the listed building was now part of the Urban Development Company and was scheduled for demolition, (soon to be replaced by an exciting complex of office blocks, retail units, and coffee shops), and all books now needed to be taken to the next nearest library some ten miles distant.

Epilogue

After the end; Yvonne is gone, the office staff are compliant, and the prole narrator is once more relegated to making ineffectual snarky comments in the chapter headings and footnotes, where no-one will ever read them.

And just in case anyone is wondering where Chapter Thirteen got to, it was dropped over superstitious concern of the number itself. If the reader is wondering where the promised information set to appear in Chapter Thirteen is now going to be, the answer will be forthcoming, in the fullness of time, after a period of quiet reflection and a full independent investigation has been carried out, and all criteria and other miscellaneous elements which need to be fully investigated and documented have been analysed and the answers put forward without any ambiguity so that apposite action may be taken at the appropriate juncture.

See Chapter Thirteen for further details.

The following morning, Vansittart peered cautiously through the office window to check the angry Bla – the disruptive presence was gone. He noted the clear desk, straightened his back, and strode with confidence through his kingdom, smiling graciously at his remaining office staff of Helen, Felicity and Sarah who were, in truth, little more than office serfs. The empty desk may have made a lesser man feel guilty, but Vansittart knew from the quiet, dutiful atmosphere he had Done the Right Thing.

He settled himself at his desk, plump and relaxed after the weekend away at his mother's house in Tunbridge Wells, wherein Mrs Vansittart senior had performed all the domestic duties expected of her by providing (with her daughter-in-law) to her son's needs. But now he was back in the real world, and work awaited him.

He was still browsing the Internet two hours later when the call came through from his old school chum Sebastian Featherstonehaugh, MP, Deputy Minister of Culture (Regions) and self-proclaimed rising star of the government, who wanted to discreetly congratulate Vansittart on getting the funding for his marvellous project to give the public a new and authoritative account of the Greatest Man in British History, Sir Winston Churchill.

'Marvellous news, Seb, simply marvellous!' enthused Vansittart. 'And it's very kind of you to call me personally.'

'That's quite all right,' said Featherstonehaugh, breezily, though in fact he had good reason to call in person, for what he was about to say was not something he wanted written down, for things which were written could be read by anyone and thus be misunderstood.[172] 'Have you decided which author you'll be going with?'

---

[172] i.e. they could be understood perfectly.

'Well, there's an extraordinarily strong pool to choose from,' said Vansittart, his finely tuned social antennae telling him some unspoken message was hovering in the air.

'Oh, I'm sure,' twittered Featherstonehaugh, 'but representations have been made on how the writer really needs to be the right sort of chap. One who will truly communicate the greatness of Churchill himself.'

'Naturally, naturally,' smiled Vansittart, reassuring Featherstonehaugh he knew the code. 'Someone in just the right position to do the work, yes?'

'That's it *exactly*!' burbled Featherstonehaugh. 'And we do have someone in the right position, I believe, in that Terrance – er, in that *representations* have been made on how our very own Terrance Rogerson is interested in taking on the role. He's just the man, given his enormous media platform in the *Daily Crier*, and his twice weekly column in *The Explorer*,[173] as well as his weekly essay in The *Trumpet*,[174] and I know Terrance will be using those platforms judiciously to sell – to inform the public the book is on the way.'

'Ah!' beamed Vansittart, swiftly drawing the independent conclusion that Terrance Rogerson was, in fact, exactly the right man for the job. True, Terrance could be a little slow

---

[173] The biggest selling broadsheet of the day.

[174] The biggest selling tabloid of the day.

with his deadlines,[175] unconventional in his writing,[176] and maybe a touch eccentric in the research,[177] but if they hired (at Terrance's expense, to be recouped from his side of the royalties) an old school chum who was now a respected, hardworking, but above all *discreet* historian to help get the book written ... 'I think we can work with that.'

'Excellent! But do bear in mind this is unofficial; the announcement will be made next week, so until then, mum's the word!'

'Mum's the word!' echoed Vansittart as he cut the call, delighted now the future of his company was assured. Which meant he could offer young Hutchinson-Cockburn an official post and a small wage, which would undoubtedly please the boy's father, Perceval, a man who held many useful contacts.

Vansittart closed the tab *Schoolgirl Sexpots* and instead opened *Home County Classic Car Sales,* for he rather fancied himself in a Jaguar E Type. And what's more, he *deserved* a Jaguar E Type, because now his company could tell the truth of the Greatest Man of History, ensuring

---

[175] Rogerson never handed anything in on time.

[176] Rogerson's prose was often racist, hackneyed, and plain bloody awful.

[177] Rogerson skimped the research – or else simply made it up to suit his needs.

Constructing Churchill | Jon Hartless

Winston Churchill's shining light would never go out, and all could bask in the full glory of England's Greatest Hero.[178]

---

[178] And this is the self-replication of the English Establishment, monopolising not only the opportunities but the entire narrative also. Meanwhile, the people have been abandoned, UK life expectancy is falling, the pension age is rising, social mobility is heading downward, bigotry and hatred are now the norm, and all the while the news outlets, their owners, and the political classes live pretty much above the law in taxpayer-subsidised privilege.
Nowhere is it possible for the people to escape the class system, or their servitude to the capitalist state.
This is English society.
Forever.
We are all utterly fucked.